The Henna Wars

The Henna Wars

adiba jaigirdar

PAGE STREET
PUBLISHING CO.

PAGE STREET
PUBLISHING CO.

Copyright © 2020 Adiba Jaigirdar
First published in 2020 by
Page Street Publishing Co.
27 Congress Street, Suite 105
Salem, MA 01970
www.pagestreetpublishing.com

All rights reserved. No part of this book may be reproduced or used, in any form or by any means, electronic or mechanical, without prior permission in writing from the publisher.

Distributed by Macmillan, sales in Canada by The Canadian Manda Group.

24   23   22   21   20   2   3   4   5

ISBN-13: 978-1-62414-968-9
ISBN-10: 1-62414-968-5

Library of Congress Control Number: 2019948872

Cover design by Molly Gillespie, book design by Ashley Tenn for Page Street Publishing Co.
Cover illustration by Nabigal-Nayagam Haider Ali

Printed and bound in the United States

Page Street Publishing protects our planet by donating to nonprofits like The Trustees, which focuses on local land conservation.

to queer brown girls,
this is for you

content warning

This book contains instances of racism, homophobia,
bullying, and a character being outed.

"I donate my truth to you like I'm rich
The truth is love ain't got no off switch"

—Janelle Monáe, "Pynk"

1

I DECIDE TO COME OUT TO MY PARENTS AT SUNNY APU'S engagement party.

Not because of Sunny Apu and her groom, or the buzz of the wedding in the air. And not because everything about a Bengali wedding is so palpably heterosexual that it's almost nauseating.

I decide to come out because of the way Ammu and Abbu look at Sunny Apu, with a mixture of pride and love and longing. It isn't directed at Sunny Apu at all, really; it's directed at the future. At *our* futures, mine and Priti's. I can almost see Ammu and Abbu stitching it together in their heads: Castles in the air, made of deep red wedding saree dreams and lined with thick gold wedding jewelry aspirations.

I've never thought of my parents as traditionalists

before this. I'd seen them as pioneers, people who made things happen even when those things might seem impossible. They'd broken rigid tradition, and have what Bengalis call a "love marriage." Though they've never told us the story, I always imagine a movie-moment meeting, exactly like in a Bollywood movie. Their eyes meet across a crowded room, maybe at a wedding of distant relatives. Ammu's in a saree, Abbu in a sherwani. Suddenly, a song starts in the background. Something romantic, but upbeat.

My parents' "love marriage" is one of the reasons they work so well here, despite the lack of family and support. Without anything, really. They uprooted their lives one day to come to Ireland. To bring *us* here. To give us a better life, they said, even when in some ways they are stuck to the past. To Bangladesh. To everything Bengali custom tells them.

Unfortunately, one of those things is this: a wedding consisting of a bride and a groom.

But my Ammu and Abbu did make it past the customs that told them love before marriage was unacceptable, and that love after marriage was to be hidden in a locked bedroom like a shameful secret. So maybe—just maybe— they can accept this other form of love that blooms in my chest sometimes when I see Deepika Padukone in a Bollywood movie, and *not* when I see her male love interest.

So that is how I spend Sunny Apu's engagement,

trying to construct the perfect coming out moment, and wondering if that even exists. I try to think back to every movie, TV show, and book that I've ever seen or read with gay protagonists. Even gay side characters. Each coming out was tragically painful. And they were all white!

"What are you doing?" Priti asks when she spots me typing on my phone in the midst of the engagement ceremony. Everyone's eyes are turned to the bride- and groom-to-be so I thought this was the moment I could Google "gay happy endings" without someone peering over my shoulder.

I quickly slip the phone into my bag and shoot her a wide-eyed, innocent smile.

"Nothing. Nothing at all."

She narrows her eyes like she doesn't believe me, but says no more. She turns back to the bride- and groom-to-be.

I know Priti will try to talk me out of it if I tell her what I'm thinking of doing. But I also know I can't be talked out of it now.

I can't keep living a lie. I have to tell them at one point or another.

And tomorrow is going to be that point.

It's weird, but after I've made my decision I feel like I'm on borrowed time. Like this is my family's last day together and something is about to break open between us. When we're driving home from the engagement party, it's past midnight. The streetlights cast a strange glow on the road ahead, marred by the bright, full moon in front of us. It's a clear night, for once. Priti is dozing in the backseat beside me. Ammu and Abbu are speaking in a low hum, so I can barely understand what they're saying.

I wish I could bottle this uneventful moment—a flash of time when we're all at peace, together and apart at once—and keep it with me forever.

I wonder if this is what things will be like tomorrow too, after I've told them.

But then the moment's over and we're home and stumbling out of the car. Our churis jingle against each other, sounding too loud and bright in the dead-of-night quiet on the streets.

Inside, I strip my face of all the heavy makeup Priti carefully dabbed onto it just hours before. I slip out of my itchy, uncomfortable salwar kameez and bury myself in my blankets, where I pull up Google again and translate the word *lesbian* into Bengali.

The next morning, Priti flits off to her best friend Ali's house with a smile on her lips. She's promised to tell Ali every detail she can about the engagement party, and the upcoming wedding. With pictures.

There are still a few hours until Abbu has to leave for the restaurant, so it's perfect, really. I take my time making my morning tea, stirring especially slowly and going over the words I practiced last night. They seem lackluster and silly now.

"Ammu, Abbu, I have something to tell you," I finally say, trying to breathe normally but somehow forgetting how breathing works.

They're sitting at the kitchen table with their phones in their hands, Abbu reading the Bengali news, and Ammu scrolling through Facebook—so reading the Auntie news/ Bengali gossip.

"Yes, shona?" Abbu says, not bothering to glance up from his phone. At least my momentary breathing amnesia isn't obvious.

I stumble forward, nearly spilling my tea, and somehow make it to the chair at the top of the table.

"Ammu, Abbu," I say again. My voice must sound grave because they finally look up, twin frowns on their lips as they take me in, trembling hands and all. I wish all of a sudden that I had spoken to Priti. That I'd allowed her to talk me out of it. I am, after all, only sixteen, and there's still time. I've never had a girlfriend. I've never even kissed a girl, only dreamed of it while staring at the cracks on my ceiling.

But we're already here and my parents are looking at me with expectation in their eyes. There is no turning back. I don't *want* to turn back.

So I say, "I like women."

Ammu frowns. "Okay, that's good, Nishat. You can

help your Khala with the wedding."

"No, I'm . . . " I try to remember the word for lesbian in Bengali. I *thought* I had committed it to memory, but clearly not. I wish I'd written it on my hand or something. Like a cheat sheet for coming out.

"You know how Sunny Apu is going to marry Abir Bhaiya?" I try again.

Ammu and Abbu nod, both looking equally bewildered by the turn this conversation is taking. I'm right there with them, if I'm being perfectly honest.

"Well, I think in the future I won't want to marry a boy at all. I think I'll want to marry a girl instead," I say lightly, like this is a thought that just popped into my head, not something I've spent years agonizing over.

There's a moment when I'm not sure they understand, but then their eyes widen, and I can see realization settling into them.

I expect something. Anything.

Anger, confusion, fear. A mixture of all of those things, maybe.

But Ammu and Abbu turn to each other instead of me, communicating something through their gaze that I don't understand at all.

"Okay," Ammu says after a beat of silence passes. "We understand."

"You do?"

Ammu's frown and the chill in her voice suggests anything but understanding.

"You can go."

I stand up, though it feels wrong. Like a trap.

The mug of tea burns into my skin as I grab hold of it and carry it upstairs, stealing glances back the whole way up. I'm waiting—hoping—for them to call me back. But there's nothing except silence.

"I told them," I say as soon as Priti slips in the door. It's just past nine o'clock. I don't even give her a chance to breathe.

She blinks at me. "You told who what?"

"Ammu and Abbu. About me. Being a lesbian."

"Oh," she says. Then, "*Oh.*"

"Yeah."

"What did they say?"

"Nothing. They said . . . 'okay, you can go.' And that was it."

"Wait, you actually *told* them?"

"I just said I did, didn't I?"

"I thought maybe . . . you were kidding. Like an April Fool's joke or something."

"It's . . . August."

She rolls her eyes and shuts the bedroom door behind her before flopping onto the bed beside me.

"You okay?"

I shrug. I've spent the last few hours trying to figure out exactly that. I'd spent years going through all of the various scenarios of coming out to my parents. None of those scenarios had included *silence*. My parents have always been forthcoming enough about their thoughts and feelings; why is now the moment they choose to shut themselves up?

"Apujan," Priti says, wrapping her arms around me and resting her chin on my shoulder. "It'll be okay. They probably just need to think, you know?"

"Yeah." I want to believe her. I almost do.

To distract me Priti pulls up a movie on Netflix, and the two of us slip under my duvet. Our heads touch lightly as we lean against the headboard. Priti loops her arms through mine. There is something comforting about having her there; I almost forget about the rest of it. The two of us must drift off to sleep because the next thing I remember is blinking my eyes open.

Priti is softly snoring beside me, her face pressed against my arm. I push her off—gently. She groans a little but doesn't wake up. I sit up, rubbing my eyes. The clock on my phone flashes *1:00 a.m.* There's a murmur of voices off somewhere in the distance. That must be what woke me.

I crawl out of bed and push my door open a smidge, letting in the air and the voices of my parents. They're speaking in low, careful voices just loud enough for me to make out.

"Too much freedom and that's what happens. What does it even mean?" Ammu says.

"She's confused, she's probably seen it in the movies, heard her friends talking about it. Let her work it out and she'll come back and change her mind."

"And if she doesn't?"

"She *will*."

"You saw the way she was looking at us. She believes it. She thinks she'll . . . she'll marry a *girl*, like that's normal."

There's a deep sigh and I'm not sure if it's Ammu or Abbu, or what it means, or what I want it to mean.

"What do we even do while she *works it out*?" It's Ammu's voice again, dripping with something akin to disgust.

Tears fight their way up my body, trying to burst out. I choke them down somehow.

"We just act normal," Abbu says. "Like nothing's happened."

Ammu says something else, but it's lower. I can't make out the words.

Abbu says, "We'll talk about it later." And the night descends into silence once more.

I push the door closed. My heart is going a million miles a minute. But before I can even think, even process, Priti flings her arms around me in an embrace. We both stumble backward, making more noise than anyone should at one o'clock in the morning after eavesdropping on their parents' conversation.

"I thought you were asleep."

"I woke up."

"Clearly."

"It'll be okay," she says.

"I'm okay," I say.

But I don't think either of us really believes that.

2

AMMU AND ABBU ARE TRUE TO THEIR WORD. THE NEXT morning it's like nothing has changed. It's like I haven't told them this huge secret that's been weighing on me for years.

"Sunny wants to know if you'll go to the parlor with her tomorrow?" Ammu says to Priti and me at the breakfast table. These are our last few days of the summer holidays so Ammu wakes up and makes us Bengali breakfasts whenever she has time. This morning it's norom khichuri with omelets. I spoon the soft, yellow rice into my mouth, but for once it doesn't really have much of a taste. I spent the rest of the night running Abbu and Ammu's words around in my head on repeat; looking at them in the morning light, I don't know how they can just ignore the truth I've told them.

"Apujan?" Priti nudges me with her shoulder.

"Huh?" When I turn, she's staring at me with a raised eyebrow. I realize she must have asked me a question. There's a spoonful of khichuri uneaten in front of me. I shove it into my mouth and chew slowly.

"Do you want to go to the parlor? Sunny Apu is going to get her henna done, so that the color is all set for the wedding."

The last thing I want to do is think about this wedding, but we're smack dab in the middle of it. All it's reminding me of now is that Abbu and Ammu think that somehow I'll come back to this. Somehow, after everything, I will be exactly like Sunny Apu. Ready to marry a Desi guy like Abir Bhaiya.

"No." I shake my head. "I don't think so. You can go if you want."

"If you're not going, I'm not going."

Ammu rolls her eyes like she's tired of our antics.

"You'll go to the wedding with no henna on your hands then?" she asks with a frown. "You're bridesmaids, how will you look?"

That's true. Sunny Apu will have henna spiraling all the way up her arms, and I'm sure the other bridesmaids—whoever they are—will be decked with henna as well. Plus, I don't think either of us have ever attended an event like this without a full hand of henna.

When we were younger, our Nanu used to spend hours

applying intricate, beautiful henna patterns to our palms. But that was years ago, when we lived in Bangladesh. Or when we visited during peak wedding season. Back then, one coat of henna could last us for at least three or four weddings of people we barely knew but were somehow related to.

"I can put henna on us?" I offer with a shrug. Ammu looks at me with narrowed eyes. I don't know what she sees, but a moment later she nods her head.

"Fine, but make sure it's nice, okay?" Ammu says. "There are henna tubes in the storeroom. I'm going to your Khala and Khalu's house."

Sunny Apu's parents aren't really our Khala and Khalu—which are titles usually reserved for your maternal aunt and her husband. But Ammu and Abbu became joined at the hip with them when they moved to Ireland a year ago. They're the only relatives we have here, even though they're very, very, *very* distantly related to us.

"We should just go to the parlor," Priti says when we get up the stairs and slip into my room. I grab a bunch of henna tubes, a piece of disposable cloth and my open laptop before spreading it all out on the bed.

"Sit."

"I'm going first?"

"I can't go first and then do your henna after. My hands will be all covered."

She casts a wary glance at the things I've laid out on the bed and then up at me.

"You know you don't have a lot of practice in this, right?"

I know. I definitely know.

I only started practicing henna last year, now that we only see Nanu on Skype every other weekend. It's something that makes me feel a little more connected to her, even though she's entire oceans away.

Though my work is nowhere close to Nanu's, I've definitely gotten better. Compared to the lopsided flowers and inconsistent vines I was drawing on Priti's ankles a few months ago, I'm practically a henna genius.

Priti shifts around on the bed for a frustratingly long time before finally settling in and holding her palm out. I take hold of her bony wrist and rest her entire hand on the old, ratty cloth I laid out on the bed.

"No shaking," I warn her, taking hold of the tube of henna. With my eyes flickering between my laptop screen and my sister's outstretched hand, I finally begin my work. I draw half of a flower on one side of Priti's hand, and if I have to say so myself, it looks pretty good. The half-circle petals are slightly uneven in shape and size, but from a distance they more or less look the same.

"Can you remind me again how Sunny Apu is related to us?" Priti asks. It isn't that we don't like Sunny Apu—

we definitely do. She's kind of like a fun, cool cousin who is also a family friend. But ever since her wedding was announced, it's like she might as well be our sister from the way Khala and Ammu are acting.

I frown. Trying to apply henna to my sister's hand while explaining complicated family dynamics to her isn't exactly ideal. But if I don't keep talking, Priti will get so bored that she'll definitely start shifting around again. She's the kind of person who can rarely sit still.

"She's Ammu's aunt's husband's cousin's daughter," I say, drawing a curved line from one of the flower petals all the way up to the tip of Priti's ring finger.

"Why are Bengali relationships so complicated?"

"Something I ask myself every single day," I mumble. It comes off a little more bitter than I want it to. I've laced it with all of the resentment I'm feeling for Ammu and Abbu. After all, it's not just Bengali relationships that are complicated, is it? It's this weird, suffocating culture that tells us exactly who or what we should be. That leaves no room to be anything else.

"Apujan." Before I know it, Priti is prying the tube of henna out of my fingers. There is a glob of henna on her hand where it's definitely not meant to be, but I can barely see it through the sudden glaze of tears in front of my eyes.

"Sorry." I sniff, rubbing my eyes and willing the tears to disappear into nothingness.

"I get it," Priti offers kindly.

She doesn't get it at all, and I don't have the heart to tell her that. I lean over to the box of tissues sitting on the bedside table and pluck one out. I wipe at her hands softly, dabbing so that only the glob of henna and any smudged parts are wiped away while the rest of the design remains untarnished.

"We don't have to keep—"

"I want to." I pick up the henna tube again. We both settle into the bed. There is something calming about the henna, something familiar and real and *solid*. It makes me forget about everything else, at least for a few minutes.

Though Priti's hand still trembles as I work away, I manage to finish her palm without any more incidents. I come away with a small smile on my face as Priti examines her hennaed hand, holding it up in front of her with some admiration.

"You know what?" she says. "You've definitely gotten better at this."

"I know." My smile widens. Priti nudges me with her non-hennaed hand.

"Don't get too cocky now."

"Okay, well. The other hand." I hold out my hand with the henna tube, waiting for her to stretch her other palm out to me.

She groans. "Can we take a break? I need to stretch my

legs." She's taking a million photos of her outstretched hand, no doubt to put up on her Instagram. That gives me a slight jolt of happiness—that my handiwork has been deemed Instagrammable by my little sister, aka my second worst critic—but it doesn't distract me from my work.

"Priti, the wedding is in a few days. If I don't get it done now, the color won't set properly. You know that."

"Fine, fine, fine," she huffs. "But don't get mad if I can't sit still."

I will get mad. She knows that and so do I. But we begin on her right hand anyway.

The wedding hall is gorgeous. It's the first wedding I've been to outside of Bangladesh, and I didn't know what to expect. Summer weddings in Bangladesh are one of two things—beautiful, expensive and luxurious to the point where you don't even realize you're in a country where it's 104 degrees out, or so hot that the thought of dressing up in your nice clothes and putting on a full face of makeup makes you want to commit some serious atrocities.

And they're abundant. During one summer visit to Nanu's house, we had to go to fifteen different weddings. Half the time we didn't even know the names of the people getting married, much less how they were related to us.

Stepping into this wedding hall feels a little like stepping into those Bangladeshi summers. There are big, circular tables filling the entire hall, each with a small vase of red and white flowers laced together. Fairy lights twinkle everywhere, winking on and off every few seconds.

"Hani Khala and Raza Khalu went all out," Priti whispers as we step inside the hall. I have to agree. It makes sense; there's no way they would have their sole daughter's wedding on a budget.

I only have a moment to wonder where everybody is before Priti and I are ushered into a back room by a woman in a black and white salwar kameez who looks like she means business.

"Sunny Apu!" Priti cries as we step inside. Because there she is, made up all beautiful like a bride in a traditional red lahenga with a pattern of gold gilded on the edges. I feel a prick of something bubbling up inside of me, some kind of anxiety that I hadn't expected, and I bite my lip to keep it at bay.

"You two look so lovely!" Khala says from behind Sunny Apu. "Absolutely stunning, don't they?"

Sunny Apu smiles nervously, nodding at the two of us, but she doesn't say anything. She looks nervous—scared, even. Priti casts a glance over at me, as if to check if I've noticed Sunny Apu's nervousness too.

"All the bridesmaids are gathering up in the other room."

Hani Khala nods at the door past the dressing table. "They're almost ready to go, I think."

Priti and I hurry toward it, giving a fleeting smile to Sunny Apu before slipping inside.

I recognize almost nobody in this room, though they're all dressed like Priti and me. It takes me a moment to snap out of the dissonance of entering a room where everybody is dressed the same and to politely murmur a hello.

"They must be Sunny Apu's friends, right?" Priti asks. "And her cousins?"

I nod, my eyes roaming over the lot of them as subtly as possible. There are two girls huddled in one corner of the room who are both white and, I'm pretty sure, Irish. The pink and gold salwar kameez that Hani Khala sent over to all of us looks oddly out of place on them.

"It washes them out," Priti says, as if reading my thoughts. I shoot her a glare to shut up. The room is small enough that they can hear her, even if she whispers.

In the other corner, there's a group of four girls. Two of them share features with Sunny Apu, but the other two don't look Bangladeshi at all.

"I think I recognize her," I whisper to Priti as low as I can. "The tall girl with the curly—don't look so obviously!" I have to cut myself off because Priti has abandoned any notion of subtlety and is staring directly at the group of girls. It's a good thing they're too deeply involved in their conversation to pay attention to us.

"She's pretty," Priti says. "I don't think I've seen her before though."

I'm trying to place her. From school? No, she looks far older than me. She must be at least the same age as Sunny Apu. Maybe I saw her at a Desi party? But she's not Desi, or at least she doesn't look it.

"I know I've seen her somewhere," I whisper to Priti, trying to stare at the girl as subtly as possible to find something that will give away how I recognize her. "But I can't remember where."

We have no more time to mull it over because a moment later, the door to the room is flung open again and the woman in black and white is giving us instructions about how to properly enter the wedding hall.

"Is that all we do as bridesmaids?" Priti whispers to me as she's handed a small bunch of red and white flowers. "Walk?"

I shrug. "I guess so."

Weddings in Bangladesh didn't have any of this bridesmaids business—not that we would have been a part of it if they did, considering how young we were and how we barely knew the people getting married.

I link my hand through Priti's.

She makes a face and says, "Did you put on deodorant before leaving the house?"

I hit her over the head with my bouquet, secretly hoping one of the thorns from the red roses gives her a little prick. Alas, no luck, because she ducks and giggles. The woman in black and white gives us a scathing look from the front of the line and I wonder if you can be thrown out of a wedding when you're a bridesmaid.

Better not risk it, I think to myself, and I elbow Priti to behave.

"I'm not having bridesmaids at my wedding," Priti says, once the wedding procession is over and we've done our bit as good bridesmaids and . . . well, walked into the wedding hall with our arms linked together. It was a bit of a letdown, though I suppose Priti and I shouldn't have expected anything else.

"Nobody could even see the henna on our hands," Priti says. "Because of these annoying flowers."

"Shh. You're going to get us into trouble again," I whisper.

She huffs, slides back in her chair and crosses her arms together. We managed to find two seats together at a table where we recognize absolutely nobody. I look around, trying to locate Ammu and Abbu, but there are so many people milling about that it's almost impossible.

"Maybe we should get up and find them?" Priti asks. It's kind of the last thing I want to do. I'm weirdly happy to be separated from them for once, and to not have our conversation hanging over our heads like a dark, unspoken cloud.

"No, we're here, we might as well stay put." I settle into my chair, setting my beaded gold clutch on the table beside me.

"Good idea, we probably wouldn't find seats together again anyway. They're about to serve the food."

"How can you tell?"

"I have a nose for these things."

I catch a glimpse of Sunny Apu on stage, with her new husband sitting at her side. They're both smiling.

"What was that in the backroom?" I ask Priti.

"What?"

I duck my head close to her, aware that the Auntie who is sitting in front of us just turned to give us an interested look. I immediately peg her as the gossiping type.

"You know, how Sunny Apu looked . . . kind of . . . I don't know, panicky."

"She's about to be married, of course she's panicky. It's a lifelong commitment." Priti's voice is louder than I'm comfortable with. The Auntie in front of us isn't looking anymore, but she's edged closer to us somehow. I have a feeling she's straining to listen.

"I know people *do* get panicky. I know why. But I just didn't think she would be." I lower my voice further.

Priti doesn't get the hint. She shrugs and says, "It's normal. Just because she already knew Bhaiya—sorry, Dulabhai—before the wedding doesn't mean she wouldn't be nervous."

Except, that's exactly what I thought would be the case. She'd known him for so long, since they were kids. If you could know someone for that long and still get nervous at the wedding, what hope did the rest of us have?

I try not to let my dejection show on my face. She looks happy now, I think, looking up at the stage. She looks happier than happy. She looks exuberant. It brings out a kind of beauty that I hadn't seen in the back room, a beauty that has nothing to do with her red and gold dress or the intricate henna pattern weaving its way up the length of her arm, or with the heavy set makeup that makes her skin twice as pale as normal and her red lips as dark and voluminous as Angelina Jolie's. It's more like a spark of happiness inside of her that's now shining through on the outside. I wonder if Dulabhai can see it too. I think he must, from the way he looks at her.

When I look away, I catch a glimpse of the girl from the back room, the one with the curly hair. She's speaking with someone she bears a striking resemblance to.

I frown, realization dawning on me.

It wasn't her that I recognized, but this other girl with the same sort of curly hair and dark brown skin. I went to primary school with her a few years back. As soon as I catch a glimpse of her, that part of my life suddenly floods back.

She turns her head all of a sudden, like she can sense someone watching. She catches my eye, and for a moment it's just the two us taking each other in from across the wedding hall. If I didn't know better I would call this my own Bollywood moment.

But I do know better, so I turn away quickly, before our gaze becomes something longer than I can explain away.

3

My absolute favorite part of the wedding distracts me from all of my worries. It even perks Priti up from her bridesmaid melancholy. Food!

For starters, the waiters bring out kebabs and sticks of chicken shashlick with green and red fried peppers stuck between the pieces of chicken. I start piling food onto my plate before the waiter has even set everything down. The Auntie sitting opposite us looks at me fearfully, like she didn't think Priti and I could be so ravenous in our hunger. I smile back at her, hoping that she's not too closely related to Sunny Apu.

I'm about to start eating when Priti stops me with a tap on my shoulder.

"You can't eat with your hands," she says with a frown.

"Why not?" But I realize the answer as I look around

and notice that everybody else has picked up the cutlery next to their plates and is politely cutting into their kebabs. Like we're Westerners and not Bengalis.

"I can't believe we're supposed to eat like white people even at a Bengali wedding," I complain in a whisper.

Priti rolls her eyes, but says nothing, probably hoping I'll get fed up with complaining and just shut up. I have more to say, but I'm far too hungry, and the Auntie at our table has piled so much food onto her plate already that I'm afraid I won't get to seconds unless I start stuffing my face right now.

I reach out for my knife and fork, but knock them over in my hurry to get to the food. They make a loud clanking noise on the way down. I catch *her* looking over out of the corner of her eyes, and my cheeks heat up with embarrassment. Does she remember me?

"This is what happens when we give in to Western traditions," I whisper to Priti before ducking underneath the table. Grabbing hold of the knife and fork, I try to stand, but due to the pencil heels I never wear, I underestimate my height and bump into the table with a loud bang.

"You're making such a scene!" Priti says in a delighted way. Like she couldn't have asked for anything better.

"Shit, shit, shit," I mumble. Priti's head appears under the table, and she extends an arm adorned with clinking gold churis. I take it, muttering, "shit, shit, shit," all the way up because my head is throbbing. This is definitely not what I need before sitting down to a lovely wedding dinner.

The Auntie opposite us gives me a filthy look as I take my seat, and I feel my face heat up all over again as I realize she must have heard me curse.

"Siss!" I cry this time. "The floor of this wedding hall is so gross, Auntie! You wouldn't believe it."

She doesn't look like she *does* believe me but I give her a smile nonetheless. Priti is in a fit of giggles beside me. I shoot her a grin before enthusiastically digging into my kebab. All of the embarrassment, and the Auntie's judgment, will be worth it if the kebab is good.

"Mmmmmm," says Priti, when she has finally gotten over her giggling fit for long enough to put some food into her mouth. I'm too busy piling more kebabs onto my plate to reply.

"You know there's a main course, right?" Priti grins after I've eaten my fourth kebab.

"Will the main course have these kebabs though, huh?" I'm feeling pretty glad that we managed to find seats separate from Ammu and Abbu.

"I wonder what the main course will be?" I ask Priti. I'm hoping for biryani. That one's easy enough to eat with cutlery. Priti rolls her eyes. As if she's not thinking the exact same thing as me.

We talked about this wedding for ages. The whole summer, really. It's the first wedding we've attended where we actually play a role—but that wasn't the part we were excited about. We were far more excited about what the cuisine at a Bengali wedding set in Ireland could be like.

"They won't have the typical Bengali wedding dishes, right?" Priti had asked one summer day—a day where the sun had decided to grace us with its presence and we were both lounging in our backyard, me with a book in hand and Priti with one earbud in her ear and one dangling down her neck.

"What? You don't like korma and polau?" I asked.

She frowned. "They're just a bit boring, aren't they?"

I rolled my eyes. Priti never complained about them being too boring when we were in the midst of wedding season in Bangladesh.

Still, one thing was clear from the get-go—for us, this wedding is all about the food.

I can barely contain my excitement when the waiter brings around the main course: Platters full of biryani that smell like heaven on a plate. Priti gives me a look that says *don't grab the biryani dish before the rest of the table have taken some,* presumably because the Auntie opposite us is eyeing the biryani with even more fervor than me. I think this is a little unfair. The Auntie is an adult and can have as much biryani as she wants any old day. I can only have it when

Ammu deems it enough of an occasion to cook us some.

Priti and I patiently wait, watching the waiter bring out more and more dishes—a bowl of steaming lamb curry, plates of naan, a small bowl of mung daal, and a plate of chicken tikka. While the Auntie spoons biryani onto her plate I grab the naan, tossing one to Priti and another onto my plate.

"Am I supposed to eat this with a fork and knife too?" I grumble under my breath, tearing at the bread with my fingers and following it with a forkful of lamb curry. It's the most unsatisfactory way of eating I've ever been subjected to. It's cruel, really, to have a Bengali wedding full of Bengalis but expect them to eat in a totally non-Bengali way. I'm almost missing the weddings in Bangladesh; at least there we were free to eat with our fingers, even if it was unbearably hot and the food was almost always korma and polau.

After our plates are hoisted away, all the guests begin to rise. The bride and groom have obviously finished their dinner and are sitting up on the stage at the front of the hall. They sit on a settee lined with gold and silver that looks more like a throne than commonplace furniture. Sunny Apu looks a little bit like a princess sitting on it in her red and gold dress, her urna draped over her head almost casually. I know from experience that it has probably been pinned into place by a stylist to maintain that casual look.

What really makes her look like a Rajkumari, though,

is the jewelry she's draped with. There are heavy gold bangles clinking on each of her hennaed wrists and a gold chain hanging from her neck, settled gently over her dress, but the bit I love most is the golden chain that clasps around her nose and stretches all the way to her ears. It seems heavy, but somehow it works on Sunny Apu. She pulls it off almost effortlessly.

I touch my own nose ring self-consciously as I look at hers. After putting on my salwar kameez earlier today I swapped out my usual stud for a golden hoop. I wonder if I can pull off a chain like Sunny Apu. I wonder if I'll ever get the chance to. You only really wear them at your wedding, after all. And with the way things are going . . .

"Will you come with me to take a photo with them?" Priti asks, cutting off my train of thought. She's already whipping her phone out of her beaded white clutch, so I know I don't have much of a choice. But right now I'm so grateful that she's here, that she's my sister, that I don't care.

"Sure." I give the Auntie at our table a smile that I hope conveys apology, condescension, and mischief all in one, and the two of us slip away from the tables and into the throng of people waiting to take a photo with the bride and groom.

"She looks so happy now," I say.

"Well, duh," says Priti, even though it's not very "duh" at all. She thrusts her phone out, nearly punching a guy in a khaki sherwani standing in front of her. He ducks out of her way, shooting us a glare while I try to give him an apologetic smile. Priti is too busy checking that she has nothing in her teeth to even notice.

"I gotta run to the bathroom to fix this." She waves her hand over her face.

"It looks okay," I say. I want to add "your face," but that might be too complimentary. And "your makeup" might make her scoff, because she probably means something specific. So I settle for adding nothing.

"Thanks, now I feel confident. Do you want to come?"

"To the bathroom?"

"No, the moon. I hear there's a really big mirror there—perfect for fixing up your makeup and taking selfies, didn't you know?"

"Okay, there's no need to get sarcastic." I punch her on the shoulder.

"I'm going, I'll be right back. Don't go up on stage without me, okay?" She turns around and whips me in the face with her urna.

"Okay," I mumble, but Priti has already disappeared into the crowd. I turn back to face the stage. The Irish girls from the back room are up there now, their faces arranged into wide grins as the professional photographer clicks away. One of them rushes off the stage, nearly tripping, and hands the photographer her iPhone, mumbling something. The photographer frowns but begins to click away with the iPhone. I wonder if photographers feel a little insulted when people ask them to do that.

"So is this what weddings in your country are usually like?"

I turn around and come face-to-face with the girl with the curly brown hair who has been dancing in the back of my mind all night. She must remember me to come up to me like this. There's a hint of a smile on her face; I can't tell if she's impressed by the wedding or if she's trying to insult it.

"Sorry?" is all I can say, though there are a million other things I could have said that would have made me seem a little more charming and a little less dumbfounded.

"You don't remember me." Her smile shifts into a smirk. It suits her, weirdly. There's a dimple that forms on her right cheek.

"I do." It comes out more defensive than I want it to, but I *do*. More clearly than I should.

"And my name?" she asks, raising an eyebrow.

I bite my lip. Then, acting braver than I feel, I say, "Do you remember *my* name?"

"Nisha." More confident than *she* should feel.

It's my turn to smirk. "Wrong."

She looks bewildered. "No, I'm . . . that's . . . " She knits her eyebrows together, like she's really thinking about this.

"That *is* your name. I remember, you're from Bangladesh. Ms. O'Donnell made you do a presentation about it in your first week in class and you were so embarrassed or shy or something that your entire face was on fire, and you stuttered through the whole presentation."

I do remember that presentation. It was my first week in school, my first month in the country. Everything was still new and everyone's words blurred together in an accent I couldn't yet understand.

"It's Nishat," I offer. "I can't believe you remember that."

"You were kind of distinctive." She's trying to bite down another smile. I can tell from the way her lips are turned up at the edges.

"Flávia," I say, and she brightens at the sound of her name, like she really didn't expect me to remember.

"You look nice in that." The words slip out, and I immediately feel heat rushing up my cheek. But she does look nice. She's wearing a salwar kameez that a Desi girl wouldn't be caught dead in at a wedding, but Flávia wears it with such nonchalance that she pulls it off. It's royal blue, with a silver floral pattern on its torso. She's wrapped the urna around her neck like a scarf, with the long end of it hanging off to the side. It's beautiful, but far too simple a design for an elaborate wedding like this.

"Thanks." This time she does smile, dimple and all.

"I like your henna. Did you do it yourself?"

I look at both sides of my right hand, filled with vines and flowers and leaves darkened to a deep red.

"Yes. I've been trying to teach myself."

"Do you find it difficult?"

I shrug. "A little. It was . . . really just for the wedding."

"Oh . . . " Her eyes leave me, and travel up to the stage where Sunny Apu and her husband are sitting with a group of people that I don't recognize.

"Do you want to go up?" she asks. "I don't really know anyone else here."

She doesn't really know *me* either. It's been years since I last saw her. She's changed so much that I hardly recognize her now. And we weren't exactly friends back in primary school, either, but now I'm kind of wishing we had been.

"Sure, yes. That'd be nice," I say.

"You haven't yet?"

"No, um . . . there's a queue." It's not so much a queue as people pushing in front of each other whenever they get the opportunity.

"I think you have bridesmaid priority. Come on." She takes hold of my hand. Her grip is soft and warm and kind of sweaty because there are a lot of people around us, but I don't really mind. I'm on cloud nine because this beautiful girl is holding my hand. I'm sure it doesn't mean anything, but my heart is beating a mile a minute and I can't help but think that this is better than the kebab. Maybe even the kebab and the biryani combined.

I'm barely aware of pushing through the crowd and onto the stage. I only realize we're there when Flávia lets go of my hand and smiles. She takes a seat next to Dulabhai and I slip into the space beside Sunny Apu, suddenly uncomfortably aware of how small the settee is.

"Congrats," I whisper to Sunny Apu, taking hold of her hand and giving it a small squeeze.

"Thanks, Nishat," she says. "Where's Priti?"

My eyes dash to my right, like I'm expecting Priti to simply appear there. It only occurs to me now that I did exactly the one thing she told me not to do.

"She's in the bathroom," I say, turning back to Sunny Apu.

"Oh," she says with a polite smile.

"She has to fix her face," I say. "Like . . . the makeup." I should have probably shut up at bathroom.

"Excuse me?" The photographer is looking at me with some exasperation. She gives a wave of her hand, indicating that we should all look ahead. There are a few clicks and flashes, and then the photographer is ushering us off the stage.

"Bye," I mumble to Sunny Apu. In a moment, my seat is occupied by a petite girl that I've never seen before. She whispers something into her ear, and I feel a weird pang of jealousy, realizing that this is probably an in-law. It feels as if Priti and I have already been replaced by Sunny Apu's new relatives.

"Coming?" Flávia asks with a tilt of her head. I nod, hoping she'll take my hand again, but she doesn't.

We're ambushed by my sister before we've even descended from the stage.

"I told you not to go up without me!" Priti cries, standing at the bottom of the stage with her hands on her hips. She looks so much like Ammu when she's angry that I have to bite back a smile.

"Sorry," I say, not really meaning it. I figure it's best not to mention how much she looks like Ammu because it'll make her even angrier. "Just . . . Flávia here doesn't know anyone." I nod at her standing beside me. "This is Flávia, by the way."

"Hi," Flávia says.

"Hello." Priti looks Flávia up and down, judgment flashing in her hazel eyes.

"She used to go to school with me," I say, and add—again—"she doesn't know anyone here."

"She has a sister. She was a bridesmaid, remember?"

"Priti." I try to squeeze a lot into her name; a warning, and some of my excitement about the fact that Flávia was holding my hand only minutes ago. And also an apology.

Priti obviously doesn't understand any of it, because

she just glowers at both me and Flávia.

"I actually better go find my sister," Flávia says, and even though I want to say, *no, stay and hold my hand for longer*, I say, "Okay, see you later."

But of course, I won't see her later. Or maybe ever again. Then all I'll have to remember her by is the way our hands fit together for those few short moments.

"You know we can go up to the stage again," I say once I'm sure Flávia is out of earshot. "It's not like there's a rule you only get to go up once!"

"I . . . I know," Priti says, some of the fight gone out of her now. "I just . . . wanted to go up together. I've never heard you mention her before."

"I told you, we went to school together. A long time ago," I say, feeling deflated. *And we probably won't see each other for a long time again. If ever.* "Well, do you want to go up then?"

Priti looks so huffy that for a moment I think she'll say she really doesn't want to. But she nods, even through her pout. I have to smile because it's kind of adorable. I even mumble an apology as we step up to the stage again, taking either side of the bride and groom.

After the photographer has clicked away for a few moments, Priti rushes toward her—heels clicking loudly—and hands over her phone.

"Can you please take a few on this?" Her voice is all sugar and sweetness.

The photographer looks a little exasperated, but nods. It's as she clicks away with Priti's phone that I realize how ridiculously forgetful I've been.

Why didn't I do this when I was with Flávia? I had the perfect opportunity to document the moments we spent together—fleeting and out of the blue as they were. But I was so busy telling Sunny Apu about Priti being in the bathroom doing her makeup that I missed my chance.

"Wow, these are definitely going up on Instagram," Priti says, flicking through the photos on her phone as we step off the stage. "You look really nice."

"I doubt it." After all, I didn't dash off to the bathroom with Priti to touch up my makeup. I haven't even looked at myself in a mirror in hours. I can't imagine what all of those helpings of food has done to my makeup.

"You do. You look even happier than Sunny Apu in this one. Look!" She holds the screen up in front of my face. It's zoomed onto my smiling face. I don't look half bad, even though my urna is half falling off of my body.

"Wait. I'm sitting next to Sunny Apu here. But I was sitting next to Dulabhai?"

"Yeah, in the picture with me. This is the one I took of you with . . . you know, that girl."

"Her name is Flávia . . . " I mumble. I can't really mean it as a reprimand when Priti has done what I naively forgot to do. I feel a strange flutter in my stomach that I know too well but don't want to know at all. "Did you take many photos of us?"

"Only a few." Priti's head is buried in her phone once more.

"Can you send them to me?"

Priti looks up at this, a frown on her lips.

"Okay, what's with you today?" she asks. "And with this girl, Flávia?"

"Nothing. I don't know what you're on about," I say. "Look! They're cutting cake!"

I cry it out loud enough for a few people in front of us to turn their heads and look at me. I don't care because Priti does look ahead at where Sunny Apu and Dulabhai have come off the stage to cut a cake that looks to have at least eight different layers.

"Oooh, what kind of cake do you think it is?" she asks.

4

FLÁVIA IS FORGOTTEN UNTIL WE PILE INTO THE CAR LATER on. It feels strange that the wedding is over and done with; all those months of planning resulted in an event that lasted only a few hours.

Ammu and Abbu are in the front of the car discussing someone they ran into at the wedding. The intricacies of the conversation are more or less drowned out by the loud music blaring from the radio.

My phone pings in my purse. I root around for it only to find a WhatsApp message from Priti. I turn to give her a questioning look. She smiles cheekily and gestures that I should read it.

For a moment I think she's being nice, though that's obviously more than I should expect from my little sister. Three photos load from the wedding, all of me and Flávia on stage with Sunny Apu and Dulabhai. I smile, until I scroll to the bottom.

So what's the deal with you and Flávia?

I frown. I really did think Priti would forget about it after the cake. I suppose the cake was lackluster; if it had been better, maybe . . .

Nothing, I type quickly. I pause for a moment before adding, *can we leave it?*

I can see Priti reading the text. She doesn't type anything back, or say anything, so I think that's that. But later, as I'm unclipping my dangly earrings and nose ring, Priti slips in through the door. She's already changed into her pajamas and stripped her face of makeup. She's fast.

"I just didn't think we kept secrets from each other," she says, like we left off in the middle of a conversation and she's just picking it up. "I mean, we haven't before."

"There's no secret." I catch her eye in the mirror of my dressing table.

"Well, then, tell me."

"There's nothing to tell."

"I know that look on your face, you know?"

"What look?" I ask, even though I know exactly the look she's talking about. Priti has lived through too many of my crushes, all of which ended in nothing. In a way, it was better, I guess. All I have left of these—probably—unrequited crushes are the dreams and memories, and that familiar feeling of butterflies in my stomach.

"Apuj—"

"She didn't know anybody there. Like I said."

"You wanted me to send the pictures."

"Just to like . . . keep, you know. *You* took them."

"You made a weird face when you said it."

I turn around. "What?"

"A weird face. Like, I don't know. It was kind of goofy. I hope you didn't make that face in front of her."

I pull a goofy face then and Priti giggles. She slips away from the doorway and plops down onto the bed.

"I didn't think she was your type," Priti says after a moment of silence.

"I don't have a type," I say, and it's true; I've never really thought about having a type. I guess my type is . . . beautiful girl. Which is a lot of them. Most of them? Pretty much all girls.

"Well, but . . . you do like her, right? That's what that was about?"

I purse my lips and sit down next to her. Do I? The butterflies in my stomach and the staring and the thinking about how holding hands with her is better than biryani would indicate yes. But maybe it was just the rush of *any pretty girl* more than *her*.

"Just . . . be careful, okay?" Priti says.

"I probably won't ever even see her again. Also, I'm the

older sister. I'm pretty sure I'm supposed to tell you that."

Priti just smiles.

I'm kind of ashamed to say that I spend a lot of time lingering over the photos on my phone. There are only three of them, and Flávia and I aren't even next to each other.

In primary school, she was one of the smallest girls in our class. She hadn't had her growth spurt yet. She was quiet, too. She liked to keep to herself, and didn't have many friends for the few years that I knew her.

I dig up one of our old school photos. She's easy to spot, but so am I. We're both darker than the rest of the girls, standing on either end of the picture. She's smiling with her teeth, showing a glint of braces. Her hair is tied up neatly in a short ponytail. Her hands hang limp by her sides, making her look uncomfortable.

At the wedding she seemed completely different. There was an air of confidence around her that I don't remember back in school. That happens, I guess. People change when they go from primary to secondary school. They take on new personas, like they're testing out a new self.

Of course, all of the things I remember about her don't appear in the school photo. Like the fact that for my first few weeks in school, Flávia was the only one who would speak to me. That when Ammu gave me rice and daal for lunch and all the other girls made fun of me, Flávia stuck up for me. That I'm pretty sure she was my first crush ever, but I'm only realizing it now in hindsight. Back then, I didn't even *think* about being gay, but I did think a lot about Flávia and the freckles that dot her cheeks.

After I've basically burned the three photos from the wedding into the back of my eyelids, I log onto Instagram and go to Priti's account. I scroll through all of the pictures she's put up just from today. I'm tagged in almost all of them. There's the photo of her and me up on stage with Sunny Apu and Dulabhai, of course. Priti looks absolutely prim and proper. I look like kind of a mess.

There's also a selfie she must have taken in the bathroom of the wedding hall, and there are photos of the wedding cake. The last photo is of Priti and me in my bedroom. It was after we'd finished getting ready, and Priti insisted that we needed a photo before we left for the wedding hall, just the two of us. She also insisted that we find a way to showcase the henna I'd spent all summer perfecting, so our hands are at awkward angles in front of us. We look totally unnatural, but in a way, it also totally captures our essence: goofy and weird. I smile. We could almost pass for twins. With our identical salwar kameezes and our thick black hair falling around us, you almost can't tell where I end and Priti begins.

It's the only picture from the night that I really love.

And then I see a comment below the photo from Flávia's account, and my smile widens.

Nice henna—your sis did a great job!

It's the last day of summer and I'm spending it thinking about Flávia Santos, a girl I'm probably never going to see again. I'm pathetic.

The sun is shining outside, as if taunting me for being the kind of person who spends more time fantasizing about an unattainable girl than living her life.

"I don't want to go back to school," Priti groans, slipping into my room and plopping herself down onto my bed. Unlike me, she's spent most of the day with her head buried in her books, at Ammu's insistence. She's a year younger than me, which means that this school year will be her first state exam. Every Irish student has to do them in their third year of secondary school.

"Well, that's too bad," I tell her.

She groans again, and turns to face me with a frown on her lips. "You're so lucky to be going into Transition Year. Getting to do fun stuff. Trying different things. Getting work experience."

"Yep, lucky . . . " The truth is that while the rest of the girls in our year have been bubbling with excitement at the idea of Transition Year, I've been feeling a sense of dread ever since I decided to go ahead with it instead of skipping ahead to Fifth Year. Transition Year is meant to be a year of doing practical things, of getting work experience and exploring the world around us, but I'm not sure I'm ready for the world yet. I much prefer stressing over exams.

"So, feeling prepared for your Junior Cert?" I know this will get a rise out of Priti. It always does.

She groans and buries her face in her hands, like I've just said the worst possible thing.

"Please, please don't start," she says. "Please, for this entire year, never bring up exams at all. I'll have enough of that from Ammu."

I can't help but laugh.

"So what do you want me to do when it's June? Just not speak to you at all?"

"You can speak to me," she says. "But just . . . not about exams. You can just avoid it. Pretend there are no exams. Pretend that I'm off for the summer with you, too."

"Okay, okay. No exam talk. Even though you didn't exactly let up on that last year."

"Are you nervous?" Priti asks then, looking at me with wide eyes. "About the results?"

I try to bite down the anxiety bubbling in the pit of my

stomach and just shake my head. If I show my nerves now, Priti will be even more nervous going into the year than she already is.

"What's done is done. Nothing I can do about it now, so there's no point being nervous, is there?"

We spend the night ironing our school uniforms and getting them ready to go in the morning, sighing complaints about each and every thing we can think of to do with school.

As I'm in the bathroom brushing my teeth before bed, Priti leans against the doorway.

"You're not going to . . . try and get somewhere with Flávia, are you?"

My mouth is full of toothpaste, so I just shrug.

"Because . . . I saw the comment she left on my Instagram photo and her Instagram profile and—"

I turn to glare at her, spitting out my toothpaste.

"Have you been stalking her?"

"It's Internet stalking, it doesn't count!"

"Priti, I saw her at that wedding and I'll probably never see her again," I say definitively, even though I've spent countless hours thinking about her since I saw her comment last night. The truth is, I did a little bit of Internet stalking of my own, and Flávia is definitely living in the vicinity. I even came up with a few scenarios where I could casually "accidentally" bump into her. I'm not serious about it—I don't think. But I'm not going to tell Priti about that.

"It's just, she seems like bad news to me."

"You don't even know her." I stuff the toothbrush into my mouth once more, hoping that's the end of that. But of course it's not.

"I've spent a lot of time . . . perusing her online presence." Priti nods proudly, like this is an admirable skill everybody should possess. "And I've learned a lot. Like . . . did you know that she had a boyfriend before?"

I frown. "And?" I try to be nonchalant about it, but the information sends my heart into a tizzy. Maybe she still has a boyfriend?

"So she's most likely straight."

"Priti. There are more sexualities than gay and straight. Just because she had a boyfriend doesn't mean anything." Although it *can* mean a lot.

"I'm just saying that she's dated before. You haven't. And she dated a boy. I'm pretty sure you're not looking to date any boys and you just don't seem compatible and she's probably straight and I don't want you to get your hopes up." She's breathing hard when she finishes, eyebrows furrowed in anger.

I'm not sure whether I should be mad or touched by her overwhelming concern.

"Nothing's going to happen anyway. You're worrying for nothing," I say even as my heart sinks a little at Priti's words. *She's most likely straight.* I had no reason to doubt that she was; taking my hand at the wedding was nothing. Straight girls do that all the time. That's why being a lesbian is so confusing.

But I had that inkling of hope, and now I feel it wither away to nothingness.

5

I WAKE UP THE NEXT MORNING TO THE TRICKLE OF RAIN outside my window. It's a pleasant sound on mornings when you can wake up lazily, listening to the steady hum of the rainwater beating against your windowsills. But when there's a looming school year ahead of you? There's nothing pleasant about it.

When I eventually get up from bed to get into the bathroom, Priti is already inside.

I rap my knuckles on the door as loudly as possible.

"HURRY UP!"

There's a low groan from inside the bathroom and I wonder for a moment if maybe Priti fell asleep inside. That image makes me feel a little better about having to get up at seven o'clock.

"Maybe don't scream at me in the morning," Priti

croaks at me a few moments later, peeking her head into my bedroom. Her hair is a right mess. Wisps of it stick up every which way, and her eyelids are still drooping with sleep.

"Sorry." I grin.

Ammu looks at us with pursed lips when Priti and I finally stumble down the stairs and into the kitchen.

"Did you even iron your skirt?" she asks Priti instead of wishing us a good morning. "It's all wrinkled up!"

"I ironed it, I promise!" Priti cries defensively, looking down at the plaid skirt and trying to smooth out the few wrinkles with her hands. "It just . . . got a bit wrinkled when I put it on, is all."

Ammu doesn't look like she believes her, but her eyes skip over Priti and her semi-wrinkled skirt onto me. She seems to take me in for a moment, and I wait for the criticism that's custom in our house. But it never comes. She turns away instead and allows us to reach for our bowls of cereal and milk.

I've never felt so horrid for not being criticized before. It feels like a slap in the face—like the ultimate criticism is this sudden lack of criticism.

I feel a lump rise to my throat as I stuff spoonfuls of cereal into my mouth. It tastes like cardboard. For a moment, I wonder if that's to do with the fact that we've spent all summer eating the breakfasts of Maharajas and now are back on a Western diet of cereal; I already miss waking up to the smell of porotas or khichuri, and eating all together in the kitchen like messy Desis, getting our hands down and dirty.

Now, I wonder if we'll ever have that again. Not just because the summer is over, but because of my revelation.

Priti and I almost miss the bus, and have to run to catch it before it leaves the stop. We're both panting as we slip onto a bus that's full to bursting.

"Should we try upstairs?" Priti asks in a deflated huff as the two of us squeeze our way through the crowd.

"Priti . . . "

"I know, I know."

We eventually manage to squeeze into a corner with a handrail within reach. The bus gives a lurch as it starts up and I almost fall onto the lap of the guy sitting in the corner seat. Priti grabs me and I give him a sheepish look.

"I'm so sorry." He shoots me a sleepy glare before going back to staring at his phone.

"This is the bane of my existence," I whisper to Priti as soon as the guy turns away.

"Buses? Falling on people? Crowds?"

"All of it!" I cry. "But . . . school. And getting there like this," I wave my hand around, but only in a small circle because I'm afraid I'll accidentally poke someone and I don't need any more glares from strangers this morning. "I'm so over it."

"We just started it, gadha," Priti says.

"Don't call me a gadha." I shoot her a glare but she just rolls her eyes. Instead of replying, she edges closer to me and lays her head on my shoulder. Despite the fact that Priti had a weird growth spurt a few years back where she actually grew taller than me, I managed to outgrow her eventually. We're still almost the same height but I have a few inches on her. I wear them with pride.

I'm tempted to push Priti off of me now since I'm not really in the mood to have 128 extra pounds on top of me this early in the morning, but knowing how Priti gets in the morning—cranky, like really, really cranky—I decide that I'll leave her be. I make the mental note to not let this become a habit.

Instead I put my arm around her shoulder and lean back against the railing. I watch the trees and buildings and people rush by outside the window, trying my best not to think about the way Ammu seemed to avoid my eyes this morning.

Something like regret weighs heavily on me, but it's not regret, exactly. It's something adjacent to it. Shame, maybe? Or the regret that something didn't happen the way I wanted it to, that things had to turn sour. Or in this case, *silent*.

As soon as we slip into school, Priti waves goodbye and runs off, no doubt to find Ali and fill her in on all of the wedding shenanigans. I watch her disappear down the hallway, weaving through crowds of girls wearing the same checkered maroon uniforms, her bag swinging behind her. Before I have a chance to turn around, somebody has wrapped me in a tight embrace.

"Nishat!" A familiar voice squeals in my ears. I turn around to find two delighted faces staring back at me. There's Chaewon, with her dark black hair at least a few inches longer than I remember it to be. Beside her stands Jess, with brand-new bangs that cover half of her face. It feels like I haven't seen them for an eternity, even though it's only been a few months.

"Hey!" I muster up the brightest smile I can offer at this time of the morning.

"We missed you!" they say in almost perfect chorus. Then I *do* smile, because I've missed this. Chaewon and Jess, joined at the hip to the point that they're finishing each other's sentences.

"I missed you too," I offer. "I have to go by the lockers and dump all of these books." I point at the giant bag swinging from my back, filled to the brim with all of my books. Maybe that's what's weighing on me, instead of the regret adjacent thing?

"We'll meet you at the assembly, okay?"

"Sure." Waving goodbye, I head toward the lockers. There are chattering girls in every single corner of the school. Leaning against lockers and walls, catching up with delighted squeals after a summer spent apart. All girls Catholic schools aren't always the most exciting places to be, but there's something enthralling about being back here and seeing everyone again after a whole summer. I bite back a smile as I swing open my locker door. I haven't even thought about what I'm going to tell Chaewon and Jess. *If* I'm going to tell them anything. Now, with that regret adjacent feeling inside of me, I don't know if I want to tell them at all. I don't know if I can stand to lose my family and friends all at the same time.

"Hey, Nishat," a familiar voice mumbles from beside me. When I turn, Flávia is opening up the locker right beside mine.

I blink.

Did I fall asleep? Did I hit my head on my locker somehow? Did my heavy bag cut off the blood flow to my brain?

"Um. Hi. Why . . . are you here?" The question is out of my mouth before I can stop it, and I can feel the heat rising up my cheeks. For once I'm glad for my dark skin, which somewhat obscures what would otherwise be a red face.

She smiles. The dimple makes an appearance.

My heartbeat escalates more than should be humanly possible.

"I just started here. Did I not mention that?"

No, she hadn't mentioned it. If she had I'd have thought about it nonstop, I'm pretty sure.

"What . . . are . . . " I'm in the middle of blurting out another nonsensical question when the crackle of the intercom interrupts me. Principal Murphy's nasally voice fills the hallway.

"*Good morning. All students should proceed to the main hall for assembly. We'll begin at eight-thirty sharp. Any latecomers will receive a late slip. Thank you.*"

Short and sweet, that's Principal Murphy's style.

"We should probably . . . " Flávia gestures with a nod of her head. Except she's nodding in exactly the opposite direction of the hall.

"Do you . . . know where the main hall is?"

It's her turn to look flustered. I notice a bloom of pink in her dark cheeks and it sends goosebumps across my skin. She shakes her head.

"I thought maybe I could pretend not to be such a newbie." She chuckles.

"It's okay. Follow me." I begin to lead the way, weaving through crowds of excited schoolgirls who are also shuffling toward the hall. My heart is still beating a little too fast and I'm trying to tell it to stop hammering, to stop getting its hopes up, to stop feeling . . . well, *feelings*.

When we enter the hall alongside a trickle of other girls, I spot Priti almost immediately. She's in a deep conversation with Ali but looks up and catches my eyes as soon as I walk in. Her eyebrows shoot up to her hairline at the sight of me. Or—probably—at the sight of Flávia by my side. I'm not looking forward to whatever she has to say later, but right now I don't really care that much.

From the other side of the hall, Chaewon and Jess wave me over. I'm about to sidle over to them but Flávia's voice stops me.

"I better go join my cousin over there," she says. And, to my surprise, she points right at Chyna Quinn. Now, *my* eyebrows shoot up to my hairline. How can Flávia, beautiful perfect Flávia, be related to *Chyna Quinn* of all people?

"Your cousin?"

"Yeah, you know her?"

I have a million anecdotes that I can offer her but I bite my tongue.

"Kind of. We're in the same year, I mean."

"Well, my mom said she would show me around today." Flávia shrugs like she has no choice in the matter. "I'll catch you later though?" And then she shoots me a smile that makes me go weak in the knees and forget all about Chyna Quinn. I nod, dumbfounded, and watch Flávia drift toward my mortal enemy.

"Who was that?" Chaewon asks when I join them, after my legs have finally solidified again.

"Flávia," I say, a little more breathlessly than I should.

I clear my throat, and repeat it again in a deeper voice that makes me sound a little like Dwayne "The Rock" Johnson. "Flávia."

"That . . . doesn't tell us anything," says Jess.

"We used to go to school together. Way back when."

"And now she's here?"

Yes, she's here and I think I've fallen in love with her. I smile and nod like my stomach isn't doing continuous somersaults. Thankfully, our conversation is cut short by Principal Murphy tapping her microphone, sending a loud crackle throughout the hall. Slowly, everyone comes to attention. Heads turn to the front as all the chatter comes to a halt.

"Welcome to the new school year," Principal Murphy begins with a tight-lipped smile. My gaze strays toward Flávia, standing side by side with Chyna Quinn, and I wonder what exactly this new school year will have in store for us.

6

CHYNA QUINN WASN'T ALWAYS MY MORTAL ENEMY. IN fact, once upon a time, we were friends. Kind of.

On our first day of secondary school, as we all flitted into this new place with butterflies in our stomachs, Chyna and I found each other. Fate—or the school administration—had decided to stick our lockers next to each other.

As we both got down on our knees to jerk open our lockers, murmuring our combinations to ourselves under our breaths, our eyes met. We exchanged a nervous smile.

She was braver than me, unsurprisingly. She stuck out her hand and said, "I'm Chyna!" in the brightest voice I'd ever heard.

"Nishat." And that was how I survived my first day in secondary school without my little sister. I was navigating an uncharted sea, but with Chyna by my side, all of it felt easier. We developed an easy friendship that was confined to school grounds, but it blossomed like any new friendship does.

The problem was that we didn't really have much in common, other than a shared anxiety of being friendless in a new school environment where we didn't know a soul.

Our school also suffers from lack-of-diversity syndrome, which basically means that in First Year I could count on both hands the number of people in our entire school who weren't white. To be accepted by Chyna—beautiful, porcelain-skinned, blonde-haired, blue-eyed Chyna—felt like starting secondary school off on the right foot.

"So I got invited to Catherine McNamara's birthday sleepover," Chyna told me during our second week. It wasn't surprising, considering she's always been more outgoing than me, more talkative, more charming, more *everything* positive. "And she was *really* exclusive about who she was inviting." Chyna looked smug about it, like tween party invites were akin to winning Oscars.

"Oh, cool," I said, trying not to sound deflated but definitely, one hundred percent sounding deflated.

"She said I could bring a friend."

"*Oh, cool!*"

She grinned and I grinned and I felt like we were going to

be friends forever and exchange friendship bracelets and, if we added two more people to our gang, do a *Sisterhood of the Traveling Pants* thing. Even if I had to be the token person of color. I was down to be the token POC.

But of course good things don't last for long, and friendships built on shaky foundations tend to fizzle out quite fast. So before we got to the stage where we were wearing friendship bracelets and exchanging magic pants, we were at Catherine McNamara's birthday party together.

It was my first secondary school party and only my second sleepover, because Ammu and Abbu are way overprotective and slow to trust white people.

I was all nerves and texted Chyna at least fifteen times before the party started.

What are you wearing?

What should I wear?

What are you bringing?

Do you think my gift is boring?

Did you tell Catherine that you're bringing me?

Are you sure it's okay for me to come?

She only responded to about five of my texts, but I couldn't really blame her for that.

Chyna was already at the front door when I arrived, ringing the bell and waving at Ammu while she backed out of the driveway with one eye on me the entire time.

"Hey," Catherine said after flinging open the door. She

was smiling at me tight-lipped, and I immediately knew the answer to half of my texts. Chyna hadn't told Catherine she was bringing me. It wasn't okay for me to come.

But I was there already, my hands full of bags, my Ammu already halfway home, and there was nothing I could do. So I swallowed my pride and stepped inside, mumbling a half-hearted, "happy birthday!" and thrusting a present into Catherine's hands.

Chyna fit into the party like the final piece in a puzzle. I fit into the party like somebody really bad at puzzles had tried to super glue a piece in out of frustration.

For a while I hovered around the edges of the party, watching Chyna be the life of it.

I texted Priti, pretending that my phone was the most interesting thing to ever exist.

This party is awful, I want to leave!!!

Priti texted back, *you have to stick it out, it's your first party with those girls!!* YOU'LL BE OKAY!

I squeezed in next to Chyna mid-conversation.

"Hi!" I tried to be bright and bubbly like I'd seen Chyna be with other people. On her, it was charming. On me? Pathetic, maybe. That's what I gauged from the way everyone in that room looked at me, with smiles that didn't reach their eyes.

"Oh, this is . . . Nishat." Chyna was smiling the exact same sort of smile as the others. She waved a hand at me as if everybody couldn't see me clearly. As if my brown skin didn't set me apart like a question mark in a sea of full stops.

"Nesha, hi, I'm Paulie," a girl with bright red hair said, sticking out her hand like we were middle-aged moms and not twelve- and thirteen-year-olds.

"Uh, hi. It's Ni-sh*at*."

"Neesha."

"Nish*at*." I tried again.

A wrinkle appeared on her forehead, like pronouncing my name was a difficult math problem she couldn't quite get right.

"Hey, can I talk to you for a sec?" Chyna was already pulling me up and away from the crowd of girls before I managed to reply to her. She pulled me into a corner of the hall, right by the door. I remember seeing a reflection of the sunset on Chyna's face—gold and orange and red.

"I think you should go."

I frowned. "You invited me here."

"It was a mistake. I thought it'd be okay but I think Catherine just said I could bring a friend to be nice."

"But I'm already here."

"Yeah, well, you can make up an excuse and leave. Tell Catherine you're feeling sick, I'm sure she'll get it."

"What about you?" I asked. I didn't think both of us could pretend to be sick and get away with it. "You'll tell her you need to go with me, to make sure I'm okay?"

Something passed over Chyna's face. A shadow, or maybe just the sunlight on its way down. But there was a shift. Not just in her expression, but in the air around us.

"I'm not coming with you."

"Why not?" But even as I asked it, reality was dawning on me. Chyna had found her place, and her place here didn't—and couldn't—include me. I was being thrown out into the cold. Literally, because it was about thirty seven degrees outside despite it being September.

"I can't go. That would be impolite."

"Oh," I said, even though it made no sense. "I guess I'll call my mom and—"

But Chyna was already turning around, already slipping into the sitting room, already grinning like she was glad to be rid of me.

As I called Ammu to pick me up, I could hear Chyna recounting the story that made her fit right into that clique of girls.

"So why is your name Chyna?" It was redheaded Paulie that asked the question. "I've never met anyone with such a unique name before."

I would have rolled my eyes into the back of my head if my hands weren't shaking as the ring-ring-ring of the phone kept fading in and out with no indication of Ammu picking up anytime soon.

"My mom went to China after she finished university, to teach English. And that was where she met my dad. They stayed there for about a year, dating, so it was like the place where they fell in love, and they decided to name me after it."

There was a round of awwws, and Chyna's face lit up.

"Have you ever been?" Catherine asked.

"Not yet, but Mom and Dad promised that someday soon we'll go so I can see for myself!"

"That's *so* exciting."

Ammu finally picked up the phone. She agreed to swing back around and pick me up, though she didn't sound happy about it. Surprisingly, Catherine came to see me off, though she still wore that tight-lipped smile.

"Shame you couldn't stay, we were going to watch a horror movie," she said, turning the lock so she could open the door. "I guess it's bound to happen though, with the food you eat."

"Excuse me?"

"Chyna said . . . you know, because Indian people eat so much spicy food, you had . . . " She leaned down to whisper the next words, like they were a dirty secret. "Some digestive issues."

"I don't have . . . I'm not . . . " But my words got lost because the next minute Catherine had opened up the front door and was pushing me out with a cheery wave of her hand.

That was how the rumor that my father's restaurant gave people diarrhea started, and spread around the whole school.

It was also the last day Chyna and I were friends.

7

I DON'T HAVE ANY CLASSES WITH FLÁVIA IN THE MORNING. At lunchtime I watch out for her, but when I catch her sitting down with Chyna and her posse I quickly put an end to my roaming eyes.

Chaewon and Jess share one of their curious looks, and I'm sure that it's about me, but I pretend not to notice.

At the end of the day, the three of us stroll into our Business class. Even though it's only the first day of the school year it already feels like we've been here forever, and I'm restless for the end-of-school bell to ring.

"The front?" Chaewon asks, resting her bag on the row of tables right in front of the teacher's desk—the seats that everybody detests but Chaewon adores for some reason.

Jess is already sidling into the back row, apparently done with sitting through teacher scrutiny at the front of the class. Chaewon purses her lips tightly but she doesn't complain. The two of us slip into chairs beside Jess, pulling our Business books out of our bags.

"Which teacher do you think we'll have for Business?" Jess leans forward on her desk to whisper to us as a slew of students trickle in, the sound of their chatter filling up the room.

"Ms. Montgomery, maybe?" Chaewon asks hopefully. Ms. Montgomery used to teach us Business back in First Year, and she always had the most creative ways of teaching. She made us think about everything practically instead of just making us read through the book and do exercises. Her classes were always just . . . fun. Although that was something First Year Business could afford to be. First Year was when exams seemed impossibly far away.

"I bet it'll be Ms. Burke, though." Jess scrunches up her face as she says this. "Open your *boooks*, girls," she adds in a high-pitched voice, imitating Ms. Burke's country-tinged accent and causing Chaewon and me to burst out into a fit of giggles.

"Settle down." Ms. Montgomery's voice comes from the front of the room. The three of us manage to stifle our giggles and look up with smiles still tugging at the corners of our lips. "Good afternoon."

"Good afternoon," we chorus back.

Ms. Montgomery smiles and slides behind her desk.

"Well, Transition Year Business . . . this is the best time to put your practical skills to use." She raises an eyebrow like she's challenging us. "So you guys can put your books away for the moment."

The entire class exchanges glances with one another. This suddenly feels like a Defense Against the Dark Arts class in *Harry Potter and the Prisoner of Azkaban*. All that's left is for Ms. Montgomery to whip out a boggart.

As I'm bent down, trying to stuff my heavy Business book into my bag, I catch a glimpse of the dark brown curls that have suddenly become so familiar to me.

Flávia.

In this class.

She's sitting quite a few rows in front of us, though. Suddenly I regret not siding with Chaewon.

"Did your head get stuck to your bag or something?" Chaewon whispers, poking me in the ribs. I sit up, feeling a blush creep up my neck once more.

"—and so," Ms. Montgomery is mid-speech, but doesn't seem to have noticed my lack of attention. "We're going to spend a significant portion of this year working on a business project." She puts more emphasis than necessary on the word project, like it's something fancy instead of something we've done for pretty much every class we're a part of.

"And we have some real businesses involved, offering prize money."

That has everyone's attention. There's a palpable shift in the mood of the class. While before it was Ms. Montgomery droning on about something, now it's Ms. Montgomery droning on about something that has prize money.

She seems to sense our increased attention, because there's a smile tugging at her lips as she peers down at us. She pauses for a beat. A long beat. Like she's trying to draw out the suspense.

"So we'll be developing our very own businesses," she says. "Groups or individuals. It's your business, so you have to make the decision. And it will count for a large percentage of your Christmas exams."

The class breaks out into a groan as she says this, but the ghost of a smile remains on Ms. Montgomery's lips. Because, of course, she's still holding back the information that we really want to know.

"The prize money . . . donated by the sponsors hosting this competition will be . . . "

We're all holding our breath. Well, I am, at least. But I can feel the anticipation of my classmates in the air.

"A thousand euros."

"A thousand euros is a lot of money," Chaewon says by our lockers at the end of the school day. "Like . . . can you imagine winning that? You could do a lot with a thousand euros."

"I could buy all of the video games I want," Jess says in a half whisper, like an endless supply of video games is her idea of heaven.

"I think I'd put my money in a bank account and use it for when I really needed it, you know," says Chaewon.

Jess and I sigh simultaneously.

"You have to be a little more creative than that. You have to treat yourself," I say.

"Yeah, you're not allowed to be such an adult yet. All this talk of banks and saving," Jess adds.

"You sound like you're forty."

"Maybe even fifty."

"Saving up is important," Chaewon mumbles.

"Okay, but these are our fantasies, Chaewon. And fantasies can be anything you want them to be."

"I guess, if I was being wild," Chaewon begins thoughtfully.

"Really wild." I nod encouragingly.

"Like, really, really wild," Jess adds.

" . . . I would go on a holiday, maybe," Chaewon says. "I mean, I'd want to go back to Korea. To visit, you know. But with a thousand euros . . . I'm not sure if that would be possible."

"You could go on a holiday to somewhere in Europe," Jess chirps happily, somehow unaware that a trip to Korea would be far more than a holiday. Even though Chaewon and Jess are best friends who keep no secrets from each other, Chaewon catches *my* eye this time. Like this is a secret we're sharing that Jess has no inkling of. It's only a moment.

Then Chaewon chuckles and says, "Yes, and I could bring the both of you, obviously."

"That would be the best holiday," Jess agrees

I'm thinking about how one grand would barely be enough for a trip to Bangladesh, too.

Priti has after-school study, which Ammu and Abbu cajoled her into doing, even though she doesn't really need it. She studies enough at home.

But it means I get to wait at the bus stop all by myself The bright orange letters of the real-time screen announce ten minutes, eleven, then back to ten again in the space of just a few seconds. Dublin bus is as unreliable as ever.

"Where's your sister?"

Flávia's voice has the usual effect on me—it sends my heart into a rhythm that shouldn't be humanly possible. What is she doing here?

If she's at the bus stop, she's probably also waiting for a bus home.

She slides onto the bench next to me, a question pasted onto her expression.

Right.

She asked me a question.

"My sister and I aren't always together." I don't know why my voice comes out defensive—apparently Flávia does something to me that makes my mind react in the strangest ways.

"I know." She chuckles, somehow not totally put off by my defensiveness. "Just . . . I feel like I haven't seen you without her. Chyna says the two of you are joined at the hip."

I'm not sure how to feel about that—first, that Flávia has been asking Chyna about me, and second that she might believe whatever Chyna tells her.

I cross my arms over my chest and glance at Flávia out of the corner of my eye, like that'll tell me exactly what Chyna has been saying about me.

"So . . . where is she?" Flávia asks after a moment.

"After-school study. She's doing the Junior Cert this year, so." I shrug.

"Wow," Flávia says, leaning back against the glass on

the back of the bus stop. "She must be just like you, huh?"

"What?"

"You don't remember? When we were in primary school, your favorite thing was sneaking off into the library when we were supposed to be in the schoolyard." She turns to look at me with amusement flashing in her eyes, and I can feel heat rising up my cheeks.

I can't believe she remembers that too. I'd almost forgotten.

In primary school, I was so terrified of the other girls. They already made fun of me for my slight accent, and for the fact that it took me a few tries to understand them because of *their* accents. They also pointed out that my food was weird, and smelled bad (though how anybody can think daal smells bad is still beyond me).

So instead of spending lunchtime in the schoolyard, hanging around by myself in a corner and alerting everyone to the fact that I was utterly alone and friendless, I would slip into the school library, hide behind a few bookshelves and bury myself in whatever I could find.

"That was different," I say to Flávia now, even though I don't want to explain how it was different. I was just trying to find a safe place for myself in that school.

Priti is just a nerd.

Surprisingly, Flávia sighs and says, "yeah," like she totally understands. "You know, it's even worse outside of Dublin." She says this like I know exactly what she's talking about.

Weirdly, I do. Because I don't think it was easy for either of us in primary school, with our pronounced differences.

"Like . . . if you think our school isn't diverse, you should see the school I went to before." She chuckles, but there's a hint of sadness to it. I can't imagine what it must have been like. Dublin is—weirdly—cosmopolitan. Maybe not so much in our little corner of it, but it is. If you go into town, the place is full of people from all parts of the world. A lot of them are Spanish students who love to block every doorway in existence—because apparently Spanish students don't come here to study English or tour Ireland, they just come to stand in front of doors and inconvenience the rest of us. But there are people from other places too—from Poland and Brazil and Nigeria, and so many other countries.

"That . . . must have been difficult," I offer, but immediately I regret it. The words don't sound like enough. Maybe they even sound a little condescending. Unhelpful.

But Flávia shrugs. "It is what it is."

"Can I ask you something?" I say after a moment of silence passes between us.

"Didn't you already ask me something?" Flávia says, raising an eyebrow. I roll my eyes, but I have to smile. It's the kind of joke I can imagine Abbu making.

"Seriously, can I?"

"Sure." She sits up, like she's ready for a serious question. She makes her face all scrunched up and somber. I have to bite back a smile.

"Why did your mom take you away?" I ask. "Why . . . didn't you stay here?"

Flávia's expression shifts—from mock serious to almost blank. Unreadable. My stomach plummets. I think for a moment that maybe I've asked a question that's way too invasive and now Flávia will be annoyed with me.

But then she says, "I think it was hard for my mom." She's looking down at the ground, toeing the dirt with the soles of the regulation black shoes that we all wear as part of our school uniform. "She came here when she was younger, and fell in love with my dad, and she thought that was it. She'd made it. She says Brazil isn't always an easy place to be in, even though she misses it. After the divorce, I think she just wanted to go somewhere where the fact that her goals had fallen apart didn't stare her in the face."

"Oh," is all I can say. I don't know why, but I'd never attributed Flávia leaving to something to do with her mom, even though obviously I heard about the divorce. We were a small class so nothing was kept under wraps for too long.

Flávia's lips quirk into something resembling a smile. "You know, she actually wanted to take me and my sister back to Brazil."

"Wow."

"I was all for it."

"Really?" I can't help the fact that my voice rises an octave. It's just that I'm not sure if I would want to go back to Bangladesh permanently, or even semi-permanently. Aside from the fact that being gay there is punishable by death, I'm also not sure where I would even fit in. I don't fit in here, but would I fit in there any better? I don't think so. I've already lost most of my Bengali, and when I sometimes talk to my cousins from there, it seems like the differences between us are akash patal—like the sky and earth.

"I've only been there when I was young and I barely remember it," Flávia says. "I thought . . . it would be good. A way for me to actually learn about where I'm from, and brush up on my Portuguese." She sighs. "But . . . it didn't really work out. I don't think my mom was ready to go back, and she says we have more opportunities here."

It's funny that Flávia and I are from such different parts of the world but our parents have the same philosophy. They shifted us halfway across the world, risking our culture, putting us in the middle of two nations and giving us an identity crisis, all because they believe it gives us more opportunities. It's strange to think about how much our parents really sacrifice for us. But then, I'm stuck on the fact that Ammu and Abbu can leave their entire world behind, yet they can't pause for a moment and consider who I am. How can they sacrifice everything for me and Priti, but they can't sacrifice their closed view of sexuality to accept me as I am?

"Well . . . I'm glad that you're back," I say. It's not like I pined after Flávia all these years, considering I didn't even realize that I had a crush on her way back then, but . . . having her here feels weird, in a nice way. She's changed so much—from her height to her hair (which she used to always straighten and put up in a ponytail), and just the way she carries herself—but then there are so many things that seem the same. She still has that warmth about her that she did in primary school, and a smile that could make anyone melt.

Flávia turns to me with that smile playing at her lips once more. "Yeah, I'm pretty glad to be back too," she says, holding my gaze for a long moment.

We're interrupted by the rushing sound of the bus zooming up, and I have to leap out of my seat to hold my hand out. If I miss this bus, I'll have to wait a whole hour to catch the next one.

Flávia stands as the bus pulls up. "I'll see you later, Nishat," she says, and she steps away from the bus stop and toward the traffic lights with the zebra crossing.

"Wait . . . you're not getting the bus?"

"Nope!" Flávia shoots me a grin. I want to ask her why she decided to stay and talk to me, but the driver is already glaring at me and I know if I don't hop on now, he'll close the doors and pull away.

So I step inside, swipe my card and hurry to the window. As I watch Flávia walk away, her curls bouncing in the wind behind her, I can't help the flutter of butterflies in my stomach.

8

"WHAT'S THAT?" PRITI ASKS LATER, AFTER BARGING INTO my room when she gets home from after-school study.

"It's a form."

"Well, I can see that." Priti reaches over and tries to grab the piece of paper out of my hands. "But . . . what's . . . it . . . for?" She stops her attempts to frown at me. "And why won't you let me look at it?"

"Remind me when this became your business?" I ask, raising an eyebrow.

She lets out a huffy breath and slumps back onto my bed. "Fine, don't tell me. See if I care."

I laugh and sidle closer to her, poking her in the ribs until she giggles. Priti is still the most ticklish person I know.

"Stop it!" she says, slapping my hands away until I'm laughing too.

"Sorry," I say once we've both settled down. "I'll tell you about the form. I need your help with this anyway."

"Maybe I don't want to help you." Priti sticks her chin out at me.

"Do you want me to tickle you again?"

She shoots me a glare, but mumbles "no," before quickly leaning toward me to read the form over my shoulder.

"Business idea?" she asks. "You're not a business person."

"Well, duh. But Ms. Montgomery is setting up this business competition for our class. Basically, we all set up our own businesses, and we have a few weeks to work on it and try to make a profit. The person who does the best job will win a thousand euros, but also it's going to be a part of our Christmas exam results."

"Oh, your first taste of Transition Year. You're going to be an entrepreneur!" She's only half serious so I roll my eyes. I don't see any entrepreneurship in my future.

"I need ideas!" I say to Priti. Chaewon and Jess have been blowing up our usually dead group chat with all of their ideas. They've already eliminated anything related to food because that'll be too much hassle, and Jess has started to consider how her obsession with video games can be made into a business venture.

But my well of ideas is dry and I have nothing to

contribute to our chat. I want to somehow swoop in with a brilliant idea that makes Chaewon and Jess think I'm a genius, though.

"You could start a food stall?" Priti suggests.

"What kind of food would I sell?"

She shrugs. "You could take some food from the restaurant? Or maybe ask Ammu to cook for you." She holds one hand out in front of her and, dragging it through the air, says "authentic Bengali food" in a dramatic whisper.

I start laughing at how ridiculous it sounds and next thing I know Priti's hitting me over the head with her English textbook.

"Okay, okay, ow. Sorry."

She finally stops and sits back down again, looking mighty proud of herself.

"English books should not be used in such ways. There's poetry in there. Very beautiful, gentle poetry." I rub my head.

"There's also all those poems about war. How gentle are those?"

"Whatever," I say. "Look, nobody's going to be interested in authentic Bengali food. For one, they don't even understand what Bengali means or where Bangladesh is. Secondly, people are just not into South Asian food right now. Dublin is currently all about burritos and donuts. And thirdly, I can't take food from the restaurant, and if I asked Ammu to cook for my business she would get so mad. Plus, wouldn't that kind of be like cheating? I'm not really doing it on my own, am I?"

"I guess not," Priti says, though she doesn't sound like she wants to admit it at all. "It's just . . . imagine Bengali street food on the streets of Dublin! Yum! It could be the next craze after donuts!"

It would be pretty cool if the next Irish food trend was South Asian. We'd already more or less flown past the Japanese food trend, and donuts are way past their shelf life. Realistically though, Bengali food is never going to be trendy in the streets here. That much I learned from Chyna, at least.

"Nobody other than you and me would be able to eat Bengali street food. Plus, can you imagine what Chyna would say if I started selling that?"

Priti frowns, and says, "Chyna isn't that bad."

I actually physically recoil from Priti at that. Not intentionally, it's just an instinct. I look at her with wide eyes. "Chyna 'your-father's-restaurant-gives-people-diarrhea' Quinn isn't that bad?" I ask.

Priti sighs, crossing her arms over her chest. "When you say it like that. It's been like . . . a long time since everything happened."

I narrow my eyes at Priti, before leaning forward and touching her forehead with the back of my hand. "You don't feel warm, but obviously you're so feverish that you're delusional."

Priti bats my arm away with a small glare. "I'm not delusional, Apujan. Oh my God. Just . . . Chyna . . . invited me and Ali to her birthday party next weekend. It was nice of her to invite us."

My eyebrows shoot up. "So . . . from the fact that you've suddenly decided Chyna is your best friend, I guess you're going?" Priti looks away, like she's really thinking about it very hard.

If you have to think about a party that hard, you probably shouldn't go. Although that's not worth much coming from someone who never gets invited to parties.

"I think so," she says finally. "I mean . . . Ali's going. And it sounds like it'll be fun . . . plus!" She suddenly turns to me with a smile and bright eyes. "It's like . . . she's extending a . . . what's the word? A hand and—"

"You forgot the word hand?"

"Shut up!" She hits me lightly on the shoulder and sits back, the smile still on her face.

"I just feel like . . . I don't know, she's changed from back then—"

It wasn't that long ago.

"And she's making an attempt, you know? To make amends. I have to meet her halfway, don't I? Isn't that my responsibility?"

Personally, I think Priti is blathering on about nothing to justify going along with Ali, but I know better than to say that.

"Did she say she was sorry?" I ask instead.

"Well, no. But it was a long time ago."

"Priti . . . remember the other day when you told me I should be careful? About the Flávia stuff?"

"This isn't the same. It's completely different." Her words tumble out so fast that they run into each other.

"Did you know that Flávia and Chyna are cousins?"

That seems to stump her because she looks up at me with wide, disbelieving eyes.

"You're lying."

"I'm not lying, Flávia told me." Which is obviously the wrong thing to say, because Priti narrows her eyes in a glare.

"You know that makes it worse, right? You hate Chyna, so by extension shouldn't you also hate her cousin?"

"You're the one going to Chyna's birthday party."

"Yeah, but that's a party, there'll be lots of people there. I'm not fantasizing about kissing Chyna."

"I'm not fan—"

"Look, I'm only going because Ali is going, okay? And she's going because her boyfriend is going and—"

"You didn't tell me Ali had a boyfriend," I say. Her first boyfriend, in fact. Priti looks away, like this isn't something she wants to discuss any further. She picks up her English book and begins to flick through it like it's the most exciting thing she's ever come across.

"You should have told me. I know it can be weird when—"

"It's not weird." Her voice comes out high-pitched, assuring me that she definitely finds it weird. "I just have to get used to him, is all."

I want to say more. I'm the big sister. I'm supposed to offer her words of wisdom. Pass on my knowledge. But it's not like I'm exactly skilled in this department.

Instead, I let the silence wash over us, reaching out and grabbing Priti's phone from beside her. I start to scroll through her phone again. She shoots me a look over the top of her book, and I return it with a cheeky grin. Neither of us comment.

I'm still scrolling through her photos when Priti shuts her English book again and says in a bright voice, "What about Bengali sweets?"

"What about them?"

"You could sell those. That would be fun, right? Jilapis. Mmmmmmm." Priti might as well have started salivating right there, right then. The look in her eye at the thought of jilapis is totally dreamy.

"I don't think so." I have to stifle a laugh. "Can you imagine the girls at school eating jilapis? They would be turned off just looking at it."

"What are you talking about? Jilapis are beautiful. They're all soft but not too soft. And golden and sweet and yummy and . . . I really want some now."

"And they're sticky and gooey and some people never want to venture out of their comfort zones. Plus, I can't make jilapis myself."

"Ammu can . . ." Priti says, before seeing the way I raise my eyebrows at her. She sighs and says, "Okay, I'll keep thinking about it."

"Thank—hey!"

"What?"

I perk up until I'm sitting straight and hold out Priti's phone toward her. There's a photo that she took of our hands joined together before Sunny Apu's wedding. We're both weighed down by rings and bracelets, but the most important feature of the photo is the deep red floral henna weaving up our arms, palms, and fingers.

"That's a photo I took?" Priti asks hesitantly.

"No, not . . ." I sigh. "The henna!"

"What about it?"

"It's good, isn't it?"

"I mean, it's okay, it's definitely not the same caliber as Nanu's but—"

"That's what I could do."

"What?" Priti's face is blank as ever. For a smart person, it takes her a very long time to catch on.

"The henna!" I exclaim.

"Yes . . . it's nice, but Nanu's is still miles better."

"Oh my God, Priti," I groan. "I could start a henna design business."

"Oh my God." Her eyes widen as my idea finally dawns on her. "You could do that. The girls at school would kill for that. I mean, did you see the comments that everybody left on my Insta when I put up that photo of my hand?"

"No?" I just remember the comment Flávia left on the photo from the wedding.

"Look!" She shoves the phone in my face. I remember when Priti took this photo, though I don't remember actually seeing the photo itself. It was right after I finished her left palm. The henna paste hadn't even hardened properly yet.

I look under the photo. 148 likes. 30 comments.

"Whoa."

"Read the comments!" Priti says. I scroll down.

Where did you get this done???

Is there a place in Dublin that does henna designs?

How much was it?

Love the design!

Gorgeous!

"Priti!" I can feel a huge grin tugging at my lips. "Why didn't you show me this?"

"Well, I didn't want you to get a big head. I mean,

the design is only okay." But she's grinning too as she puts her phone away.

"Do you really think I could do it though? I mean, I've only been practicing for a little bit. And I've only practiced on you and me. What if I mess up?"

Priti gets a serious look on her face, which causes creases between her eyebrows and makes her nose get all pinched.

"You can totally do this, Apujan," she says. "You're great at it. I mean . . . come on, look at all those comments. Some of them even came from Desi people. And they know their henna."

I smile. "You said it was only okay."

"Well, someone has to keep your ego in check," Priti says with a dramatic sigh.

"Well, can I still practice on your hands?" I ask. "And can I use your pictures to advertise?"

"Sure!" Priti's face breaks out into a huge grin. "And you should start doing your own designs, you know."

"You think so?"

"Yeah, it'll make your business so unique, don't you think?" she asks. "People can get Nishat originals on their hands. They'll be queuing up in front of your door . . . or your stall, or whatever."

I laugh because I can't imagine anybody wanting a "Nishat original," but it's a nice thought, I guess. The kind of thought only my sister could have and be excited about.

But the idea also fills me with a kind of excitement I haven't felt in a long time. So after shooing Priti off to her bedroom to finish her studies, I settle in with a blank piece of paper and my pencil in hand, trying to put together a henna design from my head.

It's hours later when I'm finished, and the page in front of me is filled with patterns of flowers, mandalas, and swirls. A mishmash of things that weirdly seem to work.

I pick up my phone from the bedside table and quickly draft a text to Chaewon and Jess about my idea. But my fingers hover over the send button. I read the message over and over again, feeling my heart beat hard in my chest.

What if they hate the idea? What if they reject it?

I delete the text as quickly as I had written it. Instead, I pull up Skype and call Nanu.

She picks up after it rings for a good few minutes, when I'm almost ready to hang up, dejected.

"Nishat?" she asks, her face appearing on screen. She looks tired. There are bags under her eyes and her skin looks blotchy. I realize I must have woken her up; I didn't even think about the time difference before placing the call.

"Assalam Alaikum," I say. "Did I wake you? Sorry. I forgot about the time difference."

She smiles, though it's a tired sort of smile. I've never

considered Nanu old before; I mean, yes she's old. She's my grandmother. But compared to other grandmothers I've seen, with wrinkles all over their faces and walking sticks and everything, I've always thought of Nanu as young and healthy. But today, she seems different altogether. Like I've caught her in a moment that I'm not really meant to see.

"It's okay. Is something wrong?"

"No . . ." I mumble, feeling deflated. I can't believe I've woken Nanu up and made her worry for pretty much nothing. I could have filled her in during the weekend when we can call during regular hours. "Nothing's wrong. I'm just . . . I'm starting to make my own henna designs, Nanu. I'm going to start my own business."

Nanu's whole face changes at that. She leans closer to the camera.

"Really?" she asks.

I nod, some of my previous excited energy coming back to me. I reach for my notebook and hold it up for her to see the design.

"That's the first one. I've been working on it all evening. What . . . what do you think?"

Nanu's eyes roam over the page I'm holding out. I can see her eyes moving, taking in all of it. Slowly and steadily.

"It's beautiful, Jannu." Her voice is soft. Quiet. Like she can't quite believe I'm the one to have done this. "It's your first one? It's amazing."

I feel pride swelling up in my chest.

"You really think so?" My voice is barely more than a whisper.

"It's so much better than any design I did when I was your age." She laughs. "Maybe next time you're here I can show you all of my sketches. I have notebooks full of them." Nanu has been decorating people's hands with henna since she was my age. She used to put henna on all of her cousins. After she got married, she applied henna on her new nieces and nephews. I can't even imagine what her sketch books look like. I can't even imagine how many she must have.

"Yes! Yes! I'd love that!" I say.

"You know, your Ammu used to be quite good at it, too, once upon a time."

"Really? She never said anything about it."

Nanu chuckles. "Yes, she wasn't very patient, Jannu. Not like you. She was great at it, but she couldn't get all of the precise details right because she would rush. She got bored very easily. After she married your Abbu and moved over there . . . well, I guess she didn't really have anyone to practice on for a long time. She lost interest and forgot about it."

I feel a pang of sadness at that thought. I imagine if Ammu had kept it up; maybe Priti and I would be experts. Maybe it would be a proper family tradition. Maybe we would already have notebooks full of original designs.

I try not to dwell on it too much as I say my goodbyes to Nanu.

9

AT THE LOCKERS THE NEXT MORNING, CHAEWON AND JESS are *still* discussing their ideas, which makes me all the more nervous about telling them *my* idea. They've already cycled through so much.

"You know, I was thinking . . . " I start, interrupting their argument about whether or not people will pay good money for Jess to draw chibi art of video game characters (Chaewon says no, but Jess insists yes). "Priti and I were brainstorming, and we came up with the idea of setting up a henna business."

"A henna business . . . " Jess repeats, like she's trying to wrap her head around it.

"You know, like . . . " I wave my henna-laden hands around in front of their faces.

"*You* did this?" Chaewon grabs hold of one of my

hands and inspects my palm. Her fingers run up and down the deep red vines sprouting leaves and flowers, sending a shiver down my spine.

"Why didn't you say so?" Jess looks impressed too as she edges closer to Chaewon and peers down at my hands like it's the first time she's seen them.

I shrug, pulling my hands away and feeling a blush rise up my cheeks.

"I didn't know you were such an artist," Jess says.

"I was just practicing over the summer. You know, for that wedding?"

"People would definitely be into this." Chaewon begins to nod so fast that she looks a little like a bobblehead. "I mean, people *love* this stuff and you're so good."

"Thanks. Jess?"

Jess gives me a nervous smile that makes my stomach drop.

"Don't get me wrong, your work is beautiful," she starts.

"Stunning," Chaewon adds.

"But . . . we don't know how to do henna. What part would we play in this?"

"The business part? Like . . . pricing, advertisement, all of that good stuff."

"Wouldn't that be unfair to you? You have to do all of the hard work?" Chaewon says, but I suspect that's not what she's worried about.

"I don't mind. No matter what we do, we're all going to have our different roles, right?"

"Right."

"That's true."

Chaewon and Jess exchange a look.

"I think we should do it," Chaewon says finally with an encouraging smile toward Jess. "It's unique. We might actually have a good shot of winning."

I grin at Chaewon like she is my favorite person in the world. Right now, she is.

"Hey," Flávia greets me with a smile during lunchtime, taking a seat opposite me. Chyna takes the empty seat beside her, looking unhappy about being seen with me. She shoots me a smile that resembles a grimace.

"You know my cousin, Chyna?" Flávia says.

"Hi, Chyna," I say, like we haven't been going to school together for the past three years. Like she hasn't single-handedly spread rumors about half the girls in this school, ruining their lives like that was something to get pleasure from.

"I wanted to show you something." Flávia extends her hands toward me on the table in front of us. For a moment, I think she's going to take my hand, until I notice it. The red wrapped around her palms, weaving up and down her skin. "You inspired me at the wedding. Well, everything there did, really. And then Chyna told me about an Asian shop in town where we could probably get a tube of henna."

Discomfort flutters around in my stomach that I don't really understand. It's how I feel when Priti comes into my room in the middle of the night and pushes into my bed and steals almost all of the duvet. Annoyance? But annoyance verging onto anger almost.

"How did you . . . ?" I begin, not sure exactly what question I should be asking.

"I just wanted to try it, you know," Flávia says, extending her palm out in front of her. She's looking at her hand and not at me anymore. She isn't even asking for my opinion, just admiring her own handiwork. "I think I did a pretty good job, what do you think?"

I frown. "I . . . I guess."

She looks at me, her smile still in place. But instead of the usual butterflies that smile sends fluttering in my stomach, the gnawing discomfort grows.

"I really thought it would be a lot more difficult than it was," she says. "But once I had that picture your sister put up on Insta . . . it was simple, really."

The gnawing grows from annoyance to all out anger. Flávia can't just *do* henna because she saw it at the wedding, and because she saw Priti's Instagram picture. How can she sit in front of me and act like there aren't a million things wrong here?

I have to stop myself from saying what I'm really feeling. What I'm really thinking. I don't even know how to form the words. And I *know* Chyna won't take it well.

"Flá is this amazing artist," Chyna chimes in. "She *always* has been. I knew she'd be amazing at making henna tattoos. Look." She inches her arms forward and there it is, inked onto her hands. The same identical design in a garishly red color. It looks odd and out of place on her white skin.

I can't explain the lump that begins to rise up my throat, or the tears prickling behind my eyes. Before I can even think, I stand. The chair makes a loud scraping noise. Flávia is looking at me with a frown on her lips, maybe looking for some sort of an explanation. But I can barely look at her. I *definitely* can't look at Chyna.

"I have to go." I dash across the room and out the door.

"Hey, Nish—" I barely hear Chaewon's voice as I walk out of the room as fast as I can, muttering *don't cry, don't cry, don't cry* to myself in my head.

"Apujan." Before I know it, before I realize what exactly is happening, Priti is pulling me into one of the bathrooms. "What's wrong, Apujan?"

"Nothing." I'm rubbing at my eyes, barely realizing

that I've begun to cry for real. And for possibly the most ridiculous reason ever. I never thought that I'd be one of those people who holed up in the school bathroom to bawl their eyes out; most of my crying is reserved for the privacy of my bedroom. And the only person allowed to see me cry is Priti.

"You're crying!" Priti exclaims. I somehow manage to put my tear-dampened hand onto her mouth to hush her.

"MM-HM-HM-HM-HMHM!" Priti's voice is muffled against my hand. I'm still crying, but silently. Each sob sends a jolt of pain through me.

Priti *hmms* something else onto my hand. I can see her glaring at me through my blurry vision. I know what comes next, but I'm too slow; she bites my hand before I can pull it away.

"I'm trying to help you!" she says.

"You're . . . being . . . very . . . loud," I say between sobs.

Priti's still glaring at me, but she leans forward and wraps her arms around me. I bury my head in her school sweater.

"You want to tell me what happened?" she asks.

"I . . . don't know."

"You don't know?"

"It doesn't make much sense."

"I'm used to that. Tell me, okay?"

"It's Flávia . . . and Chyna." I hiccup.

Priti sighs. I'm half expecting her to burst into her usual, "I told you so," routine, but she doesn't.

Instead, she says, "What did Flávia do?"

"It's not . . . imp–important." My voice is both muffled by Priti's sweater and coming out in a weak stutter. It's a wonder that Priti can understand me at all.

"Nishat." Her voice is stern in a way that reminds me of Ammu.

I pull my head away from her shoulder and rub at my puffy, red eyes. Feeling ridiculous and pathetic and horrible all at once.

"Flávia stole the henna design on your hand." My voice is barely above a whisper. "From your Instagram."

"That bitch!"

"Priti!"

"Okay, sorry." She looks sheepish, but only for a moment. "Still though, that was your first original design. I didn't put it up so she could steal it. Where did she even get henna?"

"She said she got it from some Asian shop, but Priti . . . Chyna had it too." That's what makes it all the worse. Chyna, who spent the past three years of school coming up with the most horrendous, racist rumors about me and my family that she could think of, is now sporting henna on her hands like it's nothing.

"I did tell you about her . . ." Priti says, like she's treading the waters before pulling the haughty "I told you so."

"I know." I don't need her to say "I told you so." I feel foolish enough as it is. I look at the faded red henna on my hands. Not a single person at school has even noticed that Priti and I are decked with henna. Not a single person has commented on it.

The bell rings and Priti picks up her backpack from where she dropped it on the floor when we came in.

"Are you going to be okay?" There's concern in her eyes, though I can tell that she wants to be snooty about being right. I appreciate that she can put her pride aside to comfort me.

"Yeah," I say.

But for the whole day, I can't get Flávia out of my head— and not in the way she's been on my mind lately. It's like somebody flipped a switch and changed everything. Like I can't see her the same at all anymore. No matter how much I try to stifle my anger, my upset, it keeps bubbling up inside of me. Over and over and over again.

On the way home, Priti soothes me like only a sister and best friend can.

"You're too good for her anyway," she says. "She's like . . . I don't know." She crinkles up her nose, presumably thinking of Flávia. "She seems kind of cold, doesn't she? And she's Chyna's cousin."

"You're still going to Chyna's birthday party," I point out.

"That's *different*. I'm barely even going to see her there. It's a big party, there'll be a lot of people."

"So all of that stuff you said about Chyna extending a hand and you meeting her halfway was bullshit."

Priti looks at me with narrowed eyes but doesn't deny what I've said. "Maybe it's not the most accurate portrayal of my feelings . . . I know what Chyna's like."

Everybody in our school *knows* what Chyna is like. She single-handedly runs the rumor mill. It started with the lies she spread about me, but it grew into something larger than life. Or, at least, larger than all the people in our year.

What I can never understand is why people stand by her despite the rumors she spreads. She's not exactly a credible journalist; half the things she says are outright lies, but people still accept them like decrees from the Pope himself. To the people at St. Catherine's Secondary School, Chyna Quinn basically is the Pope, and you don't go up against her.

At home that evening, I spend hours poring over blank pages, trying to perfect more original henna designs.

"You need to actually practice, you know," Priti says when she slinks into my room with her math book.

"Are you offering your hand as a canvas?"

She examines her hand with careful eyes, like it's about to reveal the answer to my question. Like it's a sentient being instead of part of her body.

"I suppose I must make this sacrifice to aid my sister." She sticks her hand out in front of her. "I offer up this hand to—"

"Oh, shut up." I can't help but smile. If there's one person who can take my mind off of miserable things, it's my little sister.

We plop down on the bed together, her with the math book propped up in front of her, and me with a stick of henna in my hand once more. It feels like we're in the summer days again, when Priti and I did this so often. Lazing about. Spending all of our days together, cooped up in this room with nobody to bother us.

I wish it could last forever.

"Do you think helping you with this competition, a.k.a. sacrificing my hand to this worthy cause, is an excuse to not have my math homework done tomorrow morning?" Priti asks.

"Definitely not."

She frowns and brings her math book closer, muttering, "I hate math."

10

After I've finished applying henna to Priti's hand, she actually looks more than a little impressed. She doesn't say anything, but I can tell from the way her eyebrows shoot way up into her hair. She purses her lips because she's usually not one to give compliments; she prefers backhanded ones, if she absolutely has to. The fact that she can't come up with anything fills me with warmth inside. I've almost forgotten about the incident at school. And Flávia.

I admire my handiwork for a second as Priti digs around, searching for her phone. It's one of my original designs—and for once I don't want to criticize it. I worked hard to perfect this design and clearly it's paid off. I spent so long applying it to Priti's hand though that most of the henna has already dried off.

It's a more intricate design than the one I attempted for the wedding. It starts with the basic mandala—a circle with flower patterns extending out of it. But then I filled in the main circle with another and another, each getting smaller and smaller. Outside of the flower petals I drew the leaves, weaving and wrapping around Priti's fingers, surrounded by dots, getting bigger and smaller and bigger and smaller.

Everything is as it should be. There are no smudges, no inconsistencies like before.

"You have to put it up on your Instagram," I say to Priti when she's finally retrieved her phone and is aiming the camera at her hand.

She lowers the phone to look at me with a frown.

"On *my* Instagram?" she asks. "It's *your* business."

"Yes, but you know what my Instagram is like." By that, I mean small and unpopular. I only have fifty followers and I think half of them are random guys who try to chat up random girls and actually have no interest in what I post.

"Because you never post on it!" I don't want to tell her that it won't matter if I post on it or not. *She's* the likable sister. The pretty, perky one. The smart one. The sociable one. Everyone loves Priti. Unlike her, I don't exude natural likeability. I might be the older sister but Priti always shines brighter than me. If the photos go up on her Insta, more people will like them. More people will *care*. And Flávia and Chyna can steal it again, a voice whispers in my head. But I brush it off. Once I'm officially competing, they wouldn't dare.

Instead of all that, I say, "You already have a lot of followers. We can capitalize on that."

She presses her lips together and says, "No."

I frown. "Seriously? I'm asking you for help with this one thing."

"One thing?" Her voice rises slightly in a way that I don't hear very often. "Hello?" She waves her hennaed hand in front of my eyes. "Did you not ask me to abandon my studies so you could practice your henna designs? Did I not spend half the morning calming you down in the bathroom at school?"

"I didn't ask you to do that."

"Well, I did it. Because that's what sisters do. But you can't just expect me to let you use my Instagram all willy-nilly because you don't have any followers and I do." She's waving her hands around wildly as she speaks. I'm afraid that she'll hit something and smudge the henna that I've carefully perfected over the last few hours. I grab her wrist just below where the henna stops.

"Careful."

She rolls her eyes.

"This is important to me, you know." My voice is quieter than I mean it to be. It fills the room's silence in a way I didn't expect it to. It softens Priti's eyes.

"I know." She picks up her phone again. I'm hopeful—even though we've just had an argument about it. "And my Instagram is important to *me*."

I frown. I know that Priti has spent time cultivating her Instagram page. Her couple thousand followers are her weird pride and joy. I don't understand it, really, but I've never had the natural charm Priti does. I've also never had that need to be *liked*.

"You can't use my Instagram for this. But . . . I can help you out with yours. You could start a new one for this whole business you're going to have. You could share it with Chaewon and Jess. That'll be better. More professional," Priti adds after a moment of silence.

It's a compromise I'm willing to make, so I nod.

"You'll have to come up with a name, though," she says. She's already typing away on her phone.

"*Who* are you texting?" I make a swipe for her phone. She extends it out of reach.

"Your business partners, Chaewon and Jess, *of course*," she says like it's the most obvious thing in the world.

"Of course? How do you even have their phone numbers?" Even though Chaewon, Jess, and I have been friends for the past few years, we aren't exactly joined at the hips. It's strange to think of my little sister having a texting relationship with them.

"We have a group chat. We need a way to vent about

you," Priti says, still holding her phone away from me.

"Priti!" I exclaim.

She faces her phone toward me. "You sent them a text through my phone that one time. I'm just asking them if it's okay for me to set up an Instagram account for you guys. We don't *really* talk about you."

For a moment there, I really feared that they did.

"What did they say?" I ask, instead of admitting my own naiveté.

"Nothing, they're not texting back. Maybe we should wait a while to set this up?"

I know waiting and asking them would be the right thing to do, but I also know that the sooner we can start getting publicity for this, the better.

"Let's set up a preliminary name. Then we can change it, right?"

"Right," Priti agrees. "Nishat's Mehndi?"

I wrinkle up my nose. "That's a little cheesy, isn't it? And it's not just mine."

"But it's a *preliminary* name. And it's cute, if a little cheesy."

I think about it for a second. It does say exactly what it is; who is applying the henna. So I say yes and Priti does her magic and sets up the account.

Afterwards, she turns on all the lights in her room and holds her henna-decked hand out for me.

"*You've* got to take the photo if we're using my hand," she says, nodding at her phone.

"But . . . I'm no good at taking photos," I remind her. "Remember that time we ran into Niall Horan and all I managed to do was take a blurry photo where you can barely make him out?"

"Don't remind me . . . " She held a grudge over that for ages. Anybody would have done the same. But that's how bad I am at taking photos—even the thought of proving to everyone that we had randomly bumped into Niall Horan didn't make me any better. Or maybe it made me worse.

I pick up the phone and click a few quick photos. When I show them to Priti, she frowns.

"I think you have like tone deafness but for photography," she says. "Picture blindness."

"Wouldn't that just be blindness?"

"Picture askew-ness?"

"Okay, I have picture askew-ness." I smile and thrust the phone out for her. "Your turn?"

She shakes her head. "You have to do it if we're going to get a decent picture." That feels like a total paradox. "Look, just hold it straight and . . . try not to move."

It's easier said than done. I try to take a few more pictures. They don't come out perfect, but Priti smiles when she sees them this time.

"I can work with this." She clicks out of the camera and

into the Instagram app. A few minutes later, she shows me the finished product. She's changed the lighting so it looks brighter. The design stands out against everything else, stark and intricate and . . . dare I say it, kind of beautiful.

I try to tell myself that pride is a sin, but I can't help the glowing feeling growing inside of me. I should be able to feel proud once in a while, right? Is that not something you earn after a whole lifetime of insecurity and secrets?

"Post it." I watch as she hits the button and turns to give me a wide grin.

"I guess we're open for business."

I feel a flutter in the pit of my stomach. I don't know if it's fear or excitement, good or bad, but I find myself not caring for the first time ever.

I wake up the next morning with all the fluttery feelings gone from my stomach. Instead, they're replaced by a hole; it's a type of panic I haven't felt in a long time. My mind conjures the worst-case scenarios: nobody liked our Instagram post, or they all commented on how horrible my designs are.

"Have you checked your Instagram yet?" Priti asks when I come down for breakfast. Ammu eyes us both with some disdain.

"What is this Instagram tinstagram?" she asks with narrowed eyes. The only thing Ammu knows about social media is checking her Facebook for the latest photos from weddings and dawats and who knows what else. Mostly she likes to judge what everyone is wearing, even though she always tells us that we shouldn't judge people.

"It's just social media." Priti rolls her eyes, even though Ammu definitely won't know what that is. She narrows her eyes further, like she's trying to process Priti's words but it's taking her a while to get there.

"You don't need social media tedia." There's a frown on her lips. "Priti, you should be studying for your exams." She turns her glare to me, like I'm responsible for Priti's lack of focus—which, I guess I am—and says, "Don't distract your sister. She needs to study."

It's the most that Ammu has said to me since I came out to her a few weeks ago, and it sends a jolt of pain through me that I hadn't expected. I guess you never really get used to your parents treating you like you're worth nothing.

"I know," I say, staring down at my shoes at the same time that Priti exclaims, "I can study and do other things at the same time!" Priti's voice drowns out mine, and I don't think Ammu hears me at all. She doesn't say anything else, turning away instead.

"So, did you?" Priti whispers to me as we're heading out the door.

"Huh?" I'm still thinking about the fact that Ammu barely looked at me all through breakfast, like she couldn't stand to. What *am* I to her now? A ghost that occupies her house?

"Your Instagram?" That snaps me out of my thoughts. "Have you checked it?"

"Not yet." There's a hole in my stomach, growing bigger and bigger with every passing second. "Have you? Is it bad? Don't tell me."

Priti pulls out her phone as soon as we've boarded the bus and made it through the throngs of people and into a corner. She thrusts the screen in front of my face.

523 likes. 97 comments.

"It's not quite viral. But it's proven to be pretty popular among the people from school."

"We don't even have five hundred people at school." Clearly the wrong thing to say because Priti groans.

"Of course we have five hundred people at school," she says. "I can't believe how bad you are at math."

I scroll through the comments. Each of them makes my heart beat faster and faster.

Omg, when are you starting up?

How much will it cost for one tattoo?

What other designs do you have?

So excited!

So pretty!

Love it!!!

I feel elated. Or . . . I feel like I *should* feel elated. This is what I *wanted*. I've been anticipating this moment since Priti opened up the Instagram account last night. But with Ammu's stony silence in the back of my mind, all I can feel is that hole in my heart getting bigger and bigger. I keep scrolling through the comments, reading them over and over and over again, hoping that they'll somehow fill it.

My fingers brush against the top of the screen and before I know it I'm on Priti's Instagram feed. And then I see a photo that makes my heart stop.

Priti snatches the phone out of my hand before I can stare for too long. She knows me too well. She must have recognized the look on my face.

"Holy shit." Her voice is low, but still one of the ladies beside us shoots her a glare that she doesn't even notice. "I can't believe her."

Priti puts her hand on my shoulder, a calming presence that I can barely feel for once. "Apujan," she says. "It's not a big deal. She doesn't even have as many likes as you."

"It's nicer. So much nicer."

"That's just . . . she's used to it, you know. She's probably been taking pictures of her art for ages. She has hundreds of posts. She has a bigger following than you." Priti's voice is gentle and soothing but it doesn't make me feel better in the slightest. Whatever happiness I'd talked myself into feeling is gone. Disappeared into thin air.

"She's going to do better than me," I say. "She already has a customer base and I have nothing."

"It's not a competition," Priti says.

"That's literally exactly what it is! A competition!"

"Yes, but—"

"And she's going to win."

"But is winning really that important?"

I know Priti agrees with me. There's no way I'm going to beat Flávia. It doesn't matter that I have authenticity on my side.

By the time we make it into school, I've already burned Flávia's photo into my head. I can't stop seeing it—hands linked together, their henna weaving together like webs. Hand to hand to hand. In a circle. The patterns sharp. All edges. So different from my mandala full of circles and flowers and leaves.

I jostle open my locker, feeling emptiness growing inside of me, wider and wider with every minute. But I'm not going to break down—not today.

I catch sight of Flávia out of the corner of my eye. She has her phone open, and I can see the photo splashed colorfully across her screen. There are people gathered around her. Their faces are wide with appreciation and glee. There's Chyna, and all her friends. I wonder if it's their hands in the photo, or if it's other people's. The hands in the photo are all pale, flushed a light pink—probably from the chill that's set in.

"When will you get started for real?" I hear Chyna asking.

Flávia smiles. "As soon as I get my supplies. I need to make a trip to the Asian shop in town."

The Asian shop in town. Like there aren't multiple, each selling different brands. Some better, some worse. Glitter henna. White henna. Regular henna paste.

Suddenly, it's like there's a light bulb illuminated in my head.

That's my advantage. I know henna. Even in the areas I don't, I know the people who do. There's no way Flávia is going to take advantage of my culture because of Chyna's popularity, because she has white friends who'll make her henna look chic and adaptable to Western culture.

I might not be able to get Ammu to look me in the eye anymore, but I *am* going to beat Flávia's henna business. Come hell or high water.

11

By the time the weekend rolls around, I have a battle plan at the ready. And I haven't shared it with anyone—not even Priti.

Saturday afternoon I stroll into the house with an armful of henna tubes, and Priti looks at me with raised eyebrows.

"Isn't this a little . . . ambitious?" she asks.

I shrug. "Raj Uncle gave me a discount."

"Probably because you bought up the entire shop." She pauses, looks at the smile stretched across my lips, and says, "Why did you go to Raj Uncle's shop?"

"Well, I heard Flávia speaking to some of her friends last week. I figure Raj Uncle's shop is the only one she knows."

"So you decided to buy up *all* of his henna?" Priti's voice rises by an octave. She rubs the bridge of her nose, the same way that Abbu does when he's annoyed but doesn't want to show it by shouting at us. "You know that's not going to work, right? He's just going to place another order for more henna. It's really not that difficult."

"I know. I'm not that thick. But it is going to slow things down for her, and by the time she's figured out that it's going to take her at least a few days—if not weeks—to get the henna tubes she needs, I'll hopefully have already taken some of her customers."

Priti smiles. "Seems like you've planned this out."

"In depth."

"Well . . . Sunny Apu is here."

I haven't seen Sunny Apu since her wedding a few weeks ago, even though over the summer we saw each other on an almost daily basis. Bengalis are like moths to a flame during weddings; and if they're not all gathered together, spending all of their time talking and planning and dancing and singing, does a wedding even take place?

"What's she doing here?" I peer into the sitting room only to find it deserted.

"She's in your room . . . " Priti trails off. She doesn't meet my eyes, tracing the groves of wood on the floor with her toe instead.

"Priti, what's going on?"

"She said she wants to talk to you." Priti shrugs, like she has no idea what's happening. I know that something else is at play, something that Priti isn't telling me, but with so many henna tubes weighing me down and Sunny Apu waiting up in my room, I'm not really in the mood to try and wheedle it out of her.

I push past her and up the stairs, henna tubes jiggling in my arms like jelly. When I push open the door of my room with my toe, Sunny Apu is inspecting my bookshelf. She stands up straight as soon as I appear, a practiced smile pasted on her lips.

"Nishat! Assalam Alaikum."

"Walaikum Salam . . . " I mumble, tossing the henna tubes on my bed.

"That's a lot of henna."

"I'm running a business," I say, as if that's an explanation. I know she wants more from the way she arches her eyebrows, but I want to know why the hell she's here, staring at my bookshelf and smiling at me like I'm a stranger and not someone who stood by her side as she got married.

She gently sits down on my bed, moving a henna tube aside. "Come, sit."

I frown, because it's my room and my bed and *my* right to offer *her* a seat, but she's come in here and asserted herself like she's in charge. But I do as she says, sitting down next to her. There's enough space between us to fill an ocean.

"How's school?" Her voice is irritatingly chirpy.

"Fine."

"What classes are you taking?"

"Sunny Apu . . . why are you here?"

She sighs. The bed creaks with the weight of it.

"Khala and Khalu spoke to me." Ah. So that's what this is about. I'd been wondering if we would ever talk about it straight out; I guess sending in a "relation" who's not really a relation at all is as straightforward as they're willing to get. This is a family matter—*I* am a family matter—but one for them to discuss with the family, not with me.

"I don't want to—"

"You have to hear me out, Nishat," she interrupts before I can say anything else. "Khala and Khalu are really worried about you. Even Amma and Abba are worried. They've been so upset . . . and they didn't even want to tell us, really, but it's good they shared so that we can *help* you."

"I don't *need*—"

"You have a problem Nishat, you just don't realize it. You've seen this on TV and in films, and you've read about it in your books and—"

"Is that what you were doing? Looking through my books to see if I have any lesbian ones in my collection?" I turn to her with narrowed eyes. She flinches at the word *lesbian*, like it's something disgusting instead of just a part of who I am.

"You're young, you're confused."

I shake my head, even though she's turned away from me and can't see it.

"I'm not confused." If I was, I would have never put myself through this scrutiny and judgement. This silence.

"Girls like you aren't . . . aren't . . . " She trails off like the word lesbian is too much for her to handle. Like her lips can't shape it.

"They are. I am."

"You're *Muslim*."

I snort. "That's not how it works, Sunny Apu."

"Muslims aren't gay," she whispers, like this is a hard and fast rule. She's still turned away from me, looking out the window like the outside world will have some solution to my lesbian problem. I would laugh if this weren't such a ridiculous claim. Because *of course* Muslims can be gay. How can anyone even think otherwise? The two aren't mutually exclusive. I am living, breathing proof.

"Sunny Apu, you don't even pray namaz," I say instead, because it seems like a more palpable bridge to build. "When was the last time you even went to the mosque? Or just prayed?"

She frowns, like she's thinking really hard about this. If you have to think *that* hard about the last time you prayed to Allah, I don't think you get to hate gay people on the basis of God.

"That's not important," she says finally. "What's important is that this . . . this is a sickness and—" I shoot up from the bed, feeling the blood rush to my head so fast that I stumble.

"I think you should leave."

"But—"

"Please leave." I want to say more. To scream, shout. Tell her that everything—every single thing—she has to say about my sexuality is hypocritical. Judgmental lies based on nothing. That she has no business coming to my room and telling me that I have a sickness. But I don't. The words clog up my throat and I realize that they wouldn't make a difference anyway.

I just want it to stop.

She stands up too and turns her whole body toward me. She has only a few inches on me but it feels like she's towering over me. I realize this is the first time she's looked at me—like *actually* looked at me—since I walked into this room. I wait for her to say something more but she doesn't. Instead, she shakes her head and slips out the door. I can hear the sound of her footsteps descending the stairs, and then Ammu's murmurs.

I close my door before I can decipher what they have to say to each other.

I'm too tired to hear them discuss me. I'm too tired to hear them judge me.

I'm too tired.

An entire hour has passed by the time Priti barges into my room. It's strange, because if things were the other way around I would already be in Priti's room, asking her to fill me in on all of the details. Instead, I've just been sitting alone in my bed, going over henna designs and stewing in my own misery.

When I look up at her though, I realize why she is only entering my room now. She has her hair up in a bun, prepared to get ready for tonight's party, and a nervous smile on her lips.

"Do you want to talk about it?" she asks, but I already know that *she* doesn't really want to talk about it. She's already in the headspace of the party and hanging out with Ali.

I shrug. "I'm okay."

"Sure?"

I wonder how much of Ammu and Sunny Apu's conversation she heard; she's an expert eavesdropper, very light on her feet. But if she *did* hear their conversation, she doesn't say anything about it.

"Well, do you want to come with me to Chyna's birthday party tonight?" she asks after a moment of silence. The smile on her face has disappeared and she's staring intently at the carpet.

Chyna's birthday party is the last place I want to go. And it's the last place I want Priti to go as well.

"I thought you were going with Ali?"

"I am."

"So what do you need me for?"

She shrugs. "I just thought . . . it'll be better than you hanging around here all evening by yourself."

"I have things to do, you know," I say, even though that's a lie. I'm probably going to spend the night watching something cheesy on Netflix, trying not to think about the fact that nobody in my family can look me in the eye anymore.

"This will be fun!" She's smiling again but there's something in her eyes, her tone, that tells me maybe she's not as invested in this party as she would have me believe. Maybe this is *Priti* asking for a helping hand. If she goes to the party with only Ali as company, will she be safe? What if Chyna decides it's the perfect time to say more horrible things? At least in school Priti and I always have each other. We might not be in the same year, but we're always within reach, and we always have each other's backs.

"Okay." I sigh.

12

I KNOW I'M NOT GOING TO LIKE THIS PARTY EVEN BEFORE we step inside. There's music blasting so loud that I can feel the walls and the ground shaking, and even through that I can hear laughter and screaming.

Priti rings the bell and we stand on the doorstep, waiting. I wonder if it's in vain. I mean, how could anybody have heard the bell through this blaring music? Priti is shivering beside me from the cold air. She's wearing a thin, pink dress that doesn't even reach her knees. I smile, smug that I decided to dress more casually in jeans and a black sweater.

Surprisingly, after we ring the bell for the second time, an excited Chyna opens the door. A shadow passes over her face when she sees us, but she quickly reverts back to being upbeat.

"Hey!" Her eyes shift from Priti to me. "You . . . brought your sister."

"Is that . . . okay?" Priti asks. As if there's anything to be said about it now when I'm already on her doorstep. Not that I would put it past Chyna to suggest leaving me out in the cold.

But she doesn't. She smiles. Her pretty red lips look like blood against her pale skin.

"Of course. *Nesha*, right?" She asks it like she hasn't spent the last three years spreading racist rumors about me around the school. Like we weren't friends once.

"Nishat." I give her a smile of my own, but it probably doesn't look very friendly.

"Come on in." She opens the door wider and allows the two of us to step inside.

"Happy birthday!" Priti says brightly once Chyna has closed the door behind her. She thrusts a pretty floral bag at Chyna and throws her arms around her neck. It's an awkward, uncomfortable hug; even before Chyna and Priti disentangle from each other I wonder what exactly Priti was thinking.

Chyna smiles. "Thanks. I think Ali is around here somewhere. The kitchen, maybe."

"Great, I'm going to go . . . find her." Priti gives me a look, her eyebrows raised asking if I'm joining her as she turns around. I'm about to follow but Chyna says, "nice sweater," and I stop.

I look down at my plain black sweater and smile.

"Thanks." I'm not sure if she's being serious or mocking.

"I saw your new Instagram account. About your henna business?"

I sigh.

"You're not going to do better than us, you know. Flávia is the best artist in our entire school. You really think you can beat her? You don't even take art as a subject anymore."

I dropped the subject after First Year, opting for Home Economics and Business instead. Art, at least the form of it we learned in school, was definitely not my forte. But henna isn't a form of art we learned in school. It's something I've been brought up with, and I'm not about to back down just because Chyna thinks she and Flávia have some form of claim over it.

"We'll see," I say with the politest smile I can muster.

Chyna smiles back before sauntering off toward one of the rooms with music blasting from it, leaving me alone in the empty hallway. I take a deep breath and lean back against the off-white wall.

Chyna's house is not like I imagined it. It's sparse and clean and empty, or at least this part of it is. It barely looks lived in. It's so vastly different from our house, which is brimming with things: knick-knacks and photos, old toys that Priti and I used to play with years ago but are too sentimental to throw out, and the things we always pick up when we go to Bangladesh—a silver rickshaw, a wooden baby taxi, stitched dolls of brides and grooms, a dhol, a latim. So many things sprawling and spreading everywhere.

I take another deep breath and walk toward the door Priti disappeared through. The brightly lit kitchen is already filled with people chatting and eating and drinking. A few of them look up as I enter. I recognize most of them from school, but not all of them. They don't seem bothered by the presence of someone new. Priti and Ali are in the corner, their heads bowed together.

I hesitate for a moment, wondering if I should interrupt whatever conversation they're in the middle of. Then I remember that if it wasn't for Priti, I would be home in bed right now, wearing my PJs and binge-watching a show on Netflix. I march right over.

"Hey!"

They break apart and turn to me, Ali with a frown on her lips and Priti looking sheepish.

"Hey Nishat." Ali's pale red hair, which is usually straight, is falling in curls around her face. It looks almost exactly like Priti's. I wonder if they planned this, or if they're so close that these things simply happen. Like they have some kind of telepathy going on.

"Most of your classmates are in the sitting room, I think?" Ali says.

I know a brush off when I hear one, but I still glance at Priti, wondering if she'll ask me to stay. After all, she asked me to come. But she says nothing. She doesn't even look at me; she just stares at the ground. At her pretty pink shoes and the cream-colored tiles.

"I guess I'll head over there, then," I mumble, turning away. I feel a hole opening up inside me. I wouldn't have come to this party if I'd known this was how things were going to go.

I guess I shouldn't be totally surprised though. Ali and Priti might be best friends, but Ali's never been my biggest fan. I always chalked it up to jealousy; Priti and I are close, obviously, and in the teen scheme of things—where you need that one BFF, the one you share half a heart necklace with—I'm Ali's competition. If I'm honest, maybe I'm a little jealous of Ali too.

Slipping away, I peek through a crack in the door of the sitting room. It's much fuller than the kitchen. I recognize more girls from school, but there are still so many who aren't familiar to me; they must be from other schools, I'm guessing. And then there are all the boys, with pimples all over their cheeks and foreheads and AXE body spray so strong that my nostrils are overpowered from outside the room.

I spot Flávia and Chyna in a corner with a group of boys.

Flávia is looking at one tall guy with messy blonde hair with particular interest. She has an arm on his shoulder and is listening to him speak intently, though how she can hear him over the persistent *thump thump thump* of the music is beyond me.

I can't help it; I feel my stomach drop even though my little crush on Flávia is supposed to have disappeared. I guess it's not that simple to get over someone. I still have a thing for Taylor Swift, after all—even though I hate all of her white feminism nonsense.

Maybe this is good for me. Flávia is not only okay with stealing my henna ideas, she's also not interested in me. She's interested in a gangly, pimply lad who is definitely *not* in her league. I guess I shouldn't judge, because I'm not in her league either.

I close the door and edge away from the sitting room, trying to get the image of Flávia and that guy out of my head. Even though they weren't doing anything, there was definitely some kind of attraction. I could see it in the way she was looking at him. The way she was touching him. The way *he* was looking at *her*. God, when did I become this girl? Obsessing over someone I never had a shot with anyway?

I sit down at the bottom of the stairs, halfway between the kitchen and the sitting room, and slip my phone out of my pocket.

There is still only the single image on my business

Instagram. It hasn't racked up many more likes since that first day—unlike Flávia's photos. She's been posting new ones on the daily, all pictures of Chyna and her friends' hands with henna designs on them. Some pictures show the dark brown henna paste, some the aftermath, when it's dried to a dark red color.

I've been trying to feel optimistic every time she posts a photo. The more henna she uses up on her friends, the less she'll have for customers. And I know it will take Raj Uncle at least a little while to get a new shipment in.

I send a quick text to my group chat with Chaewon and Jess. *This is the worst party ever.* But of course, all three of us knew it would be. What did I expect?

They don't respond, probably too busy living their lives and actually enjoying themselves.

I consider leaving the party as I scroll through my Instagram feed, barely paying attention to the pictures. Ammu and Abbu said they would swing by to pick us up later, but I'm sure I can just wander around outside until that time comes. We're in the middle of Dún Laoghaire, one of the poshest neighborhoods in Dublin. I doubt I'll be in any danger if I wander by myself for a while.

I'm pulling out my phone to text Priti about leaving, even though I'm still angry with her for bringing me here and abandoning me, when the sitting room door swings open. The loud blare of music that had been drowned out by the closed door spills out again. Along with Flávia.

I freeze, like that will somehow make me vanish. I'm far enough away that I think she'll miss me, especially in the dimness of the hallway and with me wearing clothes that don't exactly make me stand out. But she spots me almost instantly.

I try to keep my heart from leaping out of my chest at the sight of her face breaking out into a grin, and the way her curls bounce wildly as she hurries over and sits down right next to me on the narrow staircase. I'm too aware of the fact that our arms are pressed together and our legs are touching; I'm so distracted that I must miss the first time she says "hey."

"Nishat?"

"H-hi." I mumble, looking toward the door and not her. This is just infatuation. It's nothing. It means nothing.

"I saw you open the door. How come you didn't come in?"

I shrug. "There are a lot of people in there."

"Well, duh. It's a party."

When I don't reply, she heaves a sigh.

"It's not exactly your type of party, then?"

"I guess not."

"So what *is* your type of party?"

I think about it for a moment. I'm not sure if I've ever been to my type of party, and really I'm not sure if parties are my thing at all. But if I was going to throw a party there would be real Desi food everywhere. There would be samosas and fuchka and shingara and dal puri and kebabs.

"There would be better food at my type of party," I say.

She laughs. It's a small and jittery laugh, but still feels too loud in the empty, dimly lit hallway.

"You're right. The food here is awful. Though I think there's talk of pizza, and obviously some birthday cake. There's even some *brigadeiro* that I made special for today." She takes a sip from the plastic cup she's nursing in her hands.

"*Brigadeiro?*"

She nods. "It's a Brazilian dessert. You *have* to try it. We're going to have it after we cut the cake."

"I'm not sure I'll last that long."

"You're thinking about leaving already?" Her eyebrows shoot up. From where I'm sitting—too close to her—I can make out the dark browns of her eyes and the freckles that are almost hidden away.

"I don't really know a lot of people here."

"So it's like me at that wedding." She smiles. "You kept me company there, I can keep you company here, if you want." She bumps her knee to mine and it sends a jolt of electricity through me.

"That's okay . . . thanks." My voice must come out drier than I intend it to, because she frowns.

"Is something wrong?" she asks.

I don't mean to say it, really, but when she asks that question it's like she opens the floodgates.

"Yes. You're starting your own henna business for class."

Surprisingly, she smiles.

"What, you're afraid of a little friendly competition?"

"No." It comes out more defensive than I mean it to. "But . . . it was my idea. It's my culture. It's my thing."

"It's a type of art—that can't be a person's thing." She furrows her eyebrows together like this conversation is too much for her to fathom.

"It's not just a type of art. It's a part of my culture. Just because you went to one wedding that was South Asian, where you didn't even know anyone, by the way, doesn't mean you just get to do henna now."

"It's art!" Her voice has risen significantly. "I'm sure watercolor was also part of some particular culture once, but now we all do it. That's what art is. It doesn't have arbitrary boundaries."

"That's not how it works. It's not the same thing."

"Is this why you ran off the other day when I showed you my henna tattoo? Because you were annoyed I had, what, borrowed from your culture? You were offended?" She sounds offended at the idea of me being offended.

"Yes!" I say. "I mean . . . no. I was upset because . . . henna is important to me."

"How important can it be? You said you only started trying it for the wedding!"

"That's just something I said."

Flávia shakes her head. "Look, I get that you're defensive and don't want to compete and all, but . . . this is how art works. I think you don't really get it because you're not an artist."

I have a million thoughts screaming in my head. Nasty thoughts that I have to swallow down because I know I'll regret voicing them.

I silently stand instead.

"I better go." I half hope Flávia will stop me as I head toward the door, already texting Priti about leaving the party. But she doesn't. A moment later, I open the front door and step outside into the cold air.

13

FLÁVIA'S WORDS RUN THROUGH MY HEAD FOR THE WHOLE night as I toss and turn. I'm still curled up in bed the next morning, seething with anger about all of the things Flávia said, when Priti barges into my room.

"Thanks for leaving the party in a huff yesterday," she says with a glare. "Everybody was making fun of you after you left. Somebody said that it was because you'd never seen a boy before so you freaked out."

"Oh, hilarious. The Muslim girl has never seen a boy. We're not even properly practicing. That's not even good racism."

"Racism is never good."

"Maybe not good but at least it could be geographically and culturally accurate!"

Priti slips under the covers, curling up right next to me.

"Was it that bad?" I ask.

"It could have been better," Priti mumbles against my shoulder. "They were saying all of these things about you and asking me ridiculous questions. Like had you really never seen a boy? Is it illegal? Are we going to be married off when we turn eighteen? Did we have to sneak out to even go to the party?"

"Did Ali stand up for you? She was there, right?"

"She was too busy being glued to her boyfriend's face," Priti says in a small voice. Guilt hits me like a punch in the gut. How could I have just left my sister there to deal with everything and everyone? Just because Flávia made me upset, I abandoned her.

"Priti . . ."

She shrugs, but she's blinking her eyes a little too rapidly. I wrap my arm around her, and she presses her face into my shoulder harder. I try to ignore the feeling of dampness against my pajama top, and the sound of her whimpering sniffle.

"It's . . . not . . . a big deal," she says through choking sobs. Of course it's a big deal though. How did I miss this, when I'm her older sister? When I'm supposed to always protect her? I've been so caught up with my own drama . . .

"It's just because it's her first boyfriend." I try to reassure her even though I have no experience in this department. "She'll come around. *You're* her best friend.

That's way more important than some boy."

She finally pulls away from me and begins to rub at her eyes.

"It's fine. Really. I'm just . . . getting used to it." I feel like there's more to it, something she's not telling me. But she gives me a watery smile and says, "So why did you leave? I mean, I know you're a lesbian so boys aren't exactly your cup of tea, but I'm pretty sure you don't flee at the sight of one."

I sigh. Even though most of my anger has subsided now that Priti is here, I still feel it simmering inside me.

"I spoke to Flávia."

"Uh-oh."

"She was just . . . I just . . . I tried to explain to her, you know? About the whole henna thing? But she just didn't get it. And she was so . . . condescending about it as well."

"What did she say?"

"Something about how art doesn't have any arbitrary boundaries, so, because henna is art, she can do whatever she wants. She said that I'm just afraid of competing with her and—hey! She was there when they were saying all of that stuff about me, right? She *knew* why I left."

But Priti shakes her head. "I think she left around the same time you did. Chyna was kind of mad about it."

"Maybe we shouldn't go to parties anymore," I suggest. "We're not the best at them."

Priti scoffs. "We're great at parties. Other people are bad at them. *They're* the problem."

"Yeah, I guess that's true. We're pretty great."

"We're fantastic." Priti agrees with a smile.

The rest of Saturday passes by without incident. Priti spends a lot of time holed up in her room, studying for an upcoming math test. I want to talk to her more about what happened with Ali, but I'm afraid of making her upset again. Priti is definitely not someone who is prone to crying, so seeing her like that this morning has me shaken.

I spend a lot of time taking test photos of henna designs to put up on my Instagram page. I wonder if it'll get the same pull as Flávia's if I do a henna design on Jess and put *that* up on my page. Jess and Chaewon haven't said much about the Instagram page, but I'm sure I can convince Jess to hand model for pictures.

Ms. Montgomery wants to see our business plans on Monday to help us get started as soon as possible so I'm feeling extra nervous. I need everything to be perfect.

On Sunday morning Priti knocks on my door, which is a surprise in and of itself. Priti and I are not the type of sisters who knock on each other's doors and respect each other's privacy. We barge into each other's rooms (and lives) without a second thought.

"Ammu wants to talk to you," she says, cracking the door open and peeking through.

"She wants to talk . . . to me?"

"To you. That's what I said."

"To me? Are you sure?"

"She said, 'Can you tell Nishat to come over?'" Priti's trying to be all light-hearted and charming, but I can see from the way her eyes roam around the room, never landing on me, that she's just as nervous as I am. Ammu and I have barely spoken since I came out to her. She hasn't even looked me in the eye since that fateful day. What could she want with me now?

"Did she say what she wanted to talk about?" My mind is running through a million worst-case scenarios. My palms are sweaty, my heart is as fast as a hummingbird's, and I'm pretty sure I'm shaking. What if this is it? The end? What if they're done skirting around the topic and now they want to do something drastic? I can't stop thinking about all of the gay people thrown out of their homes.

Priti shakes her head, her eyes finally landing on me. She gulps and it makes me gulp.

"She just said to call you. She's in her room. Do you . . . do you want me to come?"

I mumble, "no," even though I want to say yes, yes, a thousand times yes. But if Ammu *does* want to do something drastic, I don't want Priti to sit there and take it all in.

"I'll be okay." I try to make my voice as reassuring as

I can, but it still wavers. Pushing past Priti, I walk toward Ammu and Abbu's room. It feels like the longest walk ever, even though the corridor takes only a few steps to cross. I actually begin to *pray* during the walk. Which is probably hypocritical, but I don't care. I keep thinking, *Ya Allah, if you are there please please please please* please *let my parents still love me.*

"Ummm . . . " I poke my head through the door. Ammu is sitting on her bed and there's a half-knitted scarf in front of her that she's slowly stitching together. She looks up at me for only a moment before bowing her head again. Like she can't look at me for too long.

She reaches out her hand and pats the empty space beside her. "Come, sit."

My heart is hammering so loudly that I'm surprised Ammu can't hear it, that it hasn't somehow burst out of my chest. I gingerly walk to the bed and sit down, peering at her hunched form. It's the closest I've been to her since that day at the breakfast table. She's just had a shower— I can tell because her hair is still slightly damp and she smells like coconut oil.

"Did I ever tell you the story of how me and your Abbu met?" she asks. This is the last thing I expected her to ask. I'm so stunned that I only keep staring at her. I want to say something. Words! Where are my words? My tongue is dry and my mind has gone blank.

Ammu doesn't need me to prompt her, though. With the knitting needles in her hands weaving up and down on the scarf, she heaves a sigh and starts speaking again.

"It was summer and I was studying at university. I had traveled up to Dhaka to study, and I was living with your Aarti Khala and Najib Khalu. Your Nanu used to worry about me all the time. She still lived in our house in the village back then, and your Nana was still alive. They would call every day, even if it was just for five minutes, to check up on *me* specifically. They were worried that, well . . . what happened would happen. That I would meet someone, fall in love, shame the family." She pauses and sits up straight.

For a moment I think she'll look at me, finally.

I *will* her to look at me, but she doesn't.

"It wasn't some big romance or anything," she continues. "Your Abbu and I shared a class together, so we started talking, even though both of us knew we weren't supposed to. I wanted to tell your Aarti Khala about it, but I didn't think she would have understood at the time. I think she would have tried to talk me out of it, and I probably would have let her talk me out of it. So we used to sneak around, knowing that what we were doing was wrong. That your Nana and Nanu would be horrified to know that I had been defying the request they made of me—*to not* have a romance, not fall in love."

"But why?" I croak out. Ammu's eyes snap to mine.

Only for a moment, and then she's back to looking at her blue and white wool scarf. I wonder who it's for, if it's for anyone at all or just something to do while she's recounting this tale.

"Because there's shame in it, Nishat. I didn't realize it then, everything that your Nana and Nanu had to go through because of *my* mistake. How they had to listen to people talk about me and what I had done. I brought shame on them. That's something that lives with you forever, that follows you around no matter where you go."

"So you regret it?" I always thought Ammu and Abbu were proud for defying tradition, not ashamed of it. Can you be both proud and ashamed at the same time?

Ammu shakes her head. "Regret isn't the right word."

"The right word is . . . ashamed?"

"For doing that to your grandparents, yes. For tainting our family, yes. Shame runs deep in our lives, Nishat. It can taint you forever. Do you know what people say about us living here? That we moved to a country where people are immoral, where the gays are allowed to marry. Where a gay is the president and—"

"He's the prime minister," I mumble, even though that is definitely not the point and I feel like Ammu is physically stabbing me in the heart with a knife of her own making.

"That's a choice we've made. We're living with it. Now, you've made a choice—"

"It's not a—"

"And when people find out, that shame is going to be on *us*, Nishat." She's finally looking at me, *pleading* with me. "Your Abbu and I need you to make a different choice."

I swallow down my words about how none of this is a choice. That I can't change the way that I feel. How do I make her see that? How can she not see that?

"Nishat," she says, before I can say anything else. She puts aside the half-knit scarf and needles, and wraps her arms around me. This is the first time my mother has touched me in weeks and I flinch even though I don't want to. Either she doesn't notice my reaction, or she doesn't care, because she lays my head down on her shoulder. "Your Abbu and I love you." That's all I've wanted to hear since I told them the truth. That's all I've ever wanted to hear from them. But not like this. "But that means you have to make the *choice* to not be . . . this."

This, meaning a lesbian.

This, meaning the person that I am.

The choice she wants me to make isn't between being gay and straight, it's between them and me. Who do I choose?

I pull away from her, biting down the tears rising through me like a tidal wave. This time, I'm the one who can't look her in the eye. If I do, I think I'll break.

"Can I go?" I manage to ask.

"Think about it, Nishat."

"Can I—" I'm already standing up, but Ammu grabs hold of my hand, jerking me back.

"Have you . . . " She takes a deep breath. "You haven't . . . with a girl . . . "

I shake my head frantically while pulling her fingers off of mine. Though at this stage, I'll say anything just to get away.

"Good," she says. "*Good.*" That's the word that follows me out of her bedroom and into mine.

Priti is sitting on my bed, scrolling through her phone. Her head snaps up the moment I enter, but I don't have the energy or the words to talk to her. I just collapse on the bed and let the waves of misery crash through me.

Priti must lay down next to me, because next thing I know, her arm is wrapped around me. The two of us lie there on my bed for what feels like hours, me with tears dripping down my cheek and nose and chin, her rubbing soothing circles into my back.

When my tears finally run dry, Priti turns to face me with a frown on her lips.

"Can I ask you something, Apujan?"

"About what Ammu said?"

"No . . . " She trails off. "About . . . you. Why did you . . . I mean . . . what made you tell them? You could have kept it a secret, right? It wouldn't have made a difference. It's not like you're with someone."

I don't know where to begin or how to explain it. I'm not sure if I really understand it myself. But I'm also not sure if I regret it, after everything.

"It was because of Sunny Apu's wedding."

"Because . . . ?"

"Because of the way they looked. Happy. Like . . . you know, they couldn't wait until that was you and me. Like . . . I don't know, like they had these dreams for us. And I knew that I couldn't give them that. I know that. I just . . . I'd rather they knew. Sooner, rather than later."

"If you give them time . . . " Priti starts again. The same old mantra. But I'm not sure if time is what they need. If time will make any difference at all.

"At least they have you," I say. "They get to be proud of you. You bring home the good grades and one day you'll marry a guy that they approve of."

"How do you know they'll approve of him?"

"Because he'll be a guy, at least."

She smiles at that. "He could be an *awful* guy."

"I bet he will be. And they'll still like him better than anyone I bring home. If I'm even allowed to bring someone home," I say it jokingly, but there's a sad truth to it.

"I love you, you know?" Priti says after a moment of silence passes between us. "Like . . . if I had to choose between an awful guy that Ammu and Abbu approved of and you, I would choose you every time."

"I don't think you'll feel that way forever."

"I will." Priti nods very solemnly. "I promise to love you the most, no matter what. Even when we're old and disheveled and dying and you're somehow more annoying than you already are, I'll still love you."

I reach over and wrap my arms around her. At least I'll always have Priti.

As I'm getting ready for bed on Sunday night, my phone beeps with a message.

You bought out all of the henna from Shahi Raj?

She doesn't sign the message off with her name, but I know it's Flávia. I wonder how she got my phone number. It had to be from Chyna, and I'm not sure exactly how I feel about that.

I type back quickly, *I need it for my business*

Flávia: *Every single tube?*

Me: *Yes, I'm planning to make a profit, I don't know about you.*

Flávia is typing . . .

She types for a long time. I wait with my phone in my hand, my heart beating fast. Finally, after what feels like hours, a new message pops up.

Flávia: *I thought you were the kind of person who would*

play fair but I guess I misjudged you.

Flávia: *Game on*

It feels like someone has lodged a rock in my throat. She *misjudged* me? How can you misjudge someone who you barely know?

My fingers type out a reply almost of their own accord. My words are more confident than I'm feeling.

May the best woman win.

14

On Monday morning I have a renewed purpose. If Ammu and Abbu aren't going to accept me, that's fine. If the girl I have a crush on is going to compete against me using my own culture, that's fine too. But I'm tired of being ashamed. My choice is clearly laid out in front of me. I'm going to choose me. And I'm going to beat Flávia.

I walk from the bus stop to the school with a renewed fervor. If Priti notices it, she doesn't say anything, but she does look at me skeptically before waving goodbye and heading off toward her locker.

"I have a plan for how to beat Flávia and Chyna." It's the first thing I say to Jess and Chaewon, who are huddled together by our lockers, speaking in hushed whispers.

"Well, good morning to you too." Jess turns to me with a smile.

"And what are you talking about?" Chaewon adds.

"You didn't see?" I'm already slipping my phone out of my bag and flicking to Flávia's Instagram page. I thrust it in front of their faces. The page is filled with pictures of henna. Different designs, different people. How does she already know so many people at this school?

"Oh." Jess peers closer at the photos, like she's trying to take in all of the intricacies of the henna designs, every pixel of the pictures. "Did you know?"

"Of course I didn't know. If I had known, I would have said something."

"Well, I thought she was your friend?" Chaewon says, unhelpfully.

"I knew her in primary school, but barely. I don't know her."

"Well . . ."

Jess and Chaewon share a look that is full of . . . something. Some meaning or some history. The kind of look Priti and I share sometimes. Or Ammu and Abbu share all the time.

"We've been talking this weekend, you know? About the business project," Jess says.

"Competition." I correct her.

"The business *competition*, right. And we were thinking . . . maybe the henna thing isn't the best way to go. And with this, Flávia or whatever, doing the same thing, I think it means we should try something else."

I take a step back and study them. Chaewon is fidgeting with the collar of her shirt and Jess is looking everywhere but in my eyes. They must have been discussing this for some time. They just decided not to clue me in.

"What's wrong with the henna business?"

"It's just . . . " Jess looks to Chaewon as if asking for help. "*We* don't really feel involved. Your sister set up the Instagram page over the weekend when we weren't there to help. And you even named the business after yourself. This feels like *your* thing, not ours."

"It can be all of our thing," I insist.

"But it isn't, is it?"

"And we don't want to do the same thing as someone else," Chaewon chimes in with a smile. Classic Chaewon, but for once her sweetness rubs me the wrong way. Like she's being fake and charming to get her way, not just because of who she is. "We should try and work together to find something we're all interested in. That nobody else has done. Jess and I have a few ideas."

I laugh. I can't help it, it just bursts out of me. But it's not humorous or light-hearted. It's harsh and not like a laugh at all.

"Of *course* you've already talked about it. I'm sure you already know exactly what business idea you want for the competition, and no matter what I say or think, the two of you will get your way anyway."

Jess frowns. "That's not fair. We're a democracy."

"Except, you two are basically the same person." I wave my hands over them as if there could be any mistake who exactly I'm talking about.

"We're not—" Chaewon starts, but she's cut off by the loud sound of the bell going off. It's the warning bell, which indicates that we still have a few minutes to make our way to class.

"We can talk about this later," Jess says. Before I have a chance to respond, she grabs hold of Chaewon's hand and drags her away. They steal one last glance at me, like I'm someone they've never seen before.

I spend the whole day trying to decide what I want to tell Chaewon and Jess. Or rather, how I can convince them that we *need* to beat Flávia. That we *need* to run a henna business. That *I* need this.

But how can I do all of that without telling them why? How can I convince them that right now, the business competition, the henna, the urge to win, is the only thing keeping me going? That it's the only solid thing in my life right now? When everything else feels up in the air, out of control?

I can't say any of those things. So at lunch I settle for approaching them with my brightest (fakest) smile and two of the finest chocolate bars you can purchase at the school's tuck shop.

"Hey." I sit down, offering them the bars. They accept, sharing a bewildered look but peeling the wrappers off and beginning to nibble at the ends anyway.

"Look, I'm sorry about earlier." I say. "I was just . . . upset."

"Clearly," Jess says. Chaewon looks at her chidingly, before leaning forward, her face softening.

"Look, we understand why you were upset. We do." I'm not sure she does. "But right now, it *does* feel like we're playing a very small part in all of this. And this project is supposed to be ours, you know?"

"And you're bulldozing over us."

"I'm not . . . " I begin a little too loudly. A little too angrily. I stop, take a deep breath, and begin again in a lower, hopefully calmer, voice. "I'm not trying to bulldoze over you guys. I'm sorry if I made decisions without really talking to you. But it's not like you haven't done the same thing."

"How?" Jess scoffs.

"By trying to come up with the idea for the business with no input from me before? And secretly deciding between yourselves that you don't really want to do this anymore? Talking about me behind my back?"

"Okay, first of all." Jess's voice rises a notch as she

leans over the table between us. "You were part of the groupchat, and it's not our fault you decided not to participate. And second, we weren't talking behind your back."

"Jess," Chaewon's voice is stern.

"We weren't!"

"Maybe we were being a little unfair?" Chaewon asks, catching Jess's eye. "We should hear Nishat out. She's our *friend* and this is important to her."

I love Chaewon so much at this moment that I could kiss her. It's nice to know that she has my back a little bit.

Jess doesn't look happy at being reprimanded, but she does shut up, giving me a chance to present my case. I've been practicing this all day, mostly in my head, but I also scribbled some notes into my phone when nobody was looking. I kind of wish I could whip them out now, but that would look weird.

"Chyna is racist," I start.

Jess rolls her eyes, but Chaewon sits up straight in her chair. Like this is the declaration she was waiting for.

"You guys know she is. You know the things she says, about me and my sister. And . . . everyone else as well."

"Yes, she says them about *everyone*." Jess interrupts. "She's not racist, she's just a bitch. She's a bad person but she isn't *specifically* bad to you because of your race."

I shake my head, hoping that Chaewon will cut in again to

back me up on this, but she doesn't. I know she agrees with me, though. I'm not the only victim of her racist rumors.

"Well, regardless, she's said some stuff and now she's going around with henna on her hands. That's cultural appropriation."

Jess rolls her eyes again, and it takes everything in me to not reach across the table and punch her. I do have to ball my hands into fists so tight under the desk that my nails dig into my skin painfully. It helps. A little.

"Claiming cultural appropriation is a little ridiculous, don't you think?" Jess asks. Chaewon doesn't say anything, but her lips turn down in a frown.

"It's not ridiculous, that's what it is. Chyna and Flávia are making a profit off of my culture, and my culture is important to me. Henna is important to me. I'm not just going to let them walk all over me, and sell my culture like it's some kind of product."

"But *you* can package and sell it like a product?"

"That's different."

"And how is it cultural appropriation when they have henna in Arab *and* African countries? Flávia is . . . " She pauses, like she's thinking very hard about what words she should say next. " . . . African-American."

This time, Chaewon *does* glance at me. I have to stifle a laugh and try to keep a straight face as I say, "Flávia is Brazilian and Irish."

"Yeah, but she's . . . you know."

"Black?"

Jess shifts in her seat, like the word Black is something dirty or uncomfortable.

"*Yeah*. And they have henna in Africa."

"But . . . Flávia isn't African. It's not a part of her culture."

"And if she was African, if it was part of her culture, that would be different?"

"Obviously."

Jess leans back in her chair. For a moment, I think maybe I've actually got through to her. That she'll throw up her hands and say, "Let's do it, then!"

Instead, she says, "You're making a mountain out of a molehill. Actually, I'm not even sure there's a molehill. You're just making a huge deal out of something that's not even there. Like, you can be annoyed at Flávia and Chyna stealing your idea without playing the race card."

"The race card!" My voice has definitely risen now, if only because Jess is sounding more and more like Chyna, and less and less like a rational, sympathetic human being. But before I can say more, Chaewon is standing up and putting her hands out between us. It's a little dramatic, because it's not like Jess and I are about to attack each other. At least, not physically.

Yet.

"Maybe we should just call a truce for now. Sleep on this and come back," Chaewon says.

"We can't. We have to talk to Ms. Montgomery and finalize our plans in class today." Jess points out. "And since this is a democracy, we should vote on what we want. So if you want to abandon the henna plan, raise your hand."

She raises her own hand and turns expectantly to Chaewon. I will Chaewon not to raise her hand, even though I know that she'll always choose Jess's side over mine.

Surprisingly, though, Chaewon shakes her head. "I'm not choosing a side, and we're not voting. I'm sure Ms. Montgomery will understand if we ask for an extension because we need more time. We'll tell her that we'll take a day or two to really think about it and get back to her ASAP. We can even explain the whole Flávia situation to her. The overlap of ideas."

Theft of ideas, I want to point out, but I doubt Ms. Montgomery will see it that way either.

"If we push back starting our business, then Flávia and Chyna are going to swoop in and take all of our customers. It'll be for nothing," I say.

"Then the obvious thing to do is come up with a new idea. We already have some options brainstormed and—"

But this time I stand up. My chair scrapes loudly against

the floor, nearly toppling over. Now *that* would have been dramatic. But even this has a few people in the room staring up at us, wondering what's causing an outburst in our usually quiet, introverted group.

"I'm not interested in new ideas. I'm not interested in a compromise. I'm interested in starting this henna business and beating Chyna and Flávia for stealing from me, from us."

Jess parts her lips, probably to say something else that'll make me see red, but I'm already turning around and heading out the door.

The last thing I hear is Jess telling Chaewon how unbelievably ridiculous I'm being. I don't stop to hear if Chaewon will defend me. I already know she won't.

I'm probably paranoid, but I feel like everybody in the school knows about my disagreement with Jess and Chaewon. Like everybody's staring at me, judging. It's not like I'm the most popular kid in school—far from it. But now I've alienated the only two people who actually put up with me. Who sit with me in class and lunch. Who occasionally text me on WhatsApp.

But how can they not get that this is important to me? And if I can't trust them with *this*, how can I trust them with *me*?

I shuffle into the last class of the day—Business—with my head held as high as it can be. I'm pretty sure I'm giving myself a stiff neck, but I don't care. I just want Chaewon and Jess to know they don't bother me. That I don't regret my decision, even though there's a small part of me that keeps repeating *what did you do, what did you do, what did you do* in a berating mantra.

I take a seat at the very front of the class—where Chaewon would most definitely love to sit—and stare up ahead, waiting for Ms. Montgomery to make her appearance. The rest of the class shuffles in, some of them casting curious glances at me and then at Chaewon and Jess sitting at the back of the class, huddled together. Probably discussing me.

When Flávia walks in, glued to Chyna's side as always, she glances at me. There's a twinkle in her eye, and a smile tugging at her lips. My heart flutters at the sight of her even though I'm trying to tell it to shut up because we are rivals and she's a culture thief! But then Flávia is looking away again, and she and Chyna push past my desk to find a seat by the window.

Ms. Montgomery bounds into the classroom a moment later with a flourish.

"Good afternoon, girls!" She exclaims like we're about to set off on an exciting adventure and not a regular old business class that nobody really wants to be in.

"Good afternoon," all of us mumble back in unison. Her smile is as bright as ever as she claps her hands and declares that she's going to come around to talk to each of us about our business plans, to help us brainstorm further ideas.

"We're going to have an opening day business showcase next Monday, if all goes to plan," she says brightly, before dashing off to the first group of girls to discuss their plans. The class immediately erupts into chatter, about businesses and this upcoming showcase.

My stomach drops at the thought. Next Monday seems too close. Only one week to prepare everything, to be open for business and ready to beat Flávia.

When Ms. Montgomery comes around to me a few minutes later, there's a frown on her lips.

"Nishat, I thought you were in a group of three with Chaewon and Jessica?" She takes the seat beside me and crosses her arms over her chest.

"I was, but . . . we had . . . creative differences?"

"Hm." Her lips are pressed into a thin line. For a moment I think she'll ask what happened and make me rehash everything in front of the whole class. But she shrugs and says, "Okay. So you're going solo?"

I nod, thankful that she's decided against asking any further questions.

"Well, do you have plans? Ideas? Enough to set you up

by next Monday?"

"Yeah, I do!" I open up my book and take out all of the sketches and brainstorms that I've been working on. I hand them to Ms. Montgomery and watch anxiously as her eyes scan the pages. She sounds out the occasional *hmms* and *ahhs* as she reads, but nothing gives away her thoughts.

"You do know there is another group with a similar idea to yours?" She asks when she's finally finished reading.

"I do."

"And they're a larger group, so it might be more difficult for you to compete against them."

"I know."

"But you still want to stick with this? Alone?" She doesn't say it like she disapproves, or thinks that I should change my mind, but like she just wants to confirm that this is really what I want. That I won't have regrets later.

"I do." I give her the most confident smile that I can muster.

"Well, I'm excited to see what you can do." She doesn't say it with any malice, or hope. More like she *is* excited to see what I can achieve on my own with this idea.

She slips off to the next table. I let out a breath, running my fingers through my notes and sketches.

Monday.

One week. Barely.

I can do it. Especially now that I've successfully lost all of my friends.

15

"WHY DO YOU LOOK SO GRUMPY?" PRITI ASKS ME WHEN we're on the bus on the way home.

"I'm not grumpy," I contest, even though I don't think I can pull my lips into a smile even if I try my hardest. "I just have a lot to do this week."

"That's not your stressed face, it's your grumpy face."

I cross my arms over my chest. Priti and I don't keep secrets from each other. Ever since we were kids, we've stuck together and spilled our hearts to each other like nobody else mattered. Like there was nobody else *to* spill our hearts to.

The only secret I kept from her was my sexuality, and that only for a short time while anxiety gnawed away at me. I remember spending several nights restlessly tossing and turning because I was afraid of losing my sister.

But like always, Priti came through for me.

She listened aptly while I mumbled the words about who I was, avoiding looking at her because I was afraid of who would be staring back. Even before I had finished, she was hugging me tight and telling me she loved me.

But the thought of telling Priti what happened with Chaewon and Jess makes me feel a little nauseous. How do I tell Priti that I might have lost my only friends to this competition? A competition that hasn't even started yet? And what if she doesn't understand how important it is, either?

So I stare out the window of the bus while Priti casts curious glances at me every once in a while. When my phone pings with a new message, we're both startled out of our thoughts.

I frown before unlocking my phone. Priti's already scooting closer, trying—unsubtly—to peer at the screen over my shoulder. I push her back, and shoot her a glare.

"What are you doing?"

"I just wanna see. Include me!"

I hold the phone away from her prying eyes. "Mind your business."

She huffs but picks up her own phone and begins to scroll through her Instagram feed.

One new text, my phone's notification center declares.

Flávia: *just wanted to let you know your plan didn't work*

I frown before quickly typing back, *what plan?*

The three dots that indicate she's typing appear almost instantly. I say to my heart, *stop beating so loudly! We don't like her!* But as always, my heart refuses to listen, so I wait for her reply with an increased pulse.

Flávia: *contacted the guy at the shop and there'll be new henna tubes by the end of the week!! Will pick up first thing Monday and be ready for business*

"Ugh."

Priti looks over with a haughty smile that does nothing to make my mood better. "Trouble in paradise?"

"My plan didn't work. Flávia says Raj Uncle will have the henna tubes in by the end of the week, and we're supposed to be showcasing our businesses to the school for the first time next Monday."

"She's texting you?" Priti doesn't sound too happy about that. "How does she have your phone number?"

"Chyna, I guess." I shrug. "Anyway, the point is . . . I have to think of something else. She's already got so much interest, and wherever Chyna goes a huge crowd of people follow, so . . . "

"So you need to find a way to delay the shipment." Priti taps her chin, thoughtfully.

"I don't think I have the means to do something that big. You need to think smaller."

"Apujan." Priti gasps dramatically. "Who, in the

history of the world, has achieved greatness by saying that we need to think *smaller*?"

"Hopefully me," I say, as I quickly type out a response to Flávia. There's no way she's going to have the last word. And there's no way I'm going to let her think she's won. Even if she has. So I write, *great, super happy for you :) :) :)*, hoping that the sarcasm is obvious enough to bother her.

"You could buy out Raj Uncle again?" Priti offers when I look up from my phone.

"I can't, unless I want to take a major loss."

"You could steal the henna tubes from her!"

I don't think Priti's being serious, because she's still tapping her chin thoughtfully, but that idea somehow seems totally perfect.

"I could do that," I say. "I think . . . "

"What?" Priti turns to me with furrowed eyebrows.

"Steal the henna tubes."

"That's theft."

"Only for a short while. Long enough for it to make a difference. Think of it as . . . borrowing, not stealing."

"Apujan . . . I was just kidding. I'm pretty sure you'd get in trouble for that," she says.

"Not if I don't get caught."

"You'll get caught. You're not exactly James Bond."

"I won't get caught if you help me."

"I'm not James Bond either!"

"Please, Priti. It's kind of the exact right form of payback. She stole something from me, now I *borrow* something from her."

Priti hesitates. "And you *will* give it back?"

I don't have time to answer as the bus jerks to a stop.

"This is us!" I grab my bag and hurry down the stairs before the driver decides to shut the door and zoom off. Priti hurries after me. She must not be too bothered by the idea of me taking Flávia's henna tubes because when we slip through the front door, she's too busy glaring into her phone to repeat her question.

An hour before bed, my phone rings. It actually *rings*. The only people who have ever called me are Ammu and Abbu, and both of them are in the house with me. Not to mention I don't think either of them particularly wants to speak to me at the moment. Or maybe ever again.

For a second, I just stare at my vibrating phone. There's only a number flashing on my screen. I wait the ringing out, then go back to working on my henna designs.

But a moment later the phone begins to buzz again. One, two, three times. I let it ring out. It has to be a prank call.

When it rings a third time, though, curiosity gets the better of me.

"Finally. Where have you been?" I recognize Chaewon's low, lilty voice in an instant. "I've been calling for ages."

"You only called three times . . . whose phone are you calling from?"

"My mom's. My phone is out of credit," she says. "So . . . hey."

"Hi." Chaewon and I barely text, much less talk on the phone. We're friends, or *were* friends, as a trio, and that was it. There's a silence on the line between us, and all I can hear is Chaewon's breathing, soft and slow. I want to ask why she's calling, about what happened earlier today, about why she didn't defend me to Jess. But before I can string the words together, she breaks the silence.

"So . . . what did Ms. Montgomery say when you told her you were going to do this on your own?"

I shrug, before realizing she can't actually see me.

"She said it was fine. She didn't seem too bothered about it."

"Oh." There's another lull. I chew my lip, wondering why exactly she's calling. What it is she wants.

"What did . . . what did she say to you when you told her you wouldn't have an idea for her until later?" I ask after too much silence has passed for it to be normal.

"Well . . . " Chaewon begins. "We actually did give her an idea."

"Oh?"

"It was . . . I mean, I don't know if you read all of the texts in the group chat, but Jess and I had kind of settled on an idea before you suggested the henna business."

I try to recall what the texts in the group chat were about. I remember scanning through a few of them without really considering them. Maybe I should have taken their ideas into consideration before bulldozing in with my own but, whatever their idea is, I'm *sure* mine is better. Mine is unique. Authentic. Nobody else would have thought of it . . . unless of course they attended a South Asian wedding and decided to take all of the sparkly, nice things from our culture that they liked.

"What's the idea?"

"Well, you know how my parents have their shop in town?"

"The Korean shop?"

"Yes! Well, my mom sells these cute trinkets that she imports from Korea. They're really popular over there, so I thought we would try and sell them over here too. I think the girls in school will *really* like them. They have cute cartoon characters on them and stuff." Chaewon's voice is bright as she says all of this, like she's really excited about it. She must have been excited all along, but I didn't even consider it. I feel a stab of guilt in my stomach but I push it down.

I may not have indulged Chaewon's idea, but she hasn't

stood up for me, well . . . ever. Shouldn't we have some kind of solidarity between us? We're both Asians. We're both minorities. I would stand up for *her*.

"It sounds like a good idea," I say, trying to mean it. It's reselling products that her mom has already shipped in; not exactly the pinnacle of creativity, but it is . . . something. And I'm sure that most of the other girls in our year will be doing something similar.

Minimal work, after all.

"Thanks." There's a dip in her voice. "And I'm . . . I'm sorry about what happened earlier today."

Ah, there it is. What she really called to say.

"It's . . . " I begin to say it's okay, before realizing that really, it isn't okay. That the way things happened was far from okay. Friends shouldn't treat each other like that. "It's . . . what it is," I say instead.

"Jess was upset. She . . . was never really a fan of your idea, but she wanted to try it because you were so excited, you know? But you have to admit, you were pushing us out a little bit. It felt more like your thing than ours."

"Is this supposed to be an apology?" Because it was sounding like a defense of Jess instead.

Chaewon sighs and the sound reverberates around the phone line. "I *am* sorry but I just want you to understand that—"

"I have to go, Chaewon. I have a lot of things to do."

"Oh . . . well. Okay. I'll see you at school tomorrow?" I'm not sure if that's an invitation to sit with them at lunch and in the classes we share together; I'm not sure if I want it to be.

"Sure, see you."

16

WEDNESDAY MORNING, DESPITE REASSURING MYSELF THAT the Junior Cert means next to nothing, I feel anxiety clawing away at my insides. Today is the day we get our results.

For once, Priti doesn't say anything. She doesn't even try to lean on me and do ghesha gheshi—which roughly translates to invading my personal space. Her favorite hobby.

Instead, she smiles at me brightly when we board the bus and makes pleasant conversation about nothing.

"Can you stop being so weird?" I burst out, interrupting Priti in the midst of a tirade about her English teacher that I'd only been half listening to.

"I'm not being weird. This is called having a con-ver-sa-tion."

I fold my arms over my chest. "Yes, but you're not

being your usual annoying self and that's weird."

"Hey!" She lightly punches my shoulder. I barely feel it. "I take offense to being called annoying."

"Would you rather I called you irritating? Like an itch I can't scratch? A—"

"Delightfully quirky company." Priti breaks out into a smile. "Or, just delightful is fine."

"Yeah, okay, dream on," I say dryly, but at least this is more the Priti I know.

"You are nervous though, right?" She narrows her eyes like if I wasn't, that would be committing treason against our Asian heritage. I think it kind of would be.

"I am a little nervous," I admit after a moment's hesitation. Ammu didn't say anything as I left the house this morning, but I noticed she had taken out the jainamaz, or prayer rug, and actually said a few prayers last night.

I can't quite shake the hypocrisy of that—but I guess we're all hypocrites about one thing or the other. I feel like her silence spoke volumes. It always does.

I put Ammu out of my mind once we're in school and our entire year is being called into the hallway to receive our results. We're all lined in up in our class order. An anxiety-ridden Flávia is standing to my right. She's on her own since she didn't go to St. Catherine's last year—her results must have been mailed separately. But since they're all sent by the Department of Education, she'll be getting hers at the same time as everyone who did the Junior Cert last year. She's muttering something to herself under her breath. A prayer, maybe? But it's not in English. I've never heard Portuguese before, but I assume that's the language she's praying in.

My heart skips a beat, only because I don't think I've ever seen Flávia look so vulnerable before. Since Sunny Apu's wedding she's carried an air of confidence around her. Today she looks different.

She catches my eye a moment later and I turn away before I can watch her expression harden at the sight of me.

Ms. McNamara, the head of our year, spends so long speaking about the exams and how a good result is important but not everything that it gives my body enough time to work up a sweaty panic. By the time she hands me my envelope with a smile faker than the knock-off Calvin Klein handbags for sale in Bangladesh, my hands are drenched in sweat. I don't know if she notices. My hands are shaking as my fingers hover over the seal. People around me are already opening theirs, already taking breaths of relief. Instead of making me less nervous, their relief makes my anxiety rise.

I catch a glimpse of Flávia scanning over the piece of paper with her results on it, her eyes wide open.

I look away. There's a flutter in my stomach. To think that a piece of paper can hold so much sway, and cause so many emotions in so many people.

I pull open my own envelope with my heart feeling like it's going to burst out of my chest.

The words are a blur in front of my eyes at first before they finally come into focus.

Math – C

History – B

French – B

Irish – C

English – A

Home Economics – A

Business – A

Geography – A

CSPE – A

Science – B

I can't imagine how my parents will feel about it—it feels like the two Cs are glaring at me—but I feel the stress and anxiety leaving my body.

Before I can even react properly, before I can even look up from my results paper, somebody throws their arms around me and squeezes me in a tight hug. The hug is warm—like being cuddled in a blanket during a cold winter night—and the person hugging me smells faintly of vanilla and cinnamon mixed together.

"Sorry," Flávia breathes when she finally lets me go. I'm trying to navigate my emotions—somewhere between adoration and annoyance.

"That's okay," I say, not at all sure if it is okay.

"Just . . . we did it." She's beaming. Her eyes are bright like stars and it's too easy to get lost in them.

"I know." My heart is about to burst out of my chest again but this time for a completely different reason.

"Do you think we can put our differences aside? Just for now?" she asks, sheepishly. I nod, despite myself.

She brightens—which I didn't think was even possible.

"Are you coming to the party this Friday?"

"There's a party this Friday?"

She smiles, like she can't believe I haven't gotten the memo—though obviously it shouldn't be surprising at all.

"It's Chyna's party but it's at our place. For everybody in the year. You should come." She pauses, the light diminishing from her eyes slightly, her smile fading somewhat. "You can, um, bring your sister if you want?"

"I'll think about it," is all I say, though I already know that if I go, there's no way I'm going to bring Priti.

"I guess you're putting effort into this party." Priti leans against the door frame of my bedroom as I'm applying a coat of mascara onto my eyelashes. I accidentally stab myself in the eye with the wand and smear some of the black liquid on my cheek.

"Knock, maybe?" I say.

"Your door wasn't closed, gadha."

"Okay, chagol." I rub the mascara off my face.

"I'm surprised you're really going through with this."

"I'm going to a party, Priti. Not committing to a marriage."

"I know. But you didn't exactly enjoy yourself at Chyna's last week. You left early."

"Yes, well. This is different."

"How, exactly?"

This is a perfectly valid question, because nothing really *is* different, but something *feels* different since Flávia called a truce. Even if it's for only one day, should I not make the most of it?

Because I am eloquent and amazing at expressing myself, to Priti I say, "Because it's just different, okay?"

She comes over and stands by me so we're both reflected in the mirror. After tucking a strand of hair away, she rests a hand on my shoulder.

"This is like a scene in a Bollywood movie," I say.

"What Bollywood movie does this happen in?"

"I don't know! But I feel like there's been one!"

I can see her rolling her eyes in the mirror. I stifle a smile as she says, "It's more like a Hollywood movie, really. It's your wedding day and you're getting married. Your sister–

bridesmaid comes over to tell you how beautiful you look in your wedding dress, etcetera, etcetera."

"So . . . ?"

"So . . ."

"I'm waiting for you to tell me how beautiful I look, obviously."

"Wow, Apujan, you're so beautiful," Priti deadpans. Her face and voice are so devoid of emotion that I burst into a fit of giggles. She joins me a second later, and soon we're both bent over laughing.

Priti wipes a tear from her eye and I blink rapidly, trying to keep my tear ducts in check.

"You're going to make my makeup run," I say after the giggling has finally stopped.

"You started it!"

She catches my eye in the mirror and I'm surprised by how alike we look, even with my face full of makeup and hers without any. I am a shade darker, but we both have the same wide eyes, inherited from Ammu, and the too-round face inherited from Abbu. Perhaps the biggest difference is Priti's button nose, compared to my longer, slightly arched one.

After a beat of silence, Priti says, "You'll be careful at the party, right?"

"Yes." I'm not sure if I'm telling the truth or not. When matters of the heart are involved, it's difficult to be careful.

Even from the outside, Flávia's house is already far different from Chyna's. It's a small, narrow brick house wedged between two other strikingly similar buildings. When I climb the small steps and ring the doorbell, it emits a hollow sound.

Chyna, surprisingly, greets me with a smile and a hug when the door swings open. I can smell beer on her.

"I'm so glad you're here!" she exclaims, brushing back wisps of her thin, blonde hair.

"You are?" I ask, but she doesn't seem to hear me—or care.

She grabs my hand and drags me inside, through a pair of double doors and into a sitting room that's full to bursting.

"Last one!" She shouts loudly at the room full of people. They glance up, some utterly nonchalant, some with broad grins on their faces. They all let out a cheer that drowns out the beat of the music. I catch sight of Chaewon and Jess in a corner, and turn away. I'm not in the mood to face them tonight.

Flávia strolls up to me once the crowd has turned back to itself and Chyna has disappeared somewhere among the throng.

"I guess our entire year is here?" I shout over the music, by way of greeting.

"Yeah," Flávia shouts, a sheepish smile on her lips. "She's pretty excited that she was the one to do it."

Is that the only reason I got invited? Why Flávia called a truce? I try to ignore those thoughts. I'm here, after all. There's nothing I can do about it now.

I see Flávia's lips move but the sound gets drowned out by the music, which seems to be getting louder and louder with every passing second.

I shake my head to indicate that I didn't hear what she said. She grabs my hand, sending a jolt through my entire body, and drags me out of the room. We weave through the house—the hallway littered with people, the kitchen almost as full as the sitting room—and finally slide into a small, deserted room.

The room has a few bookshelves pressed against the wall, a small desk in one corner, and a cozy-but-beaten-down couch in the other corner. It's so small that it can barely fit the two of us in with the furniture.

"It's the study. Well, technically it's a store room my mom converted into a study." Flávia's voice seems too loud without the booming music in the background. "Sorry, I didn't think we could have a conversation in the sitting room."

She clicks the door shut and strolls over to the couch.

Settling herself into the cushions, she raises her eyebrows toward me.

I shuffle over too, wondering why exactly she brought me here. What kind of conversation is she looking for? Our last conversation wasn't exactly sunshine and daisies. Plus, I'm pretty sure we could have had a conversation in the hallway, or even the kitchen. Sure, they were crowded, but the music wasn't as loud and there were plenty of people talking there.

This setting—the two-seater couch, the deserted room, the closed door—it all feels too intimate.

When I'm settled into the couch beside her, Flávia is still watching me in a way that's disconcerting. I don't know what the expression on her face means. It's unreadable—to me, at least.

"So . . . let's get it out of the way."

My stomach sinks. Was this truce not a truce at all?

"Were you happy?" she asks.

"W-what?"

"With your results? Were you happy?"

"Oh." I let out a breath. "Yeah, I guess."

"You guess?" She smiles.

"Well, it's nothing to write home about but it's not, you know, bad," I say. "Were you happy?"

She shrugs and finally looks away from me.

"It wasn't exactly what I was hoping for, but I guess it'll

have to do." She sounds disappointed.

"What did you get?" I lean forward, trying to catch her eye.

"You can't ask that!" she says with a slight laugh. "That's like . . . against the rules of polite society."

"I'll tell you mine if you tell me yours." I can see her thinking about it.

"Okay, tell me yours."

"Okay." I take a deep breath, wondering why I offered to do this. "Two Cs, three B's, and five A's."

"Five A's!" Flávia exclaims, a smile breaking out on her lips. "That's kind of amazing. You should be proud."

"Thanks," I mumble as a blush creeps up my neck. "And you?"

She sighs. "Three A's, three B's, and four C's."

"And you're disappointed with that?"

"Did you not hear the number of C's?"

"Did you hear the number of A's?"

She smiles again, though it's hesitant this time.

"My mom isn't exactly . . . thrilled."

"Oh?"

She leans back in the chair. "Just . . . she has this thing about showing up my dad's side of the family. I guess because . . . I don't know, they never really liked her and I think it's a race thing. Like they assume that because my mom is Black and Brazilian, and still has an accent, she isn't smart enough or good enough or whatever. So she always wants me to do better."

"Than who?"

"Than . . . well, everyone, really. But especially better than that side of the family."

"So . . . Chyna?"

She nods, turning to meet my eyes. Her lips are pulled down in a frown.

"I didn't, though."

"*Chyna* did better than you?" I don't mean it to come out as surprised as it does, but it does make Flávia burst into a fit of giggles, so that's something.

"She's pretty smart, you know."

I shrug. "Just . . . she makes a habit of . . . I don't know, not putting in an effort?"

"She does. I mean, she likes to act like she doesn't care but honestly, Chyna cares a lot about this stuff. She wants to be a lawyer, you know? It's all she's wanted since we were kids."

I can see that. Chyna is definitely good at manipulating the truth, at making people see her side of the situation, no matter how wrong or twisted it is. It makes me a little terrified to think of her as a lawyer. She'd be a white Annalise Keating; all the manipulation and amorality but none of the pushback from white people. Chyna would one hundred percent get away with murder, and she probably wouldn't even have to try that hard.

Of course, I don't say any of this to Flávia. To her, I say, "You and Chyna must be pretty close, huh?"

"We . . . have a complicated relationship." She tucks a strand of hair behind her ear and gives me a smile. "We're supposed to be friends, but we're also kind of competitors."

"Because of your mom and that side of the family?"

She pulls at a loose thread in her shirt absentmindedly for a moment. "When I was younger, it didn't seem like there was a difference between us, really. But the older we get, the more aware I am of just how different we are. And I think . . . the less aware *she* is."

"Because she's white and you're Black?"

Flávia doesn't seem taken aback by the bluntness of my question. I know if it was Jess, she'd be annoyed that I was "playing the race card" by bringing up race at all. White people like to pretend that race is only as deep as the color of our skin—maybe because the color of *their* skin gets them so many benefits.

But race is so much more than that. Good things and bad things. And when you're Brown or Black, it shapes you in life. Maybe even more so for Flávia.

Flávia takes a deep breath and says, "It's like . . . I know that I have to be certain things to get by in life. I have to be smart enough and talk a certain way and adapt to what my dad's family wants. Chyna thinks that's just who I am.

I guess she doesn't really see the other side of me. Maybe because I don't show her the other side of me."

I want to ask her what exactly she means by that, what the other side of her is, but she shakes her head.

"Anyway, that's enough about Chyna. You know, you look nice tonight." Before I can reply, she reaches out and touches the sheer sleeves of my dress, running her fingers over the cloth.

My heart is going a mile a minute all of a sudden and I can hear the rush of blood in my ears, drowning out almost everything else.

"Though I didn't think this was exactly your style."

I shrug, trying to be nonchalant even though I am definitely freaking out inside.

"It's a celebration, right?" I say.

"Right." She catches my eye. "Well, I like it. And when did you get this?" This time, she reaches over to touch the gold ring jutting out of my nose. It's the same one I was wearing at Sunny Apu's wedding. "I don't remember this from primary school. It suits you."

"Thanks."

Flávia leans forward so much that our faces are inches apart. And she's touching me—albeit on the nose, which is weird and not romantic at all, but it's still making my stomach do somersaults—and I can feel how hot my face has gotten. Just from that single touch that I can barely feel.

I want to think this is just something girls do—that it means nothing. But I'm one hundred percent sure that the way she's looking at me is not the way friends look at each other. Her eyes are bright, but hooded. Intense.

She's inching forward.

Is there a heterosexual explanation for why she's inching forward?

Her hand drops from my nose, grazes my cheek, and cups my face.

And then *I'm* inching forward, though it's an unconscious decision. My heart is about to burst out of my chest.

PING!

Flávia jumps, her head nearly bumping into mine.

I slide my phone out of my pocket, mumbling apologies and trying to ignore the lump in my throat from the sudden distance between us.

Priti: *How's the party? Did they eat you alive yet?*

I have never hated Priti as much as I hate her at this exact moment.

"It's just my sister." I type a quick reply and hit send. "Checking on me."

Flávia smiles, but there's a sudden rigidity to it.

"Why is she checking up on you?"

"Well, after what happened at the last party . . . " I know immediately that this was the wrong thing to say.

"Right." The smile fades off her lips.

We sit on the couch for an awkward moment that seems to stretch out forever.

Then she stands up abruptly.

"I should probably go. I'm sure Chyna is wondering where I've gotten off to."

"Sure," is all I can say as I watch her avoid my gaze.

I feel my heart sinking as she disappears out the door.

What just happened?

17

On the bus home, I can't stop thinking about that almost-kiss. It's the late bus, which is always filled with people who are a bit too drunk and always smells faintly of cheap beer and piss. Tonight is no exception, but I barely notice as I take my seat.

I can't stop replaying the party in my head: The feel of Flávia's hands on my skin. The way she leaned forward. I'm pretty sure I've been smiling ear to ear from the moment I left the party.

I slip my phone out of my pocket and open up the text chain between me and Priti. There are a thousand things going through my head, everything rushing together to form a big mush of emotions.

I type, *she almost kissed me!!!!!!!!!!!* But once it's on the phone screen, it feels odd. Like I'm revealing something too intimate. Like I want to keep this just to myself for a little while longer. So I erase the text, put my phone back in my pocket, and stare out the window with a grin pasted on my face. I can see my reflection in the dark tint of the glass, far clearer than the blurry city zooming past. My smile looks kind of manic, but I don't care. I couldn't wipe it off of my face if I tried.

Ammu opens the door with a frown before I can grab the keys from my handbag.

"Where have you been? It's almost one o'clock, I've been calling you."

"Oh . . . I was . . . at the party. Remember?" I'm sure I told Ammu about the party, even if it was a mumbled throwaway comment because we can barely be in the same room with each other anymore.

"Yes, but you shouldn't have taken the bus to come home. Why didn't you call us?"

I shrug, because we both know why I didn't call. I think she'll reprimand me some more, that she'll punish me somehow for coming home on the late bus which, according to her, is "dangerous." But she just sighs and shuts the door behind me.

"Where's Priti?"

"She's already asleep," Ammu says. "It's really late."

"I know . . . am I not allowed to celebrate my results?"

Surprisingly, she smiles. Ammu and Abbu haven't been

angry about the results. Maybe they had low expectations, like me being a lesbian means my results matter less, or negates the Asian expectation of getting straight A's. Or maybe they just had low expectations of me from the start.

I don't know whether I should be grateful or annoyed that they haven't given me a hard time about the results. But they seem kind of . . . satisfied. Which my parents rarely are.

"You are allowed to celebrate, shona." The endearment surprises me. Sends a jolt through me. "I'm . . . proud of you. You did well."

I blink at Ammu like she's sprouted several tentacles. Honestly, it would be less surprising if she *had* sprouted several tentacles.

"You're . . . "

"You're focusing on your studies. You did well. Just . . . that's what you need to keep doing." She smiles at me, but I read between the lines. *You need to keep focusing on your studies and stop being a lesbian.* I want to tell her that I didn't make the choice she thinks I've made. That I can never make the choice she thinks I've made. But the words won't come out. Because Ammu said she's *proud* of me. She's actually speaking to me. Having a conversation that's not about how I'm bringing shame to the family. How I'm wrong. How I need to do better.

So I just nod and turn away, blinking back tears.

All of my joy from the party has disappeared as I change into my pajamas and wipe the makeup off of my face. I feel like my heart, which was soaring just moments ago, has been sliced open, and I can only put it together when I make a choice. If I want my family to be my family, if I want my Ammu and Abbu to love me, the choice can't be Flávia.

My phone buzzes on my bedside table. Two messages. I bite my lip, wondering if I should click into it. But my heart is already beating a mile a minute and my fingers move of their own accord.

Flávia: *hey*

Flávia: *would it be okay if you maybe don't mention what happened at the party tonight?*

Flávia is typing . . .

Flávia is typing . . .

Flávia is typing . . .

Flávia: *I just got caught off guard*

I stare at the screen for a moment, unsure what exactly is happening. Just an hour ago, I was floating on cloud nine. I felt like the happiest girl in the world. Like everything was going *right* for once in my life. Now . . .

My hand hovers over the on-screen keyboard but I'm not sure what there is to say to that. I'm not sure how she expects me to respond.

I won't mention it, I type out, against my better judgment.

I stare at the message for a second, feeling shame bloom inside me once more. Lately it feels like that's all I am to everyone—some secret they have to hide away. I thought that coming out to my family, at least, would negate some of the shame.

I guess I was wrong.

So I hit send, feeling an emptiness in the pit of my stomach, growing deeper and darker as I stare at my phone. I clasp it so tightly in my hands that my fingers become pale.

Flávia: *thanks*

"Knock, knock!"

"You know it's not knocking when you just say the words *knock knock*, right?"

"You're supposed to say who's there."

I turn around in my chair to glare at Priti, who apparently has the same sense of humor as a child in Montessori.

"Do you want something? I'm kind of busy." I turn to my desk without waiting for her answer.

"I've been calling you down for breakfast for like the past fifteen minutes. What are you doing?"

The truth is that I never went to bed last night. I felt too wired, with too many thoughts running through my head.

It was overwhelming. Instead of going to bed, I began to pour my heart and soul out in the form of henna patterns.

There's something oddly relaxing about the repetitive patterns—the curved lines and circles and the knowledge that this is something that's mine, something important.

All of that led to the worst realization of all.

Last night wasn't about me and Flávia at all. That almost-kiss *had* to be about exactly this—getting me freaked out and anxious, and maybe even further infatuated. All so I'd decide to give up, or at the very least be distracted.

But I'm not going to feel ashamed and heartbroken because Flávia thinks I'm someone she can play with. I won't give her the satisfaction. So I spent the rest of the night creating more designs for the Monday showcase.

"I just want to finish these designs. The showcase is getting close," I say.

I'm in the middle of drawing a particularly intricate pattern when Priti leans down beside me.

"Your eyes are all bloodshot, Apujan. Are you okay? Did you get any sleep?"

"I'm fine, Priti," I growl. "Can you just leave me alone and let me do this?"

She purses her lips and crosses her arms over her chest before slipping out the door wordlessly, which is astonishing for Priti, whose favorite thing is annoying me with all her talking.

But as much as I *know* I shouldn't be taking my anger and frustration out on my sister—aka the only person in the world who seems to care about me lately—I can't seem to help it. So instead of going down to breakfast, or making amends with Priti, I go back to my notebook. My only solace these days.

Priti and I barely talk the rest of the day on Saturday, but on Sunday morning I'm the one knocking on her door. Priti looks up from her math textbook with a frown on her lips—but she doesn't look angry at me, really. Just angry at math.

"Hey," I say. "I'm sorry . . . about yesterday."

Priti shrugs. "I guess the party wasn't what you expected it to be?"

"It could have been better," I say. I definitely don't want to rehash how Flávia made a fool out of me to Priti. Not after all of her warnings.

"Whatever happened—"

"Isn't important." I cut her off and throw my arms around her. It feels good to be so close to somebody who actually loves and understands me.

"Ammu asked us to Skype Nanu, by the way," she says when I finally let go of her. "She wants you to give her the good news about your results."

"She called it good news?" I balk at the phrase, but Priti nods enthusiastically, a small giggle escaping her.

"You did *well*, Apujan. Ammu and Abbu are proud of you."

Even though all evidence points to that, it's difficult to wrap my mind around it.

"Come on." Priti slips her phone out of her pocket and clicks into Skype. It's still early, so it should be late afternoon in Bangladesh. I hope we catch Nanu before her daily nap.

She picks up after the first ring, as if she has been waiting by the phone for this call. At first we can only see a close-up of her nostrils. Priti and I exchange a glance, trying to stifle our giggles.

"Nanu, you have to move *away* from the camera," Priti says into the phone. "We can't see your face."

Her face gradually comes into focus as the camera moves farther away. It's still at an angle, but I figure it's the best we're going to get.

"How are you, Jannu?" she asks, a smile wider than the River Shannon stretching across her lips.

"We're good, Nanu!" Priti chirps happily. "Apujan is *really* good, she has good news for you." Priti aims the phone toward me so that I'm in full view. Heat rises up my cheeks as I awkwardly wave my hands in front of me.

"Hi, Nanu, how are you?"

"How are *you*? What good news?" Her eyes are bright with hope.

"Well, I got the results from my Junior Cert."

"Junior Cert?"

"The . . . O levels?" They're the equivalent of the Junior Cert in Bangladesh. "I did . . . well." Before I can say more, Priti pulls the phone away from me.

"Apujan did amazing!" she exclaims. "She got five A's!"

"Five A's! Mashallah!" Nanu says, like five A's is all she's ever hoped and prayed for me in life. "Congratulations! Congratulations!"

My cheeks are on fire, but there is also a glow in my chest. It feels warm and nice and fluttery. It means a lot.

After we say our goodbyes to Nanu, Priti throws open my wardrobe and begins to sift through the clothes.

"Looking to borrow something?"

"Uh, no. Finding you the perfect outfit." She's smiling secretively and it makes me highly suspicious.

"The perfect outfit for what, exactly?"

"You'll see." I'm not sure I want to see, but Priti pulls out a gold and red salwar kameez, with sparkling beads threaded throughout in floral patterns. If it was a little more dazzling, a bit fancier, it could be mistaken for a wedding dress.

"I have to put this on?" I want to be my usual grumpy

self about it, but the dress is pretty enough to make me excited.

"You *have* to put it on." So I do, curiosity building up inside me the entire time.

"When do I figure out what's happening?"

"Be patient," Priti says as she lines my eyes with kohl and paints my lips a dark red. She insists on taking a billion pictures too, with my henna-clad hands laid out in front of me or held out in front of my face. I feel like I've stepped into a full-on henna modeling shoot by the time Priti has taken what must be the hundredth photo.

Maybe that's what this is? Promo!

"Maybe you should be in these photos. If this is going up on my henna Instagram."

Priti shoots me a playful glare and says, "Do you ever stop thinking about that competition, Apujan? I can't just want to take some nice photos of you?"

But I doubt Priti just woke up this morning wanting to take some nice photos of me in a fancy kameez and henna. So I'm not exactly surprised when, after our photo shoot, Priti drags me down the stairs to a house that's filled with Desi Uncles and Aunties who clap their hands and exclaim, "Mashallah! Mashallah!" and offer me flowers and presents and cards.

I blush and say, "Thank you, thank you," and hope Ammu hasn't revealed my actual results to these people

I barely know.

Even though the dawat is a surprise, a gift to celebrate my Junior Cert results, it feels like anything but as I walk around with a smile glued onto my lips. It makes my cheeks hurt but if I'm not smiling, I'll probably end up death-glaring at everyone. I have to remind myself that this is just a Bengali thing: instead of celebrating achievements the way you want to, you're made to strut around in front of people you barely know, like a prize to be shown off.

The only good thing to come of it is the fact that all the Aunties take hold of my and Priti's hands, *oohing* and *aahing* at the henna patterns weaving their way up our arms. They even ask if I'll do their henna before Eid. I tell them all about the henna business, in the hopes some of them will pay me to get their henna done.

"Looks like you have a businesswoman on your hands, Bhaiya," one of the Aunties says to Abbu.

"A businesswoman? Nishat has the results to be a doctor, taina?" an Uncle interjects, beaming at me with pride, like a doctor is the only worthwhile profession anyone could hope to have. I give him a tight smile and hope he takes it as a yes and shuts up.

"Kintu women are better as teachers, nah?" one of the other Uncles comments with a solemn nod, like a woman doctor might be a bit too much.

"Doctor, teacher, engineer, our Nishat could be anything she wants to be," Abbu says, clapping me on the back proudly. It's the most he's said to me in weeks, but there's a plasticity to his smile, a solemnness to his voice. *Nishat can be anything she wants to be, except herself.*

18

"Are you ready for tomorrow?" Priti asks me after all the Aunties and Uncles have gone and it's just me and her. I'm drawing henna designs onto every inch of empty skin that I can find on my body. Flowers and leaves and mandalas—anything and everything I've picked up.

"I think so," I say with a frown, before shaking my head and, in the most confident voice I can muster, saying, "Yes. I'm ready. I'm going to win this whole thing."

Priti lets out a small laugh. "Wow, this really has all gone to your head."

"Well, you heard everyone at the dawat today. *They* all said our henna was great, and they're all Desi. They know their henna." It's true. Since I got the approval of Desi Aunties, I'm set. They're the true henna connoisseurs.

"That's true." Priti settles down on the bed next to me,

peering at the designs spreading across my skin. "Do you need, you know, any help?"

I turn to take a long look at her. She's tapping her bare feet on the floor to a nervous rhythm, and she's not catching my eye, though it's under the guise of examining my work.

"Are you procrastinating studying or is there something else?"

She lays herself down on the bed spread-eagle and gazes up at the ceiling. "I hate the Junior Cert."

I smile. "Well, you have a celebratory dawat to look forward to once you get past it all." A dawat where everybody debates your future while you linger on the edge, trying to eat the delicious food without attracting too much attention.

"Joy."

"If you really want to help—"

"Yes, I'll offer up my skin as sacrifice!" she cries.

I roll my eyes. "I don't need your sacrificial skin. I need help figuring out a plan to 'borrow' Flávia's henna tubes."

Priti stills, looking at me with a frown. "Apujan . . . you aren't really serious about that."

"I am. I'm very serious about that."

"You can't *steal*—"

"Am I having déjà vu or did we already have this conversation?"

She stiffens at the interruption. At the sarcastic tone in my voice. Usually, our banter is playful. Back and forth. But this—this feels different. Not the sarcasm or the fact that I've interrupted her, but the atmosphere in the room. Like someone has suddenly flicked a switch and changed the energy completely.

"Ammu and Abbu wouldn't approve of this. It's not how we were raised. It's not in our principles to sabotage other people. Look after yourself and what you're doing and success will follow." She sounds so holier-than-thou that I roll my eyes. Which is the wrong move, because her frown deepens.

"Ammu and Abbu don't approve of a lot of things, so forgive me for not using them as the barometer of what I should or shouldn't do."

"This is different and it's—"

"And success won't follow, because Flávia is trying to undermine everything I do. She's trying to take this away from me. I'm not going to let her win."

"I don't know what she did to you, Apujan, but . . . you know there are certain things you shouldn't do to get ahead. It's better if you just keep your head down and think about your own business, and don't worry about hers."

"You didn't say that when I bought out Raj Uncle's shop." I know my voice is rising, and I can feel the anger palpitating through my body. It's been simmering inside of me since Flávia sent me that text. Maybe longer.

"That was different." Priti's voice is soft. It seems the angrier I get, the more vulnerable she becomes. "You know it was different. That was just . . . something small. She'll barely notice that."

"So it was a terrible idea and you just went along with it?" I'm almost shouting now.

"Apujan . . . "

"Stop!" I turn away from her. "You know what she's doing is wrong, Priti. And she's trying to sabotage me and my business at every turn. Playing games with . . . with . . . " My heart, but I don't say that. "my mind, our culture. She *stole* from us. She went to a wedding and saw the pretty henna and decided it was something she could have. She barely knew anybody there. She shouldn't be doing this."

"Just because she did something wrong doesn't mean you should do something wrong too, Apujan. I know you're better than that."

I shake my head. "I'm not."

I expect her to say more. To try and change my mind. But she doesn't.

The bed creaks as she stands and shuffles out the door. The room feels too empty, too silent, in her sudden absence.

On Monday morning, I wake bright and early feeling weird and jittery about the opening showcase. I have everything prepared—my design book, more henna tubes than I could possibly need, even a haphazard banner that declares NISHAT'S MEHNDI in bright, bold orange lettering.

I'm as prepared as I'm going to get, but there are still butterflies in my stomach, making me feel sick with worry. I may be prepared for the competition, equipped to take down Chyna and Flávia, but I'm no longer on speaking terms with my two best friends and last night I successfully managed to piss off Priti.

On the bus to school, we're both quiet. The silence between us is especially palpable amidst the throngs of people on the bus with us; their voices are a steady reminder that Priti and I are not talking.

For the entire journey I keep thinking I should say something, but I don't even know what there is to say. I want to tell Priti about all the nerves that I'm dealing with. She's the only person who would be able to make me feel better, I'm sure of it. But I don't say anything, knowing that she won't be sympathetic.

Not today, anyway.

We split up silently at the school gates. Priti doesn't even bother to glance back at me, though I watch her weave through the crowds. She pushes past Ali, to her locker. Neither of them so much as glance at each other; they don't even acknowledge each other's existence.

I feel like someone has punched me in the gut. I was so caught up with what happened at the party, with Flávia and the henna stuff, that I somehow completely missed what was happening with my sister.

She spent most of her weekend in my room, which isn't exactly unusual, but she was more excitable than usual. I chalked it up to her trying to make up for our last fight, or even for what happened at the party, though she didn't know what actually happened.

I'm tempted to blame Chyna and Flávia for this, too. After all, if it wasn't for them trying to sabotage me, to distract me, to take from my culture, I would be more focused on my sister. Or I hope I would, anyway. But I know that isn't an excuse. Priti should always be my priority. And right now, I don't even know how long she and Ali have been fighting. Or why.

If I go through with my idea to steal Flávia's henna tubes, I'll just be making things worse with Priti. I have to put that out of my mind. I have to swallow my pride and apologize to Priti.

The rest of the day goes by in a flurry. I don't know if it's just that I'm jittery and projecting it onto everyone else, but there's a buzz of excitement in the air. This is the first time we've ever done something like this in our school, and it seems like everybody is excited about it. After all, they'll all reap the benefits from our businesses during the last class of the day.

At lunchtime, there isn't as much ruckus in the room as usual. Instead, hushed whispers travel through the air, like we're all trying to keep our plans a secret from each other. Maybe we are. Maybe we should be. The last class of the day is Business, but instead of heading to room 23, our usual classroom, we all shuffle into the hall. Our hushed whispers suddenly spill into laughter and chatter as everyone begins to examine each other's stalls.

I see Chaewon and Jess hurry over to theirs, digging fairy lights out of their bags and beginning to set it up. Chyna and Flávia's stall is right beside theirs, with henna tubes spread out on the table in front of them. The two of them begin to hang up floral arrangements; pink, white, and purple blossoms will adorn their stall by the time they're done. I have to laugh at the irony of them decorating their stall in sakura, while lifting from Bengali culture, like all

Asian cultures are somehow interchangeable.

At my stall at the very end of the hallway, I tape up the bright orange banner I made and lay out my design book and henna tubes on the table in front of me. It's not much, but it'll do, I think, as I look around at everyone else in the main hall.

Emma Morrison and Aaliyah Abdi are selling handmade jewelry in the stand opposite mine. They've been making their own jewelry for forever. Emma catches my eye when I look over; she offers me a small smile that seems fake, then ducks to whisper something to Aaliyah. Aaliyah's eyes open wide and she steals a furtive glance at me.

Well, that's weird.

Even though Aaliyah, Emma and I aren't exactly friends, we've always been on friendly terms. We smile at each other in the hallways and make small talk about classes, teachers, weekends. Aaliyah even invited me to her birthday party last year, though that might have been because her parents thought she should invite the only other Muslim girl in the class to her party.

Still—I have nothing against either of them. I didn't think they had anything against me either. So why are they suddenly acting so odd?

I don't have much time to dwell on it though, as the doors to the hall open and a group of girls flood in. Their giggles and chatter fill every corner of the hall, as do the sounds of their shuffling footsteps as they peer at the different stalls.

I stand with my shoulders straight and paste a bright smile on my lips. One by one the girls pass my table. Their eyes flit past me to the table next to me. Or they duck their heads and walk toward Flávia's stall.

Within minutes, a queue forms at her stall. I wait, hoping some of them will grow impatient and come over to me. But none of them even look in my direction.

Everyone's stall has people milling about. Except mine.

I bite down the tears threatening to fall. I have to be stronger than this. But how much longer can I tolerate it? How much longer do I have to stand here by myself, staring out into this hall crowded with people who obviously want nothing to do with me, and pretend it doesn't bother me?

"Apujan?" Priti is suddenly right in front of me, staring at me with searching eyes. "Are you okay?"

I'm not, but I nod. I'm more confused by her presence than anything else.

"What are you doing here?"

She doesn't respond. She's just looking at me with wide, questioning eyes.

"Have you checked your phone?"

"Not . . . recently."

She casts a quick glance around, like she's only just

realized where she is. That we're surrounded by people.
That I'm technically supposed to be working.

"Come with me." She grabs my hand and pulls me out
from behind the table.

"What about—"

"Don't worry," she says. "Nobody will touch it. Just
come on."

She tugs at my arm and leads me out of the hallway,
which has descended into near silence as almost every
head turns to watch us leave.

"What's going on?" I ask. When I turn to face the
students looking at me, they all turn their gazes away. Like
catching my eye will spread some sort of a disease.

"Somebody sent an anonymous text to the whole
school," Priti says, when we're outside in the deserted
entrance hallway. "About . . . you."

"What did it say?"

She takes a deep breath and ducks her head. For a
moment I think she won't answer, but after a minute she
sighs and says, "That you're a lesbian. Somebody sent
around a text outing you, saying you're dangerous, that
the school shouldn't have you here, that it's against their
Catholic ethos, that it's not how an all-girls school should
be run, that—"

"Stop." I feel sick. Bile rises inside me. Who would
write such hateful things about me? Who would out me

like that? Who at this school even knew I was gay? I only ever told my sister and . . .

Flávia. She's the only person who might have suspected the truth. But she wouldn't tell anyone, would she? And if not her, who?

I feel like I'm going to throw up. Like something has been ripped from me that I can't recover.

I slide down the wall behind me to the floor and bury my head in my hands. Everything suddenly clicks into place. The reason why nobody has been coming to my stall. Why everybody has been avoiding me like I'm the plague.

Priti sits down next to me. She snakes an arm around me until I'm cradled into her shoulder.

"I'm sorry," she says. "I'm so sorry."

I shake my head. I remember how it felt to come out for the first time. What it felt like to make that decision. Fear and anxiety all wrapped together. But there was something else, too. That inkling of hope. And the joy when Priti accepted me for who I am. When she wrapped me up in her arms and told me so.

Now it feels like I've been stripped of all of that. Like I've been stripped of my choice. Of my identity, even. Like I've become passive in my own life.

"You were right about her." I sit up and blink back my tears. I rub at my eyes like that'll somehow make all of this stop. "About . . . Flávia." Her name is stuck in my throat but I somehow manage to get it out. "She was all . . . wrong for me. And now . . . this."

Priti blinks at me with wide eyes, her gaze roaming my face. Like she's trying to take this all in.

"This . . . ?" she asks.

"The only people who knew my sexuality in this school were you and her."

"You . . . told her?" Priti is looking down at the ground with wide eyes. Like she can't quite believe her ears.

"No, but she knew. And she . . . she did this." I gulp down the lump making its way up my throat once more. "She must have told . . . someone. Chyna . . . or . . . I don't know." It was clicking into place now. It had to have been Chyna. And Flávia had done nothing to stop her. Nothing to warn me when she found out.

"Yes." Priti is nodding her head frantically. "That makes sense. It must have been her. We should go to the principal. Tell her everything. I'll show her the text and they'll be suspended, probably. I mean, this is a hate crime!"

"No. That's not going to make anything better." The thought of telling someone about this feels almost as bad as the fact that it happened.

"Whoever did this deserves to be punished, Apujan," Priti says in a grave voice.

I shake my head. It's not that I don't agree with her, but these kinds of things are rarely punished. It's not as if the horrendous things said about me and Priti over the years were ever met with any consequences. The teachers couldn't have failed to hear the whispers in the hallways, like horrid secrets the girls carried with them, spilling them with glee into each other's ears. But nobody ever bothered to put a stop to it.

Telling the principal would just make everything worse. What if Ammu and Abbu got dragged into it? Would they even stick up for me? Or would they agree with whatever the text said? Would they be ashamed that so many people know now?

I can imagine their faces, red and blotchy from anger and tears—with the shame that has been brought onto our family. Shame that I have, ultimately, made the wrong choice.

I stand.

"You should go back to class," I say.

"What are you going to do?" Priti stands up too.

"I'm going to go back in there and show them that I don't care. That . . . I'm stronger than them." I'm still blinking back tears. I don't know if I'll be able to keep them at bay. But I want to stand there and look Flávia in the eye. I want to hold her accountable for everything. And I won't give any of them the satisfaction of me going home. Of appearing weak.

"Are you sure?" Priti asks in a whisper, like speaking too loudly will break me. "Do you want me to come with you?"

I shake my head. "I've got this."

"I love you, Apujan," she whispers. "And I'm so damn proud of you. I hope you know that."

19

WHEN I WALK BACK INTO THE MAIN HALL, I DON'T THINK anybody expects it. They turn to stare, their eyes boring into my sides as I walk past with my head held high, telling my tears to keep back until I'm safe at home.

I slip inside my stall and behind the table. I can hear people whispering as time passes—too slowly. Girls shuffle by my stall, their gaze averted as if lesbianism is something they can catch. There are a few girls who make their way over throughout the afternoon to show their support. Frowns settle on their mouths as they take the seat opposite me and let me apply henna to their hands.

"I'm sorry," they say, pleading with me with their eyes. "Whatever they're doing, saying, it's horrible." Some of them even encourage me to report it. To go to the principal's office. They have the text saved to their phones, they say, and will show it to her to support me. I thank them, blinking back tears. I don't even know their names. They're not even in my year.

Some of them even tell me they're queer, though they whisper it, afraid that someone will overhear. I don't blame them.

A few of them only come to find out the gossip.

"So, any idea who might have sent that text?" asks Hannah Gunter. She's in our year, and is chummy with Chyna, so I'm sure she has an even better idea than me. "Is it true?" She waggles her eyebrows at me.

"Weirdly, my business is not gossip," I say. "If you want henna, I will give you henna. If you want gossip . . . "

She heaves a dramatic sigh, but plops down anyway and thrusts her hand out to me.

"Someone said you made a move on Chyna at her birthday party. That that's why you left so abruptly. Because she rejected you," Hannah says as I squeeze henna into her hand. I try not to let the rage boiling inside of me spill into my henna art. A too-tight squeeze could ruin the whole design.

"I can honestly say I have no idea what you're talking about," is all I offer Hannah. She seems disappointed, and thankfully doesn't say any more for the rest of the time she's at my stall.

It's when the showcase comes to an end that I finally

feel relief, tinged with bitterness. As everyone around me begins to clean up, I slump down on my chair, trying not to let the despair of it all hit me, even though it comes at me in waves.

Priti pops into the hallway almost as soon as classes end. She races over to my side and gives my hand a squeeze.

"Has anybody been giving you trouble?" Her voice is serious. It's so unlike her that I burst into a fit of giggles.

"What are you going to do if they have been?" I chuckle. "Send your henchmen after them?"

She rolls her eyes, but smiles. She's looking at me with those wide eyes again, like she can't quite believe I'm smiling and laughing.

"I'm glad you're okay, Apujan."

"I'm made of sturdy stuff," I assure her, and with her at my side it doesn't even feel like a lie. "Can you help me pack up?"

We put the almost-full henna tubes away into my bag and roll up the banner. Priti shoves the blue money box that Ms. Montgomery supplied each of us with at the bottom of my bag. It barely makes a noise—since it's nearly empty.

And then it's over. As Priti and I shuffle out of the hallway I can feel everyone's eyes peering at us, curiosity flickering in their gazes. I hold my head up high, even though their stares make me want to curl up into myself or, at the very least, pick up my pace.

But I don't. Priti links our fingers together, like she knows exactly what's going on in my head, and the warmth of her—her presence itself—carries me out of the hallway.

"Where have you been?"

Ammu and Abbu are standing at the entrance to the main hall, with Principal Murphy right beside them.

"What are you doing here?" I ask, even though everything is already piecing together in my head. The text went out to everyone at school. Of course Principal Murphy found out. Of course she decided to call my parents.

"Your Principal told us." Abbu begins, before trailing off and shooting Principal Murphy the angriest glare I've ever seen. I've never seen Abbu so angry before. He's usually the calm and collected one; Ammu is the one who is freer with her rage. But now, it seems like both of them are emanating anger, feeding off each other's fury. Though Principal Murphy towers over both Ammu and Abbu in her high heels, she suddenly looks small next to them.

"Nishat, why didn't you come to me immediately?" she asks urgently.

I shake my head, unsure what she wants me to say.

"Why didn't *you* go to *her*?" Ammu turns to glare at Principal Murphy, who visibly shrinks under her gaze.

"Come on, Nishat, Priti. We are leaving." Ammu turns,

the urna draped around her neck dramatically turning with her and almost hitting Principal Murphy square in her face. She looks both taken aback and impressed as Ammu walks away, heels clicking against the tiled floor of the hallway. Abbu casts a long look at Principal Murphy before following Ammu.

Priti links her fingers with mine and gives my hand a squeeze as the two of us hurry behind our parents.

The car ride home is completely silent. Abbu doesn't even put on Rabindranath Sangeet. Priti keeps glancing at me like she's worried that I'm going to break down into tears at any moment. I just look out the window, trying not to let myself think of what's going to happen once we get home.

I thought I was ready for this. I thought I wanted Ammu and Abbu to stop with the silence about me being a lesbian, but I'm not. The silence is better than this—than the rage I saw from them in the school. What if they make a drastic decision? What am I supposed to do?

The car slows as we pull into our neighborhood. I hungrily take in the houses and trees and playground that pass by, like this is my last glimpse at the world around me.

"Priti, up to your room," Ammu says as soon as we're inside.

"But—" Priti begins, but the glare Ammu shoots in her direction shuts her right up and she shuffles up the stairs. She mouths something to me from the stairs that looks like "I love you," but it does nothing to quell my nerves.

Ammu and Abbu march into the kitchen, and I follow behind, even though they don't call me in.

"What are we going to do about this?" Ammu asks Abbu. She's standing beside the glass door overlooking the backyard with her hands on her hips, like the garden will have an answer for her if Abbu doesn't.

"I don't know." Abbu takes a seat on the kitchen table and buries his head in his hands. He looks broken in a way I've never seen before.

"Well, we have to do something, we can't just let it be."

"I know we can't."

I stand in the kitchen doorway, feeling my heart getting slower. Abbu and Ammu's words seep into my skin like poison. To them, I might as well not be here. I'm simply a problem that needs a solution. To think, just weeks ago I was sitting in this very kitchen trying to find the words to tell them the truth, to reveal myself to them. I was hoping to be accepted. To be loved. But here we are again, after weeks of silence and shame.

Finally, Ammu turns to me and lets out a sigh. Her eyes

take me in from head to foot.

"Why didn't you tell us, Nishat?" Her voice is heavy with unshed tears. "How long?"

I shake my head, unsure what exactly she's asking. Does she know about Flávia? Does everyone know about Flávia? Is that what this is about? My lesbianism isn't just a concept anymore, but a solid thing in the form of her? Something I made into reality because I gave too much weight to my heart?

"How long have the girls in school been speaking about you like this?" Ammu asks. "Principal Murphy told us about the text. Why didn't you tell us?"

I can only blink at her, astonished. That's what she's angry about?

"T-today. They found out today."

Ammu's brows crease. "Found out . . ."

"About me. That . . . I'm a . . . " I've never been more afraid of saying those words aloud than I am now, but I manage to choke them out somehow. " . . . a lesbian."

Ammu crosses her arms over her chest. "Because someone told them."

"Yes."

"Do you know who?"

I hesitate for a moment before shaking my head.

Ammu throws her hands up in frustration. "There has to be some way to find out, right?" She turns to look at

Abbu, her eyebrows raised. "Now, it's the school. Soon, it'll be everyone in the neighborhood. Then, we'll be getting phone calls from Bangladesh. We have to put a stop to this."

My heart twists again. Ammu is afraid of everyone finding out about me, not worried about me at all.

"I'll talk to Sunny, maybe she can give us some suggestions, nah?" Abbu says. Ammu nods enthusiastically, like this is the best idea.

I drift out of the room as the two of them continue to discuss their options. They don't even notice as I stumble out of sight and up the stairs, rubbing at my eyes, trying to keep the tears at bay. Why did I expect more, even for a moment?

Priti is waiting on my bed when I open the door. She looks up, her eyes filled with concern.

"Apujan, what did they say?"

I shrug. "They're trying to stop more people from finding out."

"Oh." Her lips downturn into a frown. "That's good, right? You don't want more people to know?"

What I want more than anything else in the world is to feel like being myself isn't something that should be hidden and a secret. What I want is for my parents to be outraged that someone betrayed me, not ashamed of my identity.

But I just shrug and collapse onto my bed, looking up at the ceiling and wishing this day would end.

20

I BARELY SLEEP ALL NIGHT. I DON'T KNOW HOW I'M GOING to deal with going to school and facing everyone the next day. It was bad enough during the showcase, with everybody asking questions that were none of their business, staring at me like I was a thing of curiosity and not the same person they'd gone to school with for the past four years.

Priti obviously catches onto my nervousness, because when she comes into my room that morning, she looks me straight in the eye and says, "Are you feeling okay, Apujan?"

"I'm fine, Priti," I say.

"But . . . are you sure you aren't feeling a little sick? Because I'm sure Ammu and Abbu will let you stay at home if you are." She gives me a toothy grin, like she's thought up the best idea possible. Like I haven't considered staying home today instead of facing school.

But I'm not sure which is worse—staying home with Ammu and everything she said yesterday, or going to school with judgmental Catholic schoolgirls. I suppose Catholic schoolgirls are better than dealing with Ammu alone in our house.

"I'll be okay, Priti," I reassure her. I try to give her a grin of my own, but it must come off as more of a grimace because Priti doesn't look like she believes me.

Still, the two of us change into our school uniforms and pile onto the bus, Priti casting wary glances at me the entire time like she's afraid I'm going to have a breakdown at any moment. Inside, I am having something of a breakdown. There's panic bubbling in my stomach at the very thought of stepping into the school again, but I try to bite it down. There's nothing to be done about it, and I don't want to hide myself away. I don't want anyone to think I'm ashamed. I'm definitely not.

"Do you want me to come with you?" Priti asks me at the entrance of the school, edging close like she'd attach herself to me if she could.

"You want me to ask my teachers if I can have my little sister tag along with me all day?"

"You can say that I'm like your emotional support . . . sister," Priti says.

"That's not a thing."

"If people can have emotional support dogs, why can't you have an emotional support sister? Bengali culture doesn't like dogs so that's just discrimination!"

"Priti . . . I'll be okay. I can take care of myself." I'm not sure if I'm trying to convince Priti or me, but saying it out loud gives it some solidity.

"Okay," Priti finally concedes. "Come find me if you need me, okay?"

"Okay," I promise.

Priti leans over and gives me a quick hug before disappearing into the school.

I close my eyes and take a deep breath. I can hear the chatter of girls milling around the entrance and hanging around their locker doors, getting ready for class.

"Hey."

I almost jump from surprise. When I turn around, Jess and Chaewon are looking at me with wide eyes.

"We were waiting at your locker yesterday after school. We . . . wanted to talk to you," Jess says.

"But you never showed up?" Chaewon says it like it's a question. One that I don't want to answer.

I cross my arms over my chest, trying to ignore the fact that my heart has picked up speed, like it's putting itself into defensive mode without my permission. "I had to rush home."

"We just . . . " Jess and Chaewon share a look. Then, Jess murmurs, "Nishat . . . " at the same time that Chaewon asks, "Are you okay?"

"I'm fine," I say, trying not to let my voice waver.

"I'm sorry we didn't come to you when . . . when the text went out," Chaewon says, avoiding my gaze and looking at Jess instead. "We weren't . . . we weren't sure about . . . " She shakes her head, like it's not important.

"Look, whoever sent that out, they're awful," adds Jess. "Whether it's true or not." There's a question hanging there, but I try to ignore it. "If you decide to go to a teacher, Chaewon and I have your back, right?"

"I'm not going to a teacher," I say. "I'm not . . . I'm not ashamed of it. It's who I am. I'm comfortable being a lesbian. I'm just . . . I'm not a spectacle."

Jess and Chaewon nod simultaneously, pity written all over their faces. I can feel the blood rushing to my cheeks. Then, Jess says, "So did you really try to make a move on Chyna at her birthday party? Because I thought you had better taste . . . "

"Jess!" Chaewon slaps her lightly on the shoulder and looks at me with concern. But Jess is smiling as she rubs her shoulder.

"I'm joking, relax. Obviously I know Nishat has better taste than that."

I actually feel a laugh bubble up inside me. This is the

Jess I know.

Chaewon rolls her eyes and shakes her head, but now she's smiling too.

Jess steps forward and links her arm through mine. "We'll be like your bodyguards today."

"Yeah, you two are really scary. A skinny white gamer and a tiny East Asian protecting a tiny South Asian." I roll my eyes.

Chaewon steps up and takes my other arm. "Three people are better than one."

I have to admit that having them by my side does make me feel a little safer. Their presence beside me makes everything feel normal, like yesterday didn't happen at all —even if for just a minute.

But yesterday did happen. It couldn't be any more obvious as the three of us step into the school building, and the whispers start. The stares follow us. We're a spectacle. *I'm* a spectacle.

And it doesn't stop. All day—at my locker, in classes, at lunch—it feels like there's a spotlight over me. In the classes that I share with Chaewon and Jess at least I can sit with them. But in the ones where they're not there, the other girls avoid me like they're afraid of me.

My despair turns into a boiling hot anger the longer the day progresses. It simmers and sifts inside me until I feel like I'm about to explode. In English class, I poke a hole through my notebook from pressing down on the paper too hard as I scribble. Mr. Jensen looks at me with a mixture of pity and annoyance. All I can think is, of course he knows too. Everybody knows. And if they're not being blatantly homophobic, they're looking at me with this pity, like I'm a kicked puppy. Like they can't do something to help me.

By the end of the day, I am a mixture of emotions: relief that the day is finally over, and anger at having experienced it at all. When I get to my locker, I'm in a rush to leave this oppressive place behind. Sure, home isn't exactly a safe haven, but at least Priti is there and she has my back.

As I'm stuffing books into my locker, I see Chyna and Flávia out of the corner of my eye. Chyna is waving her hands around in wild gestures as she speaks to the rest of her posse. Flávia has her back against a bunch of lockers, her eyes cast down low. Her expression is unreadable. But the sight of her, instead of filling me with the jittery excitement of a crush, reignites my simmering anger.

I guess Flávia can sense me too, because after a moment she looks up and catches my eye. All I can think of is the last time we were together—at the party on her couch. How she smelled. How she leaned forward. How I almost let her kiss me.

I turn away and slam my locker door shut, trying to bottle up the anger and despair battling inside me. Trying to ignore Flávia's gaze boring through me.

"Nishat Ahsan?" It's Ms. Grenham—the school guidance counselor and health teacher. She ushers me over from the end of the hallway with a frown on her lips.

"Um, yes. That's me." There's a waver in my voice that I try to bite down.

"Can I talk to you for a minute?"

"Um, sure," I say, even though the last thing I want to do is talk to Ms. Grenham about anything. And of course I have a feeling that I already know what it's about.

"Please, follow me."

She leads me into her office around the corner, where we take seats opposite each other with her cluttered desk between us.

I try to give her my best smile, hoping that will deter whatever conversation is about to come, but she just considers me with a frown on her face, like I'm a problem she can't quite solve.

Ms. Grenham is not exactly everyone's favorite teacher. For a guidance counselor, she often seems very unapproachable. She walks around with her eyebrows knit together, like she's having the worst time of her life. I've never really dealt with her before though.

"So, Nishat," she begins slowly, taking me in. I shift in my seat, and the chair creaks under my weight. I stare at the poster behind Ms. Grenham's head—it says "The World is Your Oyster" and has a picture of an oyster smack bang in the middle. It's only one of several motivational posters hung all over her office. They look especially odd against the bright orange walls, like the office is trying a little too hard to be happy. It just makes me feel out of place.

"Principal Murphy said you were having some trouble. Your parents brought it to her attention." She leans forward. "I hope you know that the school has a zero tolerance policy. If someone is bothering you, they'll be dealt with seriously."

I already know what their zero tolerance policy is actually like. Everyone who's spent the last few years being harassed by Chyna knows.

"I'm fine."

"There was a message sent around about you. Do you know who sent it?" Ms. Grenham slips a phone out of her pocket and shows me the bright screen with a screenshot of a text on it. It's exactly as Priti described it—the words dripping with a kind of hatred I never imagined someone could feel for me. For a moment, all I can wonder is, could the Flávia at the party really have sent this message?

"It's not important," I mumble, ducking my head and not meeting Ms. Grenham's eyes. "It was probably just a joke or something."

"In ill taste," she insists. "I can't help you, Nishat, if you don't help me."

I can't stand the way she says my name: Neesh-hat, like I'm a niche hat.

"I just think it's better if we forget about it," I say. "It'll be yesterday's news soon." There will be somebody else to taunt soon enough. I know how the food chain here works. Plus, I already know that the most Ms. Grenham will do is give Chyna and Flávia a slap on the wrist. I'm pretty sure I can do better than that.

Ms. Grenham doesn't seem particularly impressed by my decision, but she nods anyway. "If that's how you feel."

I take that as my cue to leave. I mutter a quick "thank you" and slip out of her office quickly. I'm turning the corner toward the main hallway when Priti almost runs into me. She shoots me a glare and I notice that she's huffing like she's been running.

"Where have you been?" Her voice has that high-pitched quality it always gets when she's angry. "I've been looking all over for you."

"Sorry . . . Ms. Grenham wanted to talk to me." I link my hand through hers and begin to lead us out of the school. The hallways are almost empty now—only the students participating in today's after-school activity are left behind. "It was useless."

"They didn't find the person who did it?" Priti asks, her voice suddenly sounding grave.

"We know who did it," I say. "And . . . I think I know how to get back at them."

"Get back at them . . . ?" she asks slowly. The plan is clicking together in my head slowly. I just need Priti to be on board.

"They outed me to the whole school because of this . . . henna competition. We can't just let them get away with it." The anger I've tried to suppress is still throbbing somewhere deep inside of me, growing bigger and bigger with the more weight I give it.

I'm the one who has to go into school every day and face rooms full of people who know something about me that I never told them. Something they had no right to know. Just because I had a crush on the wrong girl. Because I entered into a competition with someone who decided they could appropriate my culture and win.

I can't let them win.

"Are you sure that it was Flávia?"

"If it wasn't Flávia, it was Chyna because Flávia told her," I say. "You can't give Chyna that kind of information without her spilling it to the whole world. You know the kind of things Chyna does."

Priti frowns, looking like she's really considering it. "Does it really mean that much to you, getting back at them?" she asks.

"Why do they get to take away my right to come out,

and win a competition with my culture on display?" I ask.

Priti sighs. "Okay . . . what's your plan?"

21

THE NEXT MORNING PRITI AND I GET TO SCHOOL WAY earlier than usual, just as the doors are opened. Only a small number of people are in. Priti grumbles something incomprehensible before staggering off to her locker on the other side of the school. Rolling my eyes, I make my way to my own.

I stand in the hallway, fiddling with my phone as I wait for the rest of the school to file in. Flávia and Chyna are nowhere to be seen, and I have no idea when the two of them usually get to school. I don't even know if they come together.

But about half an hour before the start of classes, Priti sends me a text that she just spotted Flávia and Chyna making their way over. I jump up and begin to dig into my messy locker full of books. Everyone else has decked their lockers out already; I know Chaewon has pictures of her favorite K-drama stars, along with her favorite boy bands. Jess has pictures of her favorite video game characters. But I've yet to put anything up in mine. Not because I don't want to, but because it feels too much like exposing myself to my classmates. It's announcing allegiance to something, or someone. It's putting your identity on display for everyone to see—and judge.

I make a show of pulling my books out of my locker and stuffing them into my bag as Flávia strolls up and starts jiggling open her locker. I watch her heavy black lock out of the corner of my eye.

"53 . . . 2 . . . 12," she whispers. I have to stop myself from grinning. She's making this way too easy.

53. 2. 12.

It's like Flávia *wants* me to break into her locker. She's basically inviting me to do it.

"Do you have a problem?" When I tear my eyes away from Flávia, I notice Chyna standing right behind her. She has her arms folded over her chest and is glaring at me like I'm no better than the dirt beneath her shoes.

Yesterday, this would have made me burst into a fit of anger. But today, with Flávia's locker combination in my head, I only feel a quiet glee.

"Nope." I swing my door shut, shoot her the sweetest smile I can, and slip away to my first class.

By the time lunchtime rolls around, I've memorized the numbers.

53. 2. 12. I've been repeating it inside my head all morning, afraid to write it down in case it could somehow be used as evidence.

I spot Chyna, her posse, and Flávia sitting in one corner of the lunchroom. They're sitting in a circle, all eyes on Chyna as she talks about something or other. Flávia is picking at her lunch—a dry-looking sandwich, cut up into triangles—and seems to be more interested in the graffiti on the desk in front of her than whatever Chyna is saying.

Jess and Chaewon are at the front of the lunchroom. They wave me over, but I just give them a quick wave back before slipping out the door.

"You know, you've made me miss sleep and food today," Priti grumbles to me when she meets me outside the room. "This better be worth it."

"Just keep a lookout, okay?" I say. "The sooner we get this done, the sooner you can go eat your lunch."

"Okay, Apujan." She sighs heavily, like this is a very stressful thing for her.

I slip through the almost empty corridors until I get to the one where my locker is located. Right next to Flávia's.

I saw the henna tubes there this morning, stuffed into the top shelf, nearly toppling over. She doesn't have even half as many as I do, but she has enough.

My heartbeat is suddenly faster than should be humanly possible. A scene of someone catching me in the act replays in my head as I open Flávia's locker. Sure, Priti is keeping lookout, but there's only so much she can do. And if I get caught, she'll be in trouble too.

Grabbing a handful of the henna tubes, I drop them through the limited spaces between the books in my bag, until they've disappeared into the black depths of the bottom.

I've almost emptied out the locker when I hear a chorus of voices in the distance. My eyes dart toward the voices, but they're far enough away, and Priti hasn't sent me a warning text. Maybe they're turning down another hallway, or going into an empty classroom.

I should be okay, I hope.

I take the last of the henna tubes and stuff them into my bag before zipping it up.

As the group of girls round the corner—a bunch of tall, gangly sixth years who look at me with frowns as they pass—I'm jiggling open my own locker door. When they disappear out of sight, I breathe a sigh of relief.

But now I realize I have a different problem entirely. Do I have to go through the rest of the school day with these henna tubes in my bag? What if Flávia realizes they're missing and reports it? Will they search the school? Lockers? Bags?

And what if my books mess up the henna tubes? What if the henna leaks all over my school bags? Then I would be caught red-handed. Literally.

"What are you planning to do with those?" I hear a familiar voice behind me as I swing my locker door shut. Chyna is staring at me with the smuggest smile I've ever seen.

"With what?" I blink back at her innocently, my voice far calmer than I feel. There are a million thoughts screaming in my head, most of them to the tune of *when did she get here?* And *how much did she see?* And *where is Priti?*

Her smile tells me she's seen far more than I want her to. Her gaze travels down to the bag that I'm clutching in my arms. Hugging to me like it's my lifeline.

"I won't ask you to show me," she says, like she's doing me a favor. "I'm sure Principal Murphy will be more than happy to ask you to do that."

I gulp, feeling my heart sink. For a moment, time seems to stop. All I can see is the way Chyna's lips curve up into a malicious grin. It's all too familiar. I've seen it too many times, paired with disparagement of me, my heritage, my culture.

There's some irony in the fact that it's the henna in my backpack that's going to get me into trouble. What will the punishment be for theft? Detention? Suspension? Will Principal Murphy go easy on me because I'm a first time offender? Or does that not make any difference?

"There you are." Flávia's soft voice breaks me out of my thoughts. She's walking around the corner with a frown on her lips. Her eyes flit from Chyna, to me, back to Chyna. "What's going on?"

"I think your friend Nishat has something of yours." Chyna says the word, "friend," with so much venom that I'm sure she knows about what almost happened between us at the party.

Flávia's eyes rest on me now. I can't read her expression. "Nishat?"

She's staring at me with so much expectation. I open my mouth, but there's nothing to say. Not really.

I pick up my bag instead, unzipping it and digging around to find the henna tubes.

"Here." I reach out and hand them to her. She takes them wordlessly, her expression still unreadable.

I wish that she would get angry. That she would get upset. At least, with Chyna, I know she hates me. I know she's taking pleasure in all of this.

"You can report me to Principal Murphy. Whatever," I say, after all of the henna tubes are emptied out of my bag. Flávia looks at them, at me, at Chyna—who is growing smugger and smugger with each passing moment.

"Principal Murphy?" she asks.

"She stole from you. That's not tolerated in this school. Come on." Chyna waves her hand at me, motioning for me to follow her, but Flávia shakes her head.

"We're not going to Principal Murphy."

"What?" It's Chyna's turn to frown. "Why not? She stole from you."

"I don't care." Flávia shrugs her shoulder. "It's not a big deal, Chyna. We're not telling Principal Murphy."

"Flá." Chyna growls out through gritted teeth.

"Chyna, please." For a moment, they hold each other's gaze. I'm sure Chyna will argue. Will refuse to listen to Flávia. Will do something. Chyna always gets her way, after all. But she doesn't. Instead, she spins around and stomps away wordlessly. She doesn't even throw me a nasty look, like she usually would.

Flávia stares at her retreating form before turning back to me.

"Nishat—"

"I'm not apologizing." I zip my bag closed and swing it over my shoulder. And I'm not thanking her, either. Though I don't say that out loud.

"Okay." She breathes. "Just . . . did you really think that would work?"

"Whatever."

"Really? If I hadn't stepped in, you would probably be getting suspended right now." There's a throb of anger in Flávia's voice now. Somehow, it's the exact same pitch as before, but I can feel the anger resonating through it.

"Wow, thank you so much for saving me from getting suspended."

Flávia shakes her head again. Slower, this time.

"Look, I know you're angry about what happened, but you're too caught up in . . . whatever this is. Victimizing yourself. You don't even realize what a brat you're being."

I almost have to laugh at that. Whatever happened *to* me, like somebody didn't make it happen.

"I don't care Flávia, okay? Report me, don't report me. Do whatever you want." With that, I turn around and walk away. My footsteps echo a little too loudly in the empty hallway. My heartbeat is still trying to find its normal pace as I search for Priti.

She's not where I left her, and not in any of the surrounding hallways either. Finally, I hear the sound of her voice coming from one of the classrooms farther away; it's choked, like she's trying to keep in her tears.

"Were you just going to pretend?"

Ali's voice doesn't sound much better, but her voice is a mix of anger and sadness. "It was a mistake!"

There's a beat of silence. Then Priti's voice comes angrier than I've ever heard it before. "I can't believe you. It's like I don't even know who you are anymore."

"I came clean to you, isn't that worth something?"

There's a cold, hard edge to Priti's voice as she says, "That's worth absolutely nothing. You've already done the damage. You can't take that back. Nobody can take that back. You don't even get what you did, do you?"

"Priti, I—"

But the next moment the door to the classroom is clicking open and Priti comes rushing out, her eyes rimmed red. She stops in her tracks when she sees me.

"Apujan," she says, blinking at me like this is the first time she's seen me.

"Are you okay?" I ask, even though it doesn't feel like enough. From her broken voice, her blotchy face, I know that she isn't okay.

Priti rubs at her eyes as Ali appears from the classroom behind her. She looks at us both warily before dashing away to the other side of the hallway.

Priti watches her for a moment before shaking her head. "I'm fine. I'm . . . " she pauses, looking up at me with wide eyes. "The henna tubes. Did you get them? I'm sorry, I—"

"Don't worry about that," I cut her off. Priti obviously has bigger things to worry about, and here I was getting her involved in something that could potentially get her into trouble. I should never have asked her to help me. "Come on, let's go get some food, yeah?"

I take her hand in mine and begin to lead her toward her locker, where I know she has stuffed away her lunch box.

Priti sniffles, wiping away the last of her tears with the

hand that I'm not holding. "I don't want to talk about it." Her voice comes out a lot more definitive than just a moment ago.

"Okay," I say. "We don't have to talk. Just . . . the food?"

She nods, and the two of us settle into a corner of the hallway, lunch boxes open. I try to ignore the pang of guilt in my stomach from forgetting about Priti's problems with Ali because of what happened to me. For putting her at risk, when I should have known better. The henna competition is important, and I want to beat Flávia and Chyna. But the cost of it can't be my sister.

22

Ms. Montgomery finds me first thing the next morning, before I've even had the chance to go to my locker. My stomach drops at the sight of her because for a moment I'm afraid that Flávia and Chyna decided to report me after all. Priti awkwardly hovers beside me, clearly trying to eavesdrop on the conversation. I shoot her a glare, but she doesn't get the message.

"Nishat, I've been informed that the text sent about you might have something to do with this business competition. Do you know anything about that?"

I shrug. "I don't know. It's not a big deal." I train my eyes on my shoes instead of her.

"Nishat, this is serious. It can be good to be competitive, but this is not healthy competitiveness. It's harassment, and whoever did this will face serious consequences. If it's someone participating in the competition, I will find out and disqualify them, at best. At worst, Ms. Murphy will ensure that they face a long suspension." When I look up, she looks determined. Like she really believes she'll get to the bottom of this.

"I really don't want to draw any more attention to this, Miss," I say, shrugging my shoulders again.

"Nishat—"

"It probably wasn't because of the competition," I say. "It could have been anyone." I don't tell her that I know exactly who it was.

She studies me silently for a few moments, her frown deepening as her eyes travel around my face. I think that she'll protest, insist that she'll look into it further. Instead, she nods her head.

"Okay, well. If anything else happens, you come straight to me, okay?"

I nod, though I don't mean it. And I think something like relief flashes in her eyes as she turns away to walk back to the staff room.

Priti catches my eye as soon as Ms. Montgomery disappears from sight. There's a frown plastered on her face, but she just shakes her head and sets off toward her locker. I'm not sure if she's disappointed, or it's something else.

I sigh and head toward my first class of the day: French.

I slip into my usual seat toward the back of the room. Both Jess and Chaewon take Spanish, so I'm on my own during French, which is a shame because it's probably the most communicative subject I'm taking. Especially this year, when it seems that all we do is practice for our orals.

"Bonjour!" Ms. Kelly walks into the classroom, past the row of desks where I'm sitting to the top of the class.

"Bonjour," everyone says back with as much enthusiasm as, well, students forced to come into school at eight-thirty in the morning.

Ms. Kelly's eyes scan the classroom. I slink back in my seat, hoping that whatever she's searching for, she doesn't find it in me. Her eyes don't rest on me. Instead, they flick to the top of the class where Chyna is sitting next to Flávia. They're whispering to each other—quiet as anything. I'm surprised Ms. Kelly noticed.

But she has. Maybe because this has become Chyna and Flávia's daily routine in this class. Usually she doesn't mind, but she doesn't seem to be in the best of moods today.

"Flávia," Ms. Kelly says in her stern I'm-not-taking-any-bullshit voice. It's the voice that makes everyone behave immediately, no matter what. Because Ms. Kelly is not one to put on that voice willy-nilly.

"Yes, Ms. Kelly?" Flávia asks. She's all wide-eyed innocence. I narrow my eyes at her, even though she can't see me. I hope she can feel my glare burning through her.

"*Parlez français en cours de français*," Ms. Kelly says with raised eyebrows.

Flávia smiles sweetly. "*Bien sûr.*"

But it seems Ms. Kelly knows as soon as she turns her back, Flávia and Chyna are going to go back to speaking English again.

She heaves a sigh and says, "I want you to take your things and sit beside Nishat for the rest of the class."

The smile vanishes from Flávia's lips. She turns around, searching for me. Our eyes meet—for a moment. She looks away and frantically shakes her head.

"*Mais non*, Ms. Kelly," she says. "*S'il vous plaît. Je ne parlerai pas anglais.*"

But Ms. Kelly simply shakes her head, turning away from Flávia and Chyna's row and taking her seat behind her own desk.

I can see Chyna leaning over to whisper something to Flávia as she packs up her things. Then she slinks to the empty desk beside me. She slumps down in her seat. Doesn't look at me. Doesn't speak to me.

Ms. Kelly prattles out more instructions that I barely listen to because Chyna is looking back at me over her shoulder, shooting me a glare. Like this is my fault.

"I'm going to ask Ms. Kelly if I can move up," I say to Flávia. I'm about to put my hand up to get her attention when I feel Flávia's hand on mine. She pulls my arm down and looks at me with her eyebrows knit close together.

"Don't do that."

"You're not going to tell me what to do."

"Girls, I want to hear French, not English!" Ms. Kelly calls from the top of the class in our general direction.

"Ms.—"

"*Oui*, Ms. Kelly!" Flávia says before I can get her attention. Then she turns to me and whispers, "Ms. Kelly already moved me. If you ask her to move you she's going to know something is wrong and then the entire class will know something is up. I'm not going to let you air our dirty laundry."

"We don't have any dirty laundry."

"You know what I mean."

I see Ms. Kelly looking at us with a frown so I quickly try to switch to French—even though my French is still rusty from an entire summer of not speaking it.

"*Je m'en fous*," I say. "*Je ne veux pas tu parler.*"

"*Je me veux pas tu parler aussi mais . . .* " She slows down, her eyebrows furrowed in thought as she tries to piece together the next sentence. "*Nous . . . devons. Nous sommes . . .* stuck with each other."

I frown. There's a mix of anger and guilt gnawing me from the inside out. I guess the anger wins out because the next words out of my lips, in terrible, awful French are, *"Tu es méchant."* It's the only insult I can think of in French. It's childish and ridiculous but saying it makes me feel a weird sense of pride.

Flávia looks taken aback. She looks around like she's waiting for Ms. Kelly to step in and tell me to stop being mean to her in French. I'm pretty sure Ms. Kelly doesn't care if we're insulting each other—so long as we're doing it en français.

"Non, tu es méchant," she says.

"Wow, original," I whisper.

"Et . . . tu es un balourd."

I don't know what that means but it sounds meaner than méchant so I look at her with wide eyes. How dare she call me a balourd!

"Well, *tu es un batard,"*

"Tu es un imbécile."

I've run all out of French insults that I know, but I don't want to let Flávia have the last word.

"Tu es une commère."

Flávia frowns. *"Je ne suis pas."*

"Oui. Tu . . . as dit . . . aux gens que . . . je suis une lesbienne," I say, before dropping my voice to a whisper and adding, "You're the only person in this whole school who could have even suspected my sexuality. Don't pretend."

She blinks at me in silence for a moment. I have to say, she's a phenomenal actress, if nothing else.

"You think I sent the text?" Her voice is soft and low, like she's genuinely surprised that I think this.

"You, or Chyna. She's always happy to spread gossip about me. Or anyone."

Flávia shakes her head. "It wasn't me, I swear. I would never do that. And . . . I didn't tell Chyna anything. Not about us . . . " she trails off, holding my gaze for a long moment. That word "us" hangs between us heavily. As if there was an us, is an us, could be an us.

She looks away, back at her desk. She stares at the wooden desktop where girls from the last few years have scratched in their graffiti: Their names, random doodles, math equations obviously meant to help them cheat.

"I'm sorry." At least she has the decency to look slightly ashamed. Her head is bowed down low. I thought I would feel proud for finally confronting her, for making her feel some shame, but I don't. Instead, discomfort settles into my stomach. Making her feel shame doesn't undo what's happened. It doesn't change the shame I've been feeling for the past month . . . for my whole life, really. It doesn't change anything at all.

"Look . . . you have no reason to believe me, but I could never do that to someone else. Maybe it was Chyna, but she didn't find out from me, I promise. I'm sorry if it was her, though. And I'm sorry . . . I'm sorry for yesterday."

I don't want to believe her. I shouldn't believe her.

After everything else, I have no reason to believe her. But her words, the "someone else" echo in my head. *I could never do that to someone else.*

She's looking at me, eyes wide with expectation and a vulnerability in her expression that I've never seen in her before.

Against my better judgment, I nod my head, and my lips form the words, "I believe you."

23

FLÁVIA APPROACHES MY LOCKER TENTATIVELY DURING lunchtime. I'm still grappling with my decision to believe her. To forgive her. Because I'm still convinced that Chyna had something to do with the text, and Chyna is still Flávia's cousin and business partner.

But of course my heart starts to beat faster just at the sight of her and her hesitant smile.

"Hey." She leans back against the locker next to mine, warm brown eyes boring into mine. I look away.

"Hi."

"So . . . I was thinking. I could help you out with your henna business."

"I'm your competition."

"I know."

"You don't have to help because you pity me," I say.

When I look up, she's tucking a strand of hair behind her ear, her eyes trained on the wall opposite her instead of on me.

"That's not why I'm offering," she says. "Just . . . I'm pretty good at the whole art thing, or so I've been told. And . . . I want to help. Like with the decorations and stuff for your stall." Her eyes finally return to mine, and a small smile spreads across her lips. Her cheeks dimple, and my heart starts beating a little too fast once more.

"Sure. That would be . . . " I trail off, unsure exactly what it would be. It would be weird and strange, but nice maybe. She's offering—extending—an olive branch. Should I take it? "That would be nice."

There's a slight hesitation before she nods her head and says, "Great. How about you come around after school today?"

"Today?"

"Is that . . . a problem? Do you have plans?" She seems to be asking genuinely, obviously unaware that my plans on most days consist of homework, Netflix, and hanging out with my sister. I'm not exactly a social butterfly.

"No, no plans. I can do that."

"Oh." Flávia stands up straight now, her eyes blinking a little too rapidly like she wasn't expecting me to actually take her up on her invitation. "Great! So . . . we can walk there together? It's not too far from the school."

"Okay."

"Okay." She looks at me for a moment too long, like she's trying to figure something out. Then she smiles brightly. "I'll meet you by the entrance, yeah?"

Before I know it, I'm meeting Flávia by the gates of the school like we've been friends for a long time.

When I told Priti about my after-school plans earlier, she looked at me like I had suddenly grown two heads. Surprisingly, though, she didn't protest.

"This is some . . . keep your enemies close kind of thing, right?" she said.

"Sure." I'm not sure if I meant it. I'm still not sure what I'm doing here, walking side by side with Flávia in overwhelming silence. The only sound is the rush of wind, getting louder and stronger until, ten minutes into the walk, the gusts give way to a downpour.

"Shit." Flávia pulls an umbrella out of her backpack, spreading it open in front of us. It's astonishing that she thinks an umbrella will hold up against all this wind and rain, like she hasn't been living in Ireland her whole life. But instead of saying anything, I huddle in close to her under the small umbrella. I breathe in her scent—vanilla and cinnamon—mixed with the smell of freshly fallen rain.

Our shoulders press against each other, and even though it's impossible to be touching, really, underneath the layers of our school uniform, it feels oddly intimate. I can feel every movement of her body, vibrating against me. I'm sure she can feel mine too.

Her hands on the umbrella handle tremble. She's nervous. The realization sends a jolt of electricity through me.

Walking side by side on this deserted road, with the wind whispering all around us and the rain obscuring our vision, feels like we've stepped into our own private universe. Like the students and teachers we left behind at school don't exist anymore. Like our destination is just an idea, not an obligation or something that holds any weight. Like everything in the world has fallen away to make space for this moment, for the rhythmic breathing of the two of us, side by side. Despite the cold, the rain, and the damp, the warmth of Flávia's body is a palpitating thing next to me. The heat of her is stronger than any Irish sun.

Emboldened by the moment, my body moves of its own accord. My hand reaches out to find hers. Our fingers link together, under the cover of rain and wind.

Flávia stops in her tracks. She's been staring ahead this whole walk, but now she turns to me. Her honey-brown eyes bore into mine.

This is it. This is the moment. Possibilities surround

us, thrumming in the wind, whispering in the rain.

But before either of us can make a move, the wind gives a loud howl and turns our umbrella inside out.

The rain that felt like part of the outside world, cocooning Flávia and I inside, is suddenly too present. It's seeping into our clothes, weighing down our sweaters and soaking our white cotton shirts on the inside.

Flávia struggles against the wind, trying to bend her umbrella into the correct position again, but it's futile.

"It's not going to work." My voice barely carries through the wind and rain.

Flávia shakes her head, like she doesn't quite want to believe me.

"We're going to have to run," she says. "Like . . . fast."

She looks at me with a hint of a smile on her lips before taking off with the broken umbrella still clutched in her arms. I follow as fast as I can, cursing the wind and rain in my head.

When we get to the house, both of us are soaking wet. Flávia closes the door behind us while I try not to drip water onto the carpet, even though that's near impossible.

"I'll get us something to dry off," Flávia says. She's smiling as she takes me in. Both of us are weighed down by our wet wool sweaters, but taking them off would only reveal our see-through white shirts. I don't think I'm ready for Flávia to see that much of me.

"*Mãe cheguei!*" Flávia shouts, seemingly to no one.

A voice floats over from the kitchen, strangely similar to Flávia's.

"*Tô na cozinha!*" the voice says. It's the first time I've heard Portuguese being spoken, and it sounds both familiar and unfamiliar at the same time. It's like a strange mixture of European languages I've been hearing for most of my life.

Flávia slips off her shoes and beckons for me to do the same. Once I do, she waves me over toward a doorway at the far end of the hallway, her light footsteps barely making a sound on the carpet as she moves.

The last time I was here, it was dark and loud and full of people. Now, in the dim daylight, Flávia's house looks completely different. For the first time I notice the bright blue paint on the walls, and the odd, otherworldly pictures that line the hallway.

"Hey, Mom!" Flávia exclaims. I slip through the doorway to find a woman whose features resemble Flávia's. She has the same sharp bone structure, wide eyes, and dark hair. When she smiles, there's even a dimple on her cheek.

"*Oi filha*, who's your friend?"

"It's Nishat. We're working on something together for school, so I invited her over." It's a statement, but the words come out like she's asking for permission.

Flávia's mom's smile brightens. "Nice to meet you, Nishat." Permission granted, I guess.

"Nice to meet you too," I say in the most polite voice I can muster.

"*É essa a garota de que você te me falou?*" Flávia's mom says.

Flávia flushes, bringing a pink tinge to her already dark cheeks.

"*Mãe, por favor,*" she says under her breath.

"*Ela é linda,*" her mom says. She's smiling at me once more. I smile back, even though I have no idea what she's saying.

"*A gente tá indo pro quarto,*" Flávia says to her mom. Turning to me, she says, "Come on, let's go up to my bedroom."

I nod and follow after her. From behind us, her mom calls, "*Deixa a porta aberta!*"

"Okay, *mãe!*" she calls back to her, rolling her eyes. "This way."

We climb up the stairs, both of us dripping water everywhere. Flávia doesn't seem to mind.

Her bedroom is a mess of clothes and books all over the floor and desks. What I'm really looking at though are her walls. They are a plain eggshell color, but I can barely see it because almost every inch has been covered with paintings, drawings, and a variety of other things.

"Are they all yours?" I ask.

"Um, most of them," Flávia says. There's a slight flush to her cheeks. She pushes the door behind us but doesn't close it all the way. "They're not great. They're like . . . from a long time ago. These are the ones that aren't mine."

She points to a mishmash of pictures on the wall beside her bed. You can only peer closely at them if you climb on top of the bed. She crawls up, and looks at me with a raised eyebrow, as if asking why I'm not doing the same. So I do.

A moment later we're both standing on top of the bed, the springs creaking noisily underneath us.

"This is by Degas," Flávia says, pointing to a painting full of young ballerinas and soft colors. "And this is Frida Kahlo, obviously," she says. It's a self-portrait of Kahlo that I don't think I've seen before. "And here." She points to a painting full of colorful shapes—with a woman popping out of them. "This is by Sonia Delaunay. And this is one of my favorites." She points to a painting crowded with faces. "It's by Tarsila do Amaral."

They're all so different and amazing in their own way. I feel like every time I glance at each one, I see something new. Something I missed in my previous glance.

"We don't really have a lot of art or paintings in our house. My mom isn't a big fan. So I don't know a lot of artists, really."

"Oh." Flávia looks at me with a slight tilt of her head, sprays of water flicking off her loose strands of hair. "My mom has always been really into art. She used to paint when she was younger too. She stopped, though. My sister used to do it as well. She wanted to go to art school for a while but when push came to shove, she decided to give it up and study something more practical in university. We always get into arguments about art in our house. Especially about Romero Britto." She pauses for a moment. "There are three things you don't bring up in a Brazilian household: politics, religion, and Romero Britto."

"Romero Britto . . . " I test the name on my lips and Flávia smiles.

"He's a very controversial Brazilian artist. I don't have any of his work up here but my mom has some downstairs. I can show you later."

"So your mom likes his work?"

"Yep."

"And your sister . . . "

"Doesn't."

"And you . . . "

Her smile widens. "Still thinking about it. But I guess that's why I picked up art. My mom and sister are both so passionate about it."

"That's why I started henna," I offer. "Kind of. Because

of my grandma. When we were in Bangladesh, she'd apply henna to Priti and my hands and she used to do all of these elaborate designs. But then, after we moved here and we couldn't really go back very often, I had to try and figure it out for myself . . . " I'm not sure how much I should share. Does Flávia even care? She didn't care about what henna meant to me before she decided to start her henna business.

"I'd love to see her designs sometime," she says.

I think she's just being polite, but she has a smile on her lips.

"Which are your paintings?" I ask in an attempt to change the subject.

"Basically everything else," she says. "But . . . you don't have to look at them. Like I said, a lot of them are older and not that good. I don't even know why they're up. Do you want some tea?"

"Um . . . a towel might be nice first."

"Oh, right. Of course. Duh." Her cheeks flush again as she jumps off the bed and begins to rifle around her drawers. She throws me a fresh towel, white and blue with flowers patterned all across it. She takes one herself and scrubs at her hair, which has become flat and limp from the rain. Mine sits flat on my scalp too, with wet strands glued to my chin and cheeks. I can't imagine it's a very attractive image.

When I'm finished drying my hair—as dry as it will get, anyway—I look up to find Flávia staring at me, unblinking. She smiles when I catch her looking.

"Can I get you something to change into?"

I look down at myself. At the red sweater that's weighing me down. The checkered skirt that's still dripping water everywhere.

"Sorry . . . " I mumble, like I'm somehow responsible for controlling the way rainwater affects my clothes.

"It's okay." She begins to rifle around her drawer once more, one hand still absentmindedly drying her hair.

"I, um . . . I'm not sure if your clothes will fit me," I say, feeling heat rush to my cheeks. "We're not exactly the same size." I'm at least two sizes bigger than her—maybe more.

"Well, you can't hang around in wet clothes. You'll catch pneumonia or something." She looks at me thoughtfully for a moment, like she's taking in the size of my body—noticing for the first time that it's not the same as hers. I suck in my breath, like that will change anything. "I'm sure I can find you something."

She eventually digs up an old, gray t-shirt that is far too big for her, but big enough for me. She pairs it with old, loose-fitting pajama bottoms that may once have been bright blue but have dulled to a color that barely resembles blue anymore.

Still, it's not as if I have a choice. I can't really decline her clothes or I *will* catch pneumonia. So I slide into her cramped bathroom, staring at myself in the tiny mirror over her sink with a hollow feeling in my stomach.

Both the t-shirt and the pajama bottoms are a little too tight, making me feel uncomfortable and itchy in my own skin. They also make me look horrible, worse than my tatty maroon uniform ever did. And that's saying something, because our uniform has the superpower to make every person who wears it look unattractive. Except for Flávia. Obviously.

The thought of stepping out of the bathroom and facing her looking like this sends my heart plummeting. But then I remind myself that I shouldn't care anyway. I'm supposed to be over her. We're not even friends, really. We're just trying to call a truce, and who knows how long that will even last. Maybe this will be good. Maybe exposing myself as an unattractive lump of potato will make me get over Flávia.

But when I walk out of the bathroom I forget all about the dull clothes clinging to me, because in front me is Flávia Santos wearing a hot pink unicorn onesie.

She looks, to put it frankly, ridiculous.

I burst into a fit of giggles. Unwillingly. The laughter bubbles up all the way from my stomach, spilling out of me in big, ugly guffaws that echo across the room.

No matter how much I try to bite it down, it won't stay down.

I should probably feel self-conscious, but I don't.

Flávia turns at the sound of my laughter. To my surprise, she grins.

"It's not that funny," she says, once my giggles have finally subsided. She reaches up and runs a hand over the silver unicorn horn at the top of her onesie. "It's cute, right?"

"Why are you wearing that?"

She shrugs. "You seemed . . . I don't know, self-conscious about changing into those. I thought me wearing this might put you at ease." She avoids my eyes as she says this, like admitting she wants to put me at ease is too much vulnerability for her. It does make my heart soar in a way I definitely don't want it to. Because the whole getting-over-Flávia thing is not supposed to go like this. She's not supposed to make me feel at ease.

"I need to take a picture." I reach for my phone and turn the camera to her, but her hands fly up to cover her face.

"No way, you are not taking a photo of me like this."

"Come on, I won't show anyone!"

"Nope. No way. Not happening."

I put the phone down and heave a sigh.

"Fine, fine. I won't take a photo."

She lets her hands drop and flashes me a smile. Before she has the chance to move another muscle, I pick up my phone and snap a quick photo.

"Hey!" she cries, lunging toward me to take the phone out of my hands. I dodge, slipping out of her grasp and climbing onto the bed. I stand up tall, on my tip toes, and raise the phone above me. It almost touches the ceiling.

Of course it's pointless, because Flávia climbs up after me and she's at least a few inches taller than I am. She towers over me.

"I promise I won't show anyone!" I say again.

"I definitely don't believe you!" She lunges for the phone. Both of us topple onto the bed. The phone slips out of my grasp, crashing onto the floor, but I barely register it because Flávia is on top of me. Her face is inches away from mine. Her hair brushes against my chest, still damp from the rainwater.

"S-sorry," I mumble. She shakes her head. I can see every bounce of her curls. And when she stops, I can make out the flecks of gold in her eyes.

She inches closer until there's barely any space between us.

"Hello?"

Chyna's voice makes Flávia jump off of me as if I'm a house on fire. Chyna pushes the door fully open just as I manage to sit up. Flávia looks at her with wide eyes and a flush on her cheeks.

"What are you doing here?" Her voice comes out a little breathless.

Chyna seems to take us in for a moment, and I'm not sure what she sees. Her expression doesn't change. She turns to Flávia and says, "Why are you wearing that?"

Flávia shifts uncomfortably, not looking Chyna in the eye. "My uniform got wet in the rain and I wanted to be comfy."

Chyna doesn't look like she's completely buying it. Buying us, looking like we've been caught doing . . . what? I can't imagine what Chyna is thinking.

Her eyes drift from a guilty-looking Flávia to me, and she says, "Nishat," with a grim nod of her head.

"Chyna," I mumble.

"I'll be downstairs . . . " She toes the doorway like she's waiting for an invitation to stay. "Auntie said I could come over for dinner. . . . "

"Oh." Flávia doesn't say any more—doesn't try to stop Chyna or anything. A moment later we hear Chyna's footsteps on the stairs, the wood creaking underneath her weight.

Flávia brushes a lock of damp hair away from her eyes and heaves a sigh.

"Sorry."

I'm not sure what exactly she's apologizing for. For

trying to kiss me again? For Chyna interrupting us? I'm afraid to ask, so I just shrug and say, "It's okay."

24

CHYNA IS IN THE SITTING ROOM, WITH HER SHOES OFF AND her legs crossed on the couch. She's watching a rerun of *America's Next Top Model* like it's the most interesting thing to ever exist.

It's actually strange to see her like this—so domestic. It almost reminds me of back when we were friends. During the first few days of secondary school, Chyna had this nervous energy about her. Like she didn't quite know where she fit in, or what her role was. I thought that all dissipated after Catherine McNamara's birthday party, but watching her now, I think that maybe it didn't really. Maybe Chyna just got really good at hiding it.

"Does she come here often?" I whisper to Flávia at the bottom of the stairs.

"Every once in a while." Flávia's lips are pressed in

a thin line like she's not very impressed with Chyna for being here. "I have to go talk to my mom, can you give me a minute?"

I can't exactly say no, even though the last thing I want is to have to spend time alone with Chyna of all people, but I nod my head.

Flávia slips away toward the kitchen and I gingerly make my way into the sitting room. The episode of *America's Next Top Model* is from a few years back—I remember the faces of most of the contestants, but I've forgotten their names.

"I can't believe you still watch this," I say, before my brain reminds me that engaging in conversation with Chyna is not something I want to do.

Chyna turns to look at me with her lips pressed together in a frown.

"I can't believe you're here, hanging out with my cousin."

I roll my eyes and take a seat on the couch next to her. "You know, I knew Flávia way before I knew you."

"Yeah, so she's said. The world has a funny way about it, doesn't it?"

Funny is definitely one way to put it. I shift around in my seat, watching the screen in front of me but not really taking anything in.

I can hear Flávia and her mom in the other room, but

their words are barely audible—not that more volume would help, since I don't speak a word of Portuguese, and as far as I know neither does Chyna.

"I hate it when Flá and Auntie talk in Portuguese," Chyna mumbles, confirming my suspicions. "You know when someone is speaking in another language right near you and you're paranoid they're speaking about you?"

I have to smile at the irony of that, because Chyna doesn't really have any qualms about speaking about other people in a language they most definitely understand.

"I don't know. Sometimes, maybe. Flávia and your Auntie are probably just more comfortable speaking Portuguese than English with each other." But also, Flávia probably *is* discussing Chyna with her mom. And Chyna probably knows that too.

"Why are you here?" Chyna turns to me with a frown on her lips. I'm surprised the question didn't come sooner. "What are you doing with my cousin?"

"Chy, that's kind of a rude question," Flávia mumbles from the doorway between the sitting room and the kitchen. "Nishat and I are friends, I was helping her with something." She doesn't look at me when she says this and I feel my stomach plummet.

"You had to help her with something in your unicorn onesie?" Chyna asks.

"I told you, I wanted to be comfy. Don't act all high

and mighty like you don't have an ugly polka dot Minnie Mouse one. At least mine is cute."

"You have a Minnie Mouse onesie?" I'm already trying to figure out how I can get a picture of that. I know Priti, Chaewon, and Jess would all appreciate it.

Chyna shoots me a glare and says, "Flávia bullied me into buying it."

Flávia crosses her arms over her chest and scoffs, "As if."

Chyna directs her glare to Flávia this time and says, "Shut up."

Flávia, in turn, crosses her eyes and sticks out her tongue. I let out a giggle. Not just because it's kind of adorable and reminds me of Priti, but because I would never have expected Flávia and Chyna to act like this when they're alone together. They always seem so reserved and serious—especially Chyna. Even when Chyna and I were friends—brief as that relationship was—we never messed around like this.

"Do you want to stay for dinner, Nishat?" Flávia asks.

My watch says it's already seven o'clock. I asked Priti to tell Ammu and Abbu where I was going, but I'm sure they're wondering about me. I don't really want this strange evening to end, but I'm also not entirely sure that I want to sit through a dinner with Flávia, her mother, and Chyna.

"I should probably get going, actually."

"I'll walk you to the door," Flávia offers. We walk out

of the sitting room in silence. I'm keenly aware of her presence beside me; of our arms nearly touching, and the sound of her breathing. The sound of mine.

We swing by her bedroom, where she picks up my still-damp school uniform and slips it into a plastic bag for me.

"Will you be okay going home in that?"

"I don't really have much of a choice." I shrug.

"Maybe my mom can give you a lift? So you don't have to get the bus all by yourself, I mean."

"I don't want to bother her at dinner time. Thanks, though."

At the doorway, a heavy silence hangs between us. I'm not sure what I'm supposed to say or do. I don't know whether this will end like the party or not; whether I should be annoyed or elated.

Flávia clicks the door open but before I can slide out, she steps close. Her fingers tuck a strand of hair behind my ear, brushing against my skin and sending a jolt of electricity through me.

"You'll text me when you get home?" she asks.

And the thing is, even though this is something that countless people have asked me to do—my sister, Chaewon, even Ammu—this feels different. Flávia's voice is laced with so much concern, her eyes sparkling with something like hope, that even though it's a familiar request everything about this moment feels brand new.

I gulp down the lump forming in my throat, and nod. She smiles and I slip out the door.

It's only when I arrive home that I realize we never even worked on the decorations for my henna booth.

Priti is waiting in my bedroom, a math book open in her lap. She doesn't look happy, though whether that's because of me or math is hard to know.

"Hey." I try to be as nonchalant as possible, like I haven't been out for hours at Flávia's house. Like this isn't an unusual occurrence.

"What took you so long?" Priti sounds distinctly like Ammu.

I shrug, and this just seems to agitate Priti further.

"Apujan, you're supposed to be careful. You can't just . . . " She takes a breath and shakes her head. "You don't remember what Flávia and Chyna did to you?"

"It wasn't Flávia." I can't help the small smile that appears on my face as I say her name. I want to tell Priti more. I want to tell her about going to her house and meeting her mom and the unicorn onesie, and the almost-kiss. But what if nothing comes of it?

"How can you possibly know that?" Priti's voice is laced with suspicion.

"Because. I know," I say. "Can you trust me? Flávia and I are . . . working things out."

Priti doesn't look impressed. She purses her lips and picks her book up from the bed, standing. She's shorter than me, so she can't exactly tower over me, but it feels like she does as she looks at me with disdain blazing in her eyes. "She's given you no reason to trust her, Apujan," she insists. "You can't possibly have forgiven her so easily."

I shrug again, because there's really nothing else I can say. "Look, she's . . . " I'm unsure how exactly to finish that sentence. " . . . not what you think." I finish awkwardly. "We're working it out. You don't need to worry about it."

"If you're going to act like a lovesick fool, Apujan, don't come crawling to me when things go wrong." With that, she turns on her heels and disappears. My bedroom door slams closed behind her.

I feel all the excitement from the past few hours slip out of me as she leaves. I sink into the bed where she left her impression, and find that apparently she's also left her phone behind. The screen is open to her text messages with Ali. Before I can slip out of it, the texts catch my eye; I scroll through them, trying to wrap my mind around what Priti and Ali are talking about.

Priti: *I just can't believe you could do something so sick. That you would stoop so low.*

Ali: *I said I'm sorry, I don't know what else I can do to make it better*

Priti: *turn yourself in?? tell Ms. Grenham you sent it.*

Ali: *I'll be suspended, Priti. Maybe even expelled. I can't do that.*

Priti: *Then you shouldn't have sent the text.*

"What are you doing?"

I drop the phone onto the bed like it's suddenly caught flames. It might as well have. That would probably be better.

"You left your phone."

"So you thought that meant looking through it was okay?" Priti sounds angry but her eyes are moving nervously from my hands to where the phone has landed.

"Was it Ali?" I ask.

She looks away from me—somewhere above my head—clears her throat, and says, "Was what Ali?" Her voice is too controlled, too stoic.

"Was she the one who told everyone?"

"I thought you said it was Flávia. You said she and I were the only ones who knew."

"I said she and you were the only ones I told."

"Well, then—"

"Priti."

She looks up, holding my gaze for only a moment before looking away. "I'm never going to forgive her for it, if it makes you feel better," she mumbles.

I take a deep breath, trying to process this information. It wasn't Flávia. It wasn't Flávia. It wasn't Flávia.

It was my sister.

"How could you . . . why would you . . . tell her? That's not your right."

Priti furrows her eyebrows together and leans away from me, like I've said something she wasn't expecting. "How was I supposed to keep that to myself?"

"So you just had to go and give your best friend a piece of gossip about me? Is that what it was?"

Priti scoffs. "Of course not. But . . . you saw what was happening here. The tension, you being upset, Ammu being upset, Abbu being upset, nobody ever talking about it. It was all driving me insane. I had to talk to someone and it couldn't be you or them. It's a taboo subject. I couldn't just keep it all bottled up inside."

"You had no right to tell her. And then to lie about it, to pretend it was Flávia—"

"Look, I'm sorry. I know. I was upset and I knew you would be mad and I thought if you could just believe it was Flávia for a little while at least . . . you wouldn't be so mad. I thought I could sort it out, get Ali to fix it."

But her words barely register in my head. All this time I suspected Flávia, and my sister was lying straight to my face. She knew exactly what was going on and she was letting Flávia take the blame for it.

"I can't believe you hate Flávia that much. That you would let me hate her for nothing."

Priti frowns. "That's not . . . " she shakes her head, her eyes settling into a glare. "You really don't care about anyone but yourself, do you?"

I blink. "What?"

"You're so obsessed with this girl who doesn't even care that you got outed to the entire school. You don't even care about what's been happening here. With us. With me. Ali and I have been on the rocks for weeks. *Weeks*. And of course I couldn't tell you about it because oh no, poor Nishat is dealing with so much. We must all walk on eggshells around her, in case she gets too upset. And Nanu is sick, which you would know if you actually bothered to keep up with her on Skype like you used to before you got too smitten with some girl who doesn't even care about you. Who was obviously just using you to win this stupid business competition."

"She wasn't . . . " The words get stuck in my throat. Not that Priti is listening anyway. She has sprung up and is pacing around the room, her hands on her hips. She looks strikingly similar to Ammu.

"You want to know something? Ammu and Abbu are doing everything they can. They have been ever since we got here, but you can't see it or appreciate it. They may have messed up after you came out to them, but they just want to be able to look people in the eye when they go back to Bangladesh. Is that so, so wrong?"

There are tears pricking at my eyes, and despite me trying my best to stifle them, they somehow manage to sneak out until Priti blurs in front of me. My little sister doesn't sound like my little sister at all.

When she stops, turns, and sees me rubbing at my eyes, I expect her to come to her senses. That's how it usually goes with us: we get angry, we say things we don't mean, but then we come back to ourselves. Go back to our rhythm. To being sisters who are there for each other no matter what.

But Priti recoils from me, like my tears are something heinous. Before I know it, my bedroom door is slamming shut behind her.

25

Priti catches the early bus the next morning. Or so Ammu tells me, when I stumble down the stairs. I'm not sure how to feel about it. If anyone should be angry, it should be *me*, for how she lied to me.

"Ammu," I say, at the edge of the doorway, ten minutes before my bus.

She looks up and catches my eye, a frown on her lips. We've gone back to barely speaking a word to each other since I was outed to the whole school.

I blink back the tears prickling behind my eyes and swallow the lump in my throat.

"Is Nanu sick?" I manage to get out.

The look on Ammu's face, stricken and sad, makes me instantly regret saying anything.

"She's . . . she'll be okay."

"So she isn't now? Why didn't you tell me?"

"Who told you?"

"Priti . . . "

Ammu shakes her head. "Your sister spends a little too much time eavesdropping when she should be studying for her exams."

"There are more important things than exams, Ammu."

For a moment, I think she's going to protest, but instead she nods slowly. "I know." She looks at me with something that resembles a smile, something that softens her face, and says, "Don't worry about your Nanu. Or . . . about your sister. Go, or you'll miss your bus."

But I can't help the worry that floods my brain about both Nanu *and* Priti. How have so many things been happening around me and I haven't even noticed?

When Flávia catches my eye by the lockers I know exactly how. Priti is right. I've been so caught up with Flávia and the competition and everything else that I've forgotten to pay attention to the important things.

But as Flávia approaches me with a brown shopping bag clutched in her hand, I'm not sure I regret any of it.

"This is for you," she says as she hands me the bag. Our fingers brush as she does it. I try to tell my body to shut up, to not react, but obviously—obviously—my heart isn't very good at listening to me. It beats a million miles a minute.

"What is it?"

"Open it." She nods encouragingly.

A furled white poster paper sticks out of the top of the bag. I pull it out and unroll it—and almost gasp aloud.

It's a banner.

It has NISHAT'S MEHNDI written in colorful letters in the middle, and below it even has some words in Bengali script. It's carefully done so that it looks sharp and geometrical—not like the rounded and soft letters that my Bengali handwriting usually is.

The background is a mishmash of bright colors, and on one side there's a drawing of joined hands with henna winding down the palms.

It's far better than anything I could ever have done.

There's something lodged in my throat. I think it's my heart.

"This is beautiful," I breathe.

Flávia just shrugs like it's no big deal. It's definitely a big deal. It's a huge deal.

Trying not to steal too many glances at Flávia, I slip the banner into my locker. When I close my locker though, we catch each other's eye. She smiles, dimples and all, and I can't help the grin that spreads out across my lips too.

"So, um." She brushes back a curl that's fallen in front of her eyes. "Yesterday with Chyna . . . I'm sorry about that. Her parents are away a lot so she comes over to ours or my dad's, but . . . " She shakes her head like she's not sure if she wants to finish that thought. "Do you . . . want to come over this weekend? We could . . . work on our French homework?"

The *yes* is on my tongue, pushing its way out, before I remember that this weekend I'm supposed to set up my henna shop at a booth in Abbu's restaurant. He agreed to let me set up shop for a few hours on Saturday and Sunday, in the hopes that my customers could also become his customers. After all, if they're interested in getting henna, maybe they're also interested in eating authentic South Asian food.

"I want to but . . . I'm busy this weekend." I'm unsure if I should mention the henna shop or not. I'm still not sure where we stand, but no matter what, our competition still hangs over us uncomfortably.

"Oh." A flash of hurt appears in her eyes but disappears so fast that I'm not sure if I just imagined it.

"I'm opening up the henna shop this weekend." The words slip out of me unprompted. I know I shouldn't tell her. She's my competition. But obviously my heart prefers her, so the words are out and I can't take them back.

"Oh."

Silence hangs between us for a moment too long. It's thick with everything that's already been said and done, everything we can't change. It's broken by the loud trill of the bell.

"I should . . . "

"Yeah."

She catches my eye and gives me a smile that's half guilt and half apology. I smile back.

When I get home from school that day, Ammu surprises me by knocking on my door. At first I'm convinced it's Priti, coming to figure things out. But then Ammu leans her head in.

"You want to talk to Nanu?" she asks, holding up her phone. I can make out Nanu's face on the screen.

"Yeah!" I leap out of my chair to grab the phone. Ammu smiles and leaves me to settle into bed. I prop the phone up in front of me.

"Assalam Alaikum," I say.

"Walaikum Salam," Nanu says. Her voice sounds weaker than I remember, but maybe I'm just projecting. "Your Ammu said you were worried about me."

"Because Priti told me you're sick," I say, my voice taking on a chiding tone. Really I'm trying to keep it from breaking, because Nanu *looks* sick. She looks paler and thinner than I remember her, and there are bags under her eyes. As if she hasn't been sleeping properly.

"Only a small thing," Nanu says reassuringly, though

it doesn't reassure me at all. "The doctors say everything will be okay, Jannu. You have nothing to worry about."

Obviously that doesn't stop me from worrying, but I don't let that show on my face. I want to ask her more questions, find out exactly what's wrong, even if that means I'll spend the next several hours on WebMD learning the worst possible outcomes of whatever it is.

But before I can ask anything else, Nanu leans forward, a smile lighting up her face. She asks, "How's your henna business? Your Ammu has been telling me a lot about it."

"She has?" I ask.

"She said you've been working very hard."

I try to bite down a rush of tears.

"Well . . . it's been going okay." I shrug. "I'm going to work from Abbu's restaurant this weekend."

"Well, I'm very proud of you, Jannu," Nanu says. "And of Priti. Your Ammu said she's been helping you."

"Yeah." I nod slowly. "She's been helping me come up with ideas."

Priti must hear her name mentioned through the wall between our rooms—or because she's been eavesdropping as always—because the door to my bedroom cracks open and she peers inside.

"Is that Nanu?" she asks in a small voice.

I nod, patting the space beside me for her to sit down. She comes over, hesitating in a way that she never has in my room before. But when she turns to the screen, her face breaks out into a grin.

"Assalam Alaikum, Nanu!" she says. I put an arm around her and bring her closer to me so we're both on screen at the same time.

"We were just talking about how you've been helping me with the henna business," I tell her. "How we're both proud of you."

Priti blinks at me with some confusion for a moment, but I give her shoulder a squeeze, hoping she understands what that means.

After Nanu finally hangs up, telling us very little about herself but saying, "Mashallah," and "Alhamdulillah," and "Insha'Allah," about a hundred times in response to everything from the business competition to Priti's exams, I turn to Priti.

"I'm sorry," I say.

"*I'm* sorry," Priti says, in turn.

"Okay, I'm trying to apologize and it's rude to take over someone else's apology."

Priti burrows her face into my hair and mumbles, "Okay, apologize away."

"That was it."

She looks up at me again, a frown settled on her lips.

"That was your apology?"

"I said sorry."

"For what?"

"Being selfish?"

She blows out a breath and sits back, crossing her arms over her chest. "And . . . "

"Not . . . paying enough attention to you. You're right. I've been so caught up with Flávia that I forgot to pay attention. What's going on with you and Ali anyway?"

She shakes her head. "We're still talking about you."

"I'm just sorry, okay? You know I love you. I would never . . . I didn't mean to . . . and I know that you . . . " I sigh. "Just . . . that. I love you."

A smile tugs at her lips and she leans forward, wrapping her arms around me. "I was mean yesterday."

"Very."

"I made you cry."

"You did."

"After everything else that's happened."

I ruffle her hair and it's like I can feel the anger and resentment slip out of my body with every breath. "It's okay. I think I get it. Will you tell me about Ali?"

"She just hasn't been the same this year. She has her new boyfriend and this new attitude about everything. I told her about you and I thought she would understand, she would listen, but . . . she was weird about it. I should have told you before."

"She was weird, how?"

"Like . . . she kept asking me weird questions," Priti says, furrowing her eyebrows together like she's trying really hard to remember exactly what was said. "She asked if Ammu and Abbu would force you to marry a man. And like . . . if you would be killed in Bangladesh if you went there now."

"Well, yeah. Everyone can smell the lesbian on me now," I joke.

She smiles, but I know she's still thinking about Ali. "I don't know if Ali is a racist or a homophobe or both. But . . . she sent the text. She said it was because everybody deserved to know about you. You were deceiving them by keeping it a secret."

"I'm against Catholic ethos, not how an all-girl school should be run." I remember the words from the text that had been sent out, even though I wish I could forget them.

I suddenly remember the conversation I overheard in school between them last week. "Is that what you were talking to her about when you were supposed to help me steal the henna tubes?"

Priti nods. "I didn't know how to tell you. I thought . . . I could just make it go away. But I made it worse."

"You should have told me."

"You were already dealing with Ammu and Abbu, and Chyna and Flávia, and then even Sunny Apu was being horrible to you. I thought you had enough on your plate."

"So you were trying to protect me?" The irony of it makes me want to laugh. By protecting me, Priti hurt me more than she would have if she had just told me the truth from the start.

"I'm sorry. I thought I was helping."

I press her closer to my chest and say, "Next time, leave the protective sister act to me, okay?"

"Okay, okay," she concedes. But I already know that she won't, and I'm okay with it.

26

On Saturday I wake up with butterflies in my stomach. These butterflies are completely different from the ones I feel because of Flávia; around her, I feel anxious in a pleasant way. Like I'm going to throw up, but at least there's a pretty girl in front of me. Now I just want to throw up.

When I get into Abbu's car with all my things, Priti's already there with her schoolbag full of books.

"What are you doing?" I ask.

"I'm going to help you," she says, tapping her book bag like that should explain everything. "I'll just study there, *while* helping you."

I slip into the seat beside her, even though I know Ammu probably won't be very happy about this. But Abbu doesn't seem to mind. He even puts on Rabindranath

Sangeet and sings along for the entire drive, even though Priti and I groan and ask him to shut up.

As Abbu gets everything in the restaurant in order, I pull a curtain in front of the corner booth and stick a copy of the poster I made onto the cloth with some tape. I hung copies up around the school throughout the week, in the hopes that people would actually come down this weekend. It's a simple poster—one of the pictures from our Instagram blown up, with NISHAT'S MEHNDI on it in cursive and the date, time, and place of the pop-up shop printed neatly below. Above it I hang Flávia's banner.

"Is that—"

"Yeah."

Priti crosses her arms over her chest, and begrudgingly takes the banner in. "It's nice."

It's probably the most I'm going to get from Priti. I still haven't told her about what happened with Flávia and me at her house a few days ago.

We both slip inside the booth, and Priti takes her phone out of her pocket to snap a quick photo of the henna tubes that I've stacked up on the table.

"There. We're open for business," she says, tapping at her phone with more gusto and flourish than necessary. She pulls her books out of her bag while I lean back against my seat, waiting for the sound of customers arriving.

Five minutes pass.

Then ten.

Fifteen.

No sign of customers.

I unlock my phone and scroll through the Instagram account. The picture Priti put up has our location tagged and is captioned, *open for business!* It has a couple of likes, but no comments yet.

My phone buzzes and I click into my messages to find a new one from Flávia. It just says, *good luck today! :)*. I smile in spite of myself. Nothing has happened between us since that day in her bedroom. We haven't spoken about it, either, and I can't bring myself to ask her what it meant, if anything. I'm too afraid of the answer.

But I can't deny that we've been on better terms. We've been texting back and forth about almost everything under the sun, and every time my phone pings with a new message, I can't help the flush that spreads through me, and the way my heart picks up pace.

I want to tell myself not to get my hopes up, but it's difficult to reason with my heart when Flávia has spent the entire week smiling at me from a distance like she wished we could reverse time and go back to her bedroom on that afternoon.

I still remember the feel of her fingers in mine under the cloak of rain, and the way she smelled, and how her curls brushed against my chest when we almost kissed.

How am I supposed to think rationally when all of those memories are imprinted into my mind?

I write a quick text back: *thank you!* <3

Then I delete the heart because that seems like too much. But without it, it seems like not enough. How do people *do* this?

"Hi?" A voice on the other side of the closed curtain mumbles. I nearly jump out of my seat, dropping my phone onto the table.

"Hi!" I say, scrambling to pick up my phone and slide it into my pocket. I pull the curtain open to reveal Janet McKinney and Catherine DeBurg.

"This is where we come to get our henna tattoos, right?" Janet asks.

"Um, yes," I say. "You both want to get them done?"

Catherine shares a look with Janet.

"Is it okay if I just watch first? And then decide?" she asks.

"Sure." I'm trying not to giggle. I wonder if she knows that henna washes away in a couple of weeks.

Both Janet and Catherine slip inside the booth, taking seats opposite Priti. I close the curtain again and take my seat.

"This is Priti, my assistant." She waves brightly at the pair of them, showing off her already hennaed hands.

"We know her, she goes to school with us," Catherine

says, even though she takes Priti in like this is the first time she's seen her.

"Yes, well, she's my little sister," I say, just in case they've forgotten.

I hand them the laminated price list I created.

"These are my prices," I say, in my professional businesswoman voice. "It costs more to get a complex design. It will also take more time. And . . . " I hand them my design notebook. "These are some of my original designs that you can choose from. I can also probably do a design of your choice if you have one."

They take in my laminated price list with raised eyebrows, looking thoroughly impressed. I try not to beam with pride, because I have to be professional and I don't think grinning like a lunatic is part of professionalism.

I wait patiently as Janet and Catherine go through my design book, even though my heart is going too fast and I don't feel patient. I'm somewhere between excited and absolutely terrified.

Finally, Janet hands the notebook to me and points to one of the simpler designs. It's a cluster of flowers and leaves and swirls.

I smile. Easy.

"Great!" I say brightly. "This is the menu for the restaurant, by the way, if you want to order anything while you wait." I hand Catherine the leather-bound menu and reach for my henna tube. "Where do you want to get it?"

Janet seems to consider this for a moment, turning her hand round and round to get a good look.

"Umm . . . the back of my hand."

"Okay, can you put your hand palm down and flat on the table?" I ask.

Janet does exactly as I instruct her—wordlessly—and I get started. Catherine spends the entire time leaning forward in her chair and watching the process with wide eyes. Halfway through, Priti even snaps a few photos for the Instagram account.

When I'm finished, Janet looks at her hand with a smile on her lips. I'm smiling too, because the design came out exactly as it looks in the notebook.

"You'll have to keep it like that until it dries off. Shouldn't take more than thirty minutes, probably even less, but the longer you keep it on, the more the color will set."

"And how do I take it off of my hand?" she asks. "Is there like . . . a special chemical or something that I should use?"

I bite down a smile.

"Just brush it off over a sink. It might stain a bit—the sink, I mean—but it should wash off. Try not to wash it off with water. Your hand. Not the sink. You should wash the sink with water."

"Okay." Janet looks like she doesn't completely

understand me. "Can I take a photo for Instagram?"

"Sure! But could you tag me in it?"

"Of course." She grins, fishing around in her pocket for her phone. "Your turn, Cat."

Catherine and Janet exchange seats. Catherine is still unsure, I can tell by the way she's glancing back at Janet. "How long does it take to go away?" she asks.

"Well, assuming you let the color set properly, a few weeks. But if you don't like it and decide to wash it off, the color won't even have a chance to set."

That seems to convince her, because she nods her head.

"Do you want to look at my designs again?" I ask.

She quickly shakes her head and says, "I want the same as Jan's, is that okay?"

"Sure. Same place?"

She nods and I lay her hand on the table too, palm down. She giggles when I touch her hand with the henna tube.

I bite down another grin as I settle into the work. I get lost in it.

Fifteen minutes later, Catherine is admiring her hand the same as Janet, and I'm trying not to beam with pride.

"That'll be fifteen euros each." They both pay up happily, mumbling their *thank yous* and admiration.

I've known Catherine and Janet for years, and have never felt anything but nonchalance or even occasional dislike from them. This is the first time anything resembling respect has been aimed at me from my fellow classmates. If I'm honest, it feels good. For once, my classmates are actually admiring my culture instead of scoffing at it.

I mean, what I love about Bengali culture is much more than henna or the food, but those are things we can share here meaningfully.

I see Catherine and Janet off to the entrance of the restaurant, waving goodbye with the brightest smile I can muster while looking around for signs of any more customers.

Well, I had two. That must mean that more are on their way.

But when I slip back into the booth, Priti is staring at her phone with a look of such blazing anger that I know something is wrong immediately.

"Priti?"

She whips her head back to look at me, her face softening. "Apujan . . . " She shakes her head. "I think I know why you've had no customers."

"Racism and homophobia?" I say jokingly, but Priti only manages a weak smile.

"I mean . . . " She shrugs as she holds her phone up for me to see. It's a picture on Instagram of a garden filled with people. There's something familiar about it: the place and the people. There are so many of them that their faces blur together at first, but I pick them out: almost all of them are girls from our year. They're wearing white t-shirts, and they're covered in paint. Reds and blues and pinks. And there, front and center, is Chyna. Her blonde hair is floating around in wisps. The red of the paint stains her cheeks starkly against her pale skin.

The caption reads, *holi party with henna tattoos!!!*

I can only shake my head. This is a new low, even for Chyna.

"Holi isn't even for months and months," I say.

Priti sighs. "You think Chyna knows that? You think she knows anything about Holi other than the colors and an opportunity to get more people to pay for her henna?" There's a sinking feeling in my chest as I slip back into my seat, leaning back and letting out a deep sigh. Priti nestles up to me and says, "Don't worry, we'll get them."

But I'm just not sure anymore.

27

Priti takes the bus home, book bag in tow. She insisted she wouldn't leave me here to mope around by myself, but I promised her that if nobody else showed up in the next hour, I would get Abbu to drive me back home.

But with Priti gone and the booth empty except for me and my henna tubes, everything feels more overwhelming. Chyna is in her house, celebrating something that isn't hers—that she doesn't even understand in the slightest—and she's using it all for profit while I'm here hoping that a third customer shows up before the hour is up.

"Hey!"

When I look up, Flávia is peeking through the curtain.

"Can I come in? Are you . . . busy?"

I blink my eyes a little too fast to make sure that she's

really here. I didn't notice her in the picture Chyna had uploaded to her Instagram, but I can't imagine her *not* there. But here she is.

"Nishat? I can . . . come back later?" She looks over her shoulder, like if I say the word, she'll turn around and leave.

"I'm not busy," I say, patting the empty space beside me. She slides into the booth.

"What are you doing here?"

"Well, I saw your posts on Instagram . . . I thought I would just come down, maybe get some henna on my hands." She lifts up her palm as if to show me that she came prepared. Both her palms are surprisingly free from henna, though there are bits of faded red blobs and smudges, probably from applying it to other people. None of the stains look fresh.

I take hold of her palm, and run a finger over it.

"How come you don't have any henna on your hands?" I hold out my own palm, covered in dark brown henna. I also have henna designs all over my feet and ankles, and all the way up to my elbows. I've become my own canvas in this business venture.

"I'm not great at putting henna on myself, so I haven't really tried much."

"Right . . ."

I grab hold of my design book and hand it to her. "These are my designs, but . . . I don't know if it's a good idea to give money to your competition."

She shrugs. "I've had worse ideas."

She reaches over and begins to flip through my book. I peer at her closely, unsure how to ask about Chyna and her party.

"You're really good, Nishat." She pauses as she flips through the book, running her hands over the pages and tracing the designs with the tips of her fingers.

"I thought I didn't get art—that I'm not an artist." My words come out a little more resentful than I mean them to. But Flávia looks up with a smile.

"Have you ever had a moment when you feel like your tongue is saying words that you have no control over, and afterwards you wish you could take it all back?"

I shrug. "Maybe. Once or twice." I've definitely said and done some things I'm not proud of—especially recently.

"I'm sorry about what I said," Flávia sighs. "It was . . . I don't know. I guess I wasn't really thinking when I said those things . . . " For a moment I'm sure she's going to say more. Instead, she points to one of my drawings and exclaims, "I want this one!"

I edge closer, peering over her shoulder.

It's one of my most intricate designs. I've only attempted it once on myself, and it's since faded away. It has the base design of a peacock—one of the most common ones in Bangladesh.

"I don't have any designs like this, you know," Flávia says as I reach for my henna tube. "All of mine are a bit plain Jane. I don't know why people come to me and not you."

I pause, unsure how to respond to that. *If* I should respond to that. I take hold of the henna tube and begin to weave the design together on her hands. A few minutes of silence pass between us, with Flávia watching my work closely and me trying, and failing, to only think of the design at hand.

"Flávia . . . " I pause in the middle of my work, lifting my head to meet Flávia's eyes. "Why aren't you at Chyna's house?"

Flávia frowns. "Why would I be at Chyna's house?"

"I'm sure you know about her party."

Flávia's face falls. "How do you—"

"She put it on her Instagram."

"Oh."

"Yeah."

There's a silence that hangs heavy in the air between us for a moment. Then, Flávia heaves a sigh, shaking her head. "I'm sorry," she says, in a voice that sounds so sincere that it pulls my heartstrings a little too tight. "Chyna is . . . she's so adamant about winning this thing. She's been getting carried away."

Except this has always been Chyna. She's been "getting

carried away" with things her whole life.

"How can she even do henna without you?"

Flávia glances at me hesitantly. "She . . . has stencils."

"*Stencils?*" My voice comes out more high-pitched than I intend it to. Nothing should shock me at this point, not even that people in our school would go to a "Holi party" thrown by a white girl who applies henna with stencils. Not after everything.

Still, it does.

"I told her that I wasn't going to her party and . . . that was her solution." Flávia shrugs. "I know it's . . . bad. The whole thing is . . . " She shakes her head again, like she can't put into words how bad it really is.

"And you didn't tell her that she shouldn't? That the whole thing was offensive?" I know Chyna's not really the type of person who listens to reason, or who does something because other people tell her to. But Flávia obviously means a lot to her. She backed off after she caught me with the henna tubes because of Flávia. And the way the two of them were with each other in Flávia's house—casual and free. Chyna *listens* to her—more than she listens to anyone else, anyway.

Flávia scrunches up her face in concentration for a moment, like she's thinking really hard about something. "She told me that if she couldn't throw that party, then I couldn't do henna. That they were the same thing."

Flávia takes a deep breath. It's heavy, like the weight of the world is on her shoulders and she doesn't know how to shake it off. "And she's kind of right, isn't she? I was the person who made her brave enough to think this is okay. I get it now. Why you were angry at me to begin with. I just . . . I wasn't thinking straight, you know? I went to that wedding and I just . . . thought because I liked it, I could run with it. I didn't really think about anything else. And . . . if I'm being honest, I kind of just wanted to have something to talk to you about when school started."

"That's . . . not true." I frown. "Is it?"

"Yes, it's true. I've never really done this before, Nishat." She's looking at me with wide eyes.

"This?"

She shakes her head and with a chuckle, says, "You're kind of intimidating. I mean, you're so self-assured and confident . . . "

"You think *I'm* self-assured?" My voice rises a notch. "You think I'm confident?"

"Nishat, come on. You're the most self-assured person I know. You're so . . . you have all of these things you believe in and you don't bend from them just because it might not be cool or people might not like it about you. You always stand your ground and . . . you're so into your culture."

"That's not self-assuredness." I feel a warm flutter in my chest.

Flávia smiles like she doesn't quite agree with me.

"I wish I could be like that. Sometimes, I feel like . . . "

"Feel like . . . ?"

"Like . . . I don't know. Like I don't really feel Brazilian sometimes, you know? Especially around Chyna and her side of my family. It feels like they want me to be something else altogether, and it's just easier to conform. I want them to like me. To accept me. But . . . "

I'm suddenly aware that there's a sadness to Flávia. I didn't notice it before, but maybe it's always been there, underneath everything.

"Is that what all of this has been about? Getting Chyna and her family to accept you?"

Flávia heaves a sigh and brushes back her hair, smudging it with the half-finished henna design on her palm.

"Oh no!" she cries, trying to take the henna out of her brown curls but somehow making it worse.

I know if this was Priti messing up my hard work, I would be beyond annoyed. But it's not. It's Flávia and she looks so adorably alarmed that it makes me smile.

I reach over and grab one of the tissues I set aside for exactly an occasion like this and use it to tug at her hair. The henna has settled into her thin curls, sticking them to one another and refusing to come away.

"You know henna is really good for your hair?" I mumble.

"Yeah?"

"Yeah, it makes your hair healthier. Plus, it's a natural hair dye . . . I mean, not really for you and me because our hair is super dark already, but . . . " I'm suddenly aware of the fact that I'm holding Flávia's hair and she's inches away from me and looking at me a little too closely. I realize that pulling henna out of someone's hair is not exactly the most romantic thing in the world, but it feels oddly intimate, especially since I can hear the sound of her breathing.

Flávia grazes her fingers against my cheek, brushing back a strand of my own hair and sending a jolt of electricity through me.

This time, when we lean toward each other, there are no interruptions.

When our lips finally touch, it feels like there are a million butterflies in my stomach. Like my heart is going double its usual pace. Like there's nothing and nobody I want more than this.

When we pull away from each other, Flávia looks at me as if she's surprised. Like she didn't mean to kiss me at all.

My stomach plummets. What if she thinks this is another mistake?

Before I can wonder about it further, she leans forward until our foreheads are touching, brushing her nose against mine. I can feel her hot breath on my skin.

"You smell like henna," she says. Which is totally appropriate, I guess.

I scrunch up my nose and pull away from her. We're surrounded by the earthy smell of henna, and I'm actually not sure if the smell is coming from her or me or the tubes on the table—or all of it.

"Is that bad?"

She smiles, threads her fingers through mine, and pulls me closer.

"I love the smell of henna." She kisses me again, but it's barely more than a chaste peck. I want it to last longer. To get lost in it. In her.

But she pulls away and sighs. "I don't know what I'm doing, Nishat."

"What do you mean?"

"I mean . . . this . . . you . . . I'm . . . " She shakes her head.

"Confused?" I remember when I felt like that too. I was confused because I couldn't see the appeal of all the men that everybody else considered attractive. I could see it in an abstract, distant way I guess. But they never made my heart race the way that girls did. That girls do.

I guess I was less confused about what I felt than I was

about what other people expected me to feel.

But how can Flávia be confused after she just kissed me like that a moment ago?

"Scared," she admits finally. In a small voice. "Of telling people. Chyna."

"I'm sorry," I mumble. "I know what it's like. Telling people. My parents . . . didn't take it too well."

"I told my mom."

"You did?"

She nods. "A while ago. Last year . . . when . . . I mean. There was this girl . . . "

Something flares inside me that feels oddly like anger. Jealousy? I push it down as deep as I can, trying to appear as nonchalant as possible as I say, "Oh?"

"I mean, it was . . . different. From this, from you. Nothing happened. But I was confused and . . . I trust my mom, you know? We're close. So I told her that . . . I don't know. I said that I thought I might be bisexual."

"And . . . ?"

She smiles. "She was . . . I mean, I don't think she was expecting it. And it took her a while to wrap her head around it. But I think she's okay with it. She's never made a big fuss or anything."

"Oh, that's . . . that's good. I'm glad." I am glad, but that feeling, something like jealousy, rears its head inside of me again, crawling through my skin and clawing at my heart. This time it's not about some girl but about the way that Flávia seems so nonchalant about her mom not making a big fuss. I'm jealous that it's come so easy to her, this revelation. When it has cost me my family.

Flávia tucks a strand of hair behind my ear, and her fingers brushing against me sends heat scalding down my skin. We're still so close to each other that we could touch at a moment's notice. I have to get my thoughts back on track. Just the sight of her, the thought of her, sends me into a jumble.

"Can I ask you something?"

"Sure."

"If you knew you were bisexual . . . why were you so weird after the Junior Cert party?"

She looks down at her stained orange palms like they will have the answer to my question. "Do you know any Brazilians, Nishat?"

"I know you."

"Other than me?" She smiles.

There are a lot of Brazilians in Ireland, but in our school, Flávia is the only Brazilian girl I know of. So I shake my head slowly.

"Well . . . you know, it's not exactly easy to be Brazilian here. When people think of Brazil, they think . . . I don't know, *futebol*, Carnival, partying—whatever. And all the boys think because I'm a Brazilian girl, I'll be up for anything. You don't know the way they look at me, the things they say. And Chyna doesn't get it. She kind of encourages it. After that party, I just kept thinking how much worse it would be if it was true that I was bisexual. Brazilian and bisexual? I would never hear the end of it."

"I get it," I say, even though I don't think I really do. But I want to. I'm trying to. "Is Chyna really that important to you?"

"It's not just Chyna . . . " she says hesitantly, like she's really picking and choosing her words. "It's just that . . . my mom brought me back here because she thought it would be good for me to get to know my dad and his side of the family. Even if they're a little conservative. A little different from us. And . . . yes, Chyna and I have had this bond our entire lives. I don't know how to explain it. I can't exactly throw that away."

Flávia might not understand it, but I think I do. After seeing the way they were together, with no inhibitions; that's the way you are with people you love.

I don't say any of this to Flávia. Instead, I say, "Family can be difficult. Complicated. I get it."

She pulls me a little closer and says, "I'm sorry, Nishat. I'm going to try and take care of it."

I'm not sure if she will, or even if she can. What I do I know is that I want this moment to last, to stretch into a million moments that we share. So I nod, choosing to believe her.

28

I WAKE UP ON SUNDAY STILL THINKING ABOUT KISSING Flávia. I'm buzzing with a kind of happiness that I haven't felt in a long time. Sure, my parents are still super weird about my sexuality. And the entire school knows, and is actively whispering about me behind my back—when people aren't doing things like refusing to use the same changing rooms as me. But none of that holds much weight right now.

Later that morning, Chaewon and Jess show up at the restaurant with bright smiles. It's just me there. Priti stayed home, deciding not to emerge from her bedroom since breakfast.

"I'm ready to be beautified!" Jess exclaims, sliding into the booth and flipping through my design book. Chaewon rolls her eyes, but shoots me a grin.

"Have you had many customers yet?" she asks.

I shake my head. "Chyna . . . decided to have a party yesterday during the time my booth was open."

"Seriously?" Chaewon asks. I shrug. After all, what else is there to say?

"We need to get back at them!" Jess bangs her fist against the table, before pulling her hand back and rubbing her fingers. "Hard table," she says sheepishly.

I swallow a smile. "Come on, let's forget about it, okay? You're my first customers of the day!" Surprisingly, they drop the subject and let me apply henna to both their hands, from the back of their fingertips all the way up to their elbows. They look wedding-ready by the time I'm done. I even throw in a friends and family discount, even though they insist on paying the full price.

No other customers show up. I'm not exactly surprised, but I can't help the disappointment that floods through me.

Flávia: *Still at the restaurant?*

Flávia's text comes just as I'm packing everything up, ready to go.

About to leave! I type back. The three dots indicating Flávia is typing show up immediately, like she's been waiting for me to text her back.

Meet me in town in 15?

So that's how I find myself at Gino's fifteen minutes

later, sharing an ice cream with Flávia. It's only forty degrees outside, so ice cream probably isn't the best idea, but if the people in Ireland let the weather stop them from having ice cream they'd rarely get the chance to indulge in it.

The good thing, of course, is that Gino's is almost empty. There's just a couple in one corner that's maybe getting a little too cozy, and a family of three that's a little too loud, but nothing to disrupt Flávia's fingers intertwined with mine, or her gaze boring into me.

"Is this . . . a date?" The question tumbles out of me before I can stop it, and I immediately feel myself warm.

Flávia grins. "If you want it to be."

"You paid for my ice cream—that's date-like behavior," I mumble.

Flávia's grin widens. "Right, but the hand-holding and ice-cream-sharing are just regular friend stuff."

I kick her foot under the table and say, "I've never been on a date before. I don't know what qualifies as a date."

Flávia lets out a small laugh. "Yes, this is a date. And it's definitely one of my best ones."

"You're just saying that to make me feel better."

She shakes her head, squeezing my fingers. "Come on, Nishat." There's a lot of reassurance in the way she says it—deep and husky—like it's a secret meant only for me. A moment meant only for us.

After our ice cream—Belgian chocolate and Nutella—

Flávia loops her elbow through mine and drags me toward the Ha'penny Bridge.

"I should be getting home," I say, making absolutely no effort to untangle myself from her.

"Soon," she reassures me. I don't believe her and I don't want to.

We climb the steps of the bridge. It's a Sunday and there are still huge crowds of people passing by on each side. Flávia pulls us into the middle. On one side, we can see O'Connell Bridge, wide and sturdy, brimming with people and cars.

But Flávia turns the other way. Through the white railings of the Ha'penny Bridge we can see down the River Liffey, where the sunset is turning the city into a kaleidoscope.

"When I was little, my mom used to bring me here." Flávia lets go of my hand and stands on her tiptoes so she can take in the sunset in all its glory. I watch the colors deflect off of her, illuminating her hair, her eyes. The curve of her lips. I want to kiss her, but it feels strange in this crowded place.

"She would tell me about São Paulo while the sun set."

"Do you wish you could go there?" I ask tentatively.

She nods, though she doesn't look at me. "Yeah, sometimes. It's like I have this weird pull for a place that I barely know. I don't understand it. My sister went two years ago with her boyfriend. She says maybe we can go together when she graduates from her Master's next year."

"That would be good, right?" I think about my own time in Bangladesh; I was lucky to grow up around family, learning about my culture and my language.

"Yeah . . . " Flávia finally catches my eye. "It's just . . . it's kind of nerve-wracking too."

I slip my fingers through hers once more and press closer. The passers-by don't care about the two girls paused in the middle of the street, or the orange glow the sun has cast over us all.

"I get it. I lived in Bangladesh for so many years but I still feel anxious about going back."

Flávia smiles and turns back to the sky again. "First date watching the sunset. It's kind of cheesy."

"It's sweet."

She gives me a sheepish smile. "So . . . cheesy?"

"Romantic." The words tumble out, braver than I feel.

Her smile widens. She pulls me closer. Suddenly, it's like there is no one but us on this busy Dublin bridge as she presses her lips to mine.

29

It's our second showcase on Friday. I wake up early to get into school and set everything up before everyone else gets there. After what happened during the first one, I can't help how nervous I feel. I know I can't be outed all over again, and I should be elated about the fact that Flávia and I are . . . something. But none of that takes away the heavy feeling in my chest.

"We'll be at the school in the afternoon," Ammu reminds me as I'm about to slip out the door. I'd almost forgotten parents were invited to today's showcase; I hadn't considered my parents might want to come. Especially considering we still had barely talked since I was outed to the whole school.

"How did you know?" I know it's the wrong question to ask, but it tumbles out before I can stop it.

"We got a text."

"Abbu is coming too?"

She nods and finally meets my eyes. She parts her lips for a moment, as if she's about to say something.

"Nishat, I'm . . . " she begins. Her eyes bore into mine and I don't know what to expect. " . . . good luck today," she finishes weakly.

I wish Priti were here, but she's probably still asleep. My whole body shakes on the way to school. Ammu wished me luck, but that doesn't mean anything. Even if it is the most she's said to me in a long time.

I don't know how I'm supposed to entertain my parents in school today. I don't know how I'm supposed to face them in the same vicinity as Flávia and pretend they haven't rejected me.

I gulp down my anxiety and look straight ahead at the rain splattering the windshield of the bus. I just have to find a way to power through this day.

At school, I hang Flávia's banner up on my stall, admiring the way it fits the whole aesthetic of my business perfectly. The colors are exactly the ones that set into your skin after henna dries off.

Chaewon and Jess come around holding a box of supplies as I'm setting out my henna tubes and design book on the table in front of me.

"Whoa, nice banner," Jess comments, nodding at it

admiringly. "You did it yourself?"

"Please." I roll my eyes, because Jess should definitely know better than that.

"Priti?" Chaewon asks, taking the banner in admiringly.

I wonder for a moment how Chaewon and Jess would take it if I told them it was Flávia. What exactly they would think of that. But I just shake my head and change the topic.

"Shouldn't you two be at your stall, getting ready? It's a big showcase. Are your parents coming?"

Chaewon nods her head excitedly, like she can't wait for her parents to show up. "My mom is so excited that people at school like the stuff we're selling. She says it's big in Korea but she didn't think kids here would like it too." She grins so wide that I'm surprised it doesn't hurt her lips.

"Anyway, we're here to help you!" Jess dramatically sets down the box she's carrying on the table. "We brought over some stuff to help you out with your stall."

"Really?"

"Yeah," Jess shrugs. "I mean, you're on your own here and . . ."

" . . . it's kind of our fault," Chaewon finishes with a sheepish smile.

"We had different creative visions," is all I say, before digging into the box. It's full of fairy lights and colorful crepe paper. "Thanks."

Jess and Chaewon help me finish setting up, stringing up fairy lights, and spreading the crepe paper around until the booth looks a little magical.

The showcase starts off okay. Even though almost every other booth gets more attention than mine, a few stragglers stop over and let me paint their hands with my henna. It's not a lot—but it's the most business I've gotten since this whole thing started.

An hour into the showcase, Jess comes over, nodding at my table with approval. "We did a pretty good job."

I roll my eyes. "You did. With yours too." Their stall has had nonstop customers—mostly students and teachers, but even the early arriving parents have been drawn to it.

"Well, will you do my henna?" Jess asks, taking a seat. "The other side." She holds up her empty palm.

"Sure." I smile and show her my design book, getting everything ready as she makes her choice about what henna design to get.

Once she's decided, she places her hand flat on the table in front of me and I hover my hand over hers, henna tube at the ready.

"I wanted to say I'm sorry." The sudden outburst takes me out of my work. When I look up, she's studying me with a frown. It's the most serious I've ever seen her look.

"You've already apologized," I say.

"Not really. Not for the real stuff," Jess sighs. "Like . . . not believing you about Chyna. And leaving you out to dry instead of supporting your idea for the henna business."

"It's okay. You're supporting me now."

"How come . . . " She stops and takes a deep breath. "How come you never told us about you being gay?"

I can only shrug. Why didn't I ever tell them? It wasn't that I never thought about it, but after I told Ammu and Abbu it felt like a curtain fell over that part of me. A curtain I couldn't part, no matter how hard I tried. Every time I thought about telling them, telling anyone, I only remembered what Ammu said about making choices. I know it's not about making choices—rationally—but to tell other people would feel like confirming what Ammu was most afraid of: Me choosing to bring us shame. And I wasn't sure if I could handle rejection and loss a second time.

Jess frowns, like she's really thinking about it. I worry she'll be angry and lash out. After all, she and I haven't had the best track record lately. But she nods her head and stills her hand beneath me.

"I think I get it. I probably wouldn't have told me either, if I were you. Especially . . . after everything." I expect her to say more, to ask more questions. But she doesn't. She just looks at me expectantly with her hand thrust out in front of her.

Once I bend over to work on the henna design, it's like I've left the loud, stuffy hallway of St. Catherine's and entered a world of my own. A world where it's only me and the henna and Jess's hand. Not even Jess, just her hand—as if it's dismembered and floating. I barely feel her presence as I work away, so when she leans forward and a strand of her brown hair brushes over my shoulder, I jump in surprise. A thin, dark line of henna makes it way down her forearm.

"Sorry!" Jess exclaims at the same time I do. I grab a tissue from my table and dab her arm.

"I was just trying to get a good look." Her voice is higher than usual.

"It's okay. Look." There's a pale, fading line where I smudged the henna, but it's more or less invisible and should be gone in a few minutes.

"You're so concentrated when you're working," Jess comments. I blush, because I'm not sure if this is a compliment or an insult.

"It takes concentration."

"I know, I know. Just . . . " She takes a deep breath and sits back in her chair, brushing a strand of hair behind her ear. "I should have listened to you before. When you wanted the three of us to do this. I was . . . I didn't really understand. And you're . . . wow, you're talented." She's looking at her own henna-clad arm now. I try not to smile because that would make me seem condescending, but I also kind of want to say, "Ha! Told you so!"

Instead, I say, "Thanks."

Nobody else shows up to my booth until we break for lunch. It's been mostly lower classes let out to venture into the hallway for the morning; I'm hoping that after lunch, when more adults show up, I'll get a little more business. I try not to let the fact that there's been a constant stream of people outside Flávia and Chyna's booth bother me as I weave past them to join Chaewon and Jess for lunch.

"You *have* to look at some of the other booths when you're free," Jess says excitedly, taking a bite of her sandwich and speaking with her mouth half open and half full. "There's some really cool stuff. Did you see the stall full of handmade plushies? So cool!"

"There isn't really anybody to watch my stall if I go strolling around." I shrug. Jess clamps her mouth shut and glances at Chaewon with a guilty look. "That's not supposed to be accusing you of something," I add quickly. "I'm just saying."

Jess and Chaewon don't bring up the other stalls again during lunch, but I do text Priti to hurry up and help me with the stall when she can.

She texts back, *YOU KNOW I HAVE THE JUNIOR CERT!!!!!!!!* before immediately following that up with, *I'll be there after lunch.*

After lunch, we all shuffle into the near-empty hallway. Chaewon and Jess hurry over to their stall, and I follow, passing Flávia and Chyna. Flávia gives me a secret smile as I pass her, and I can't help the jolt of electricity that momentary smile sends through me.

Chaewon and Jess's stall is smack bang in the middle of everything. The absolute perfect spot. As soon as we get there, Chaewon begins to sort through things, ensuring everything is perfect. Jess watches her, a bemused expression on her face.

"I wish your stall was close by so we could help each other out," Jess says.

I wish that too. I could really use a helping hand.

I shrug. "It's okay. Priti's going to come over to help me."

I stroll over to my near isolated corner, and I stop in my tracks.

"Nice setup you have here."

I turn to find Cáit O'Connell smirking at me, her eyes flitting from me to the table "setup" in front of me. It's nothing like I left it earlier. The banner Flávia made me is ripped through the middle, with jagged edges where Nishat's Mehndi had been. The fairy lights Jess and

Chaewon had carefully strung around the entire table are stripped off and lying on the floor, the glass on most of them broken.

I rush toward the table, trying to push back the lump in my throat and the tears prickling behind my eyes. The henna tubes I had carefully placed on the table are slashed open, and the henna is staining the crepe paper and table, but I'm more concerned about my design book, which I had tucked away in a hidden corner.

I breathe a sigh of relief when I finally find it under the table. Whoever did this must have accidentally dropped it and not even noticed. The loose pages I had stuffed into it are spread across the dirty floor but it's otherwise unharmed. I shove the pages back in and pull the book to my chest. I have never been happier to see a book before, and I'm often very happy to see them.

But there is still the matter of my stall being trashed.

When I look up from the table, Cáit has gone back to her own stall, arranging different cosmetics into a straight line. The rest of the hallway is awash with happy noise— of work, play, excitement.

I slump down on my chair. All of my hard work—gone. Just like that.

"What the hell happened here?" Jess and Chaewon are standing over me; Jess is glaring at the bare table with furrowed eyebrows, like it's wronged her, and Chaewon is peering at me with soft eyes like I'm a kicked puppy she needs to protect.

"Someone . . . I don't know, they messed my table up." I somehow manage to get the words out even though the lump in my throat has set up camp and is showing no sign of dissipating anytime soon.

"We have to tell Ms. Montgomery!" Chaewon says, at the same time that Jess casts a glare across the hall and declares, "I'm going to kill Chyna."

"You don't know it was her." Chaewon interjects.

"Who else would it be?"

I shake my head. "It could have been anyone," I say. I think about the way Cáit smirked when I came over. Did she do this? Chyna? Ali? The list of people who hate me simply for being me is too long, and I'm not sure what I'd do about it even if I knew who did this.

30

"Apujan!" Priti's voice cuts through the throng of people darting around the hallway, eyes hungrily taking in everything that's on offer. She's grinning from ear to ear—until she takes in my sad, trashed stall.

"What happened here?" she asks.

I've been trying to clean it up. I successfully wiped up the spilled henna and cleaned up the trashed fairy lights, but there are still bits of glass and shredded crepe paper lying about. The slashed banner I folded up and slipped into my bag. It can't be salvaged, but the idea of throwing it away makes my heart hurt.

"Someone trashed my stall," I say. People passing by have been giving me sympathetic looks, but apparently they're not sympathetic enough to offer to help.

"Ali?" Priti whispers.

I shrug. "I don't know, maybe. It doesn't even matter."

"You should tell Ms. Montgomery." She looks around, but Ms. Montgomery hasn't returned from her lunch break yet. "Ok—Ms. Grenham. Ok—"

"No," I cut her off firmly. "What are they going to do?" Priti doesn't know that I've been late to P.E. almost every day since being outed because now I have to change after all the other girls have left. She doesn't know the things I hear them whisper about me sometimes. She doesn't know that there's nothing to be done about it all—just like nobody ever called out Chyna for all of the awful, racist things she has done, nobody is going to face consequences for their homophobia in this school.

"Apujan."

"Just leave it," I say.

She frowns, before casting a glance over her shoulder. "I don't know if you're going to have a choice, Apujan. Ammu and Abbu are here."

"What?"

When I look up and follow her gaze, I can make out my parents weaving their way through the crowd, sticking out like sore thumbs. Ammu is wearing a green and red saree, one that I've only ever seen her wear on Noboborsho, the Bengali New Year. Abbu has opted to go traditional too, with a collared off-white Panjabi with a subtle black and gold design along the edges. They both look far too fancy for a regular school function; I can see some of the other kids, and *a lot* of the other parents looking at them with raised eyebrows.

If this was any other day, I might be embarrassed, but right now I actually feel a swell of pride and joy. Their fancy outfits are an obvious show of support.

They stop in front of my stall with frowns on their lips and exchange a quick glance with each other. Speaking in that unique, exclusive language they've always had.

"What's this?" Ammu asks. "This is your stall?"

I know she doesn't mean it as an insult, but I wince.

"It's . . . " I'm not sure how to string the words together to tell them what happened, but before I can try, Priti chimes in.

"Somebody destroyed it!"

"What?" Abbu asks, one eyebrow raised.

I shoot Priti a glare. "I came back from lunch and all my stuff was . . . gone."

Abbu and Ammu share another look. Then, to my surprise, Ammu steps forward and plops herself down on the chair I have set up for customers. She looks small and uncomfortable—like she really, really doesn't belong, especially in her saree.

"Well?" She looks up at me. "Aren't you going to do my mehndi?"

I grab one of the only henna tubes that hasn't been slashed and begin to weave henna patterns into her hands while Abbu goes for a stroll around the hall with Priti.

"I'll scope out the competition!" Priti says with a little too much delight in her voice, while Abbu shakes his head, like he's not quite sure how he got stuck with her.

"Does this happen often?" Ammu asks after so much time has passed that I'm drawing flowers at the edge of her fingertips, and her palm and forearm are already covered in henna.

"Henna?" I look up to see her staring at me a little too intently.

"No, not henna." She nods at my bare table. "The thing that happened to your stall."

"Oh." I take hold of her palm again and draw a flower on the tip of her ring finger. "Not *this* specifically."

"But other things?"

"Sometimes, yeah." I feel the prick of tears in my eyes and blink them back. I don't want to be having this conversation with anyone, least of all Ammu when it finally seems like we're reconciling our relationship in some way.

Silence hangs between us until I finally finish her henna. Then she stares at her hands like it's the first time she's seeing them.

"You know your Nanu will try to make a museum out of your henna designs when she sees your handiwork, right?"

I bite down a smile, but I can't help the way warmth spreads all over me.

"You like it?" I ask.

"It's beautiful," Ammu says.

I'm somewhere between relief and sadness when the day finally comes to an end and I can pack up my things and head home.

"You know, the other businesses aren't as original as yours," Abbu tells me in the car, between Rabindranath sangits.

"And not as talented either," Ammu adds with a nod toward Abbu.

"They're obviously very jealous of you to have done what they did," Priti says, crossing her arms over her chest and looking out the window. She's probably talking about Ali. But I doubt any of it was because of jealousy.

"It doesn't matter," I sigh. "Only a few more weeks . . ." Considering the way my customers had swiftly dwindled from few to none, I seriously doubt I'm in the running to win. No matter how original my idea is, or how talented I apparently am.

To my surprise, a few minutes after we get home, the bell rings. When I swing the door open, Flávia is standing in the doorway, her face flushed from the cold.

"Hey . . . " she says. I saw her out of the corner of my eye a few times during the showcase today, but our stalls were so far apart, and after I found my stall trashed I couldn't face going up to hers.

"Hi."

She gives me a hesitant smile and says, "You know it wasn't Chyna. She was with me the whole day today."

I shake my head. "Come inside." I step aside to allow her through, and close the door behind us.

We stand at the threshold, taking each other in like maybe this is the last time we'll be able to. It feels far more dramatic than it should, and all I'm really thinking about is that day in her house and how she said goodbye to me in her doorway by brushing my hair behind my ear. I feel goosebumps erupt on my skin just at the thought.

"Tea?" I push past her into the kitchen.

"Sure."

I put the kettle on and pick out two mugs from the cabinet, getting them ready with tea bags.

"Do you want to sit?"

Flávia looks at the stiff wooden chairs against the dining table and nods. She slips into one, looking out of place and uncomfortable. I bring the tea to her, and take my place on the opposite side of the table.

"So . . ."

"So . . ."

She cradles her mug in her hand, but doesn't take a sip. I didn't even ask her how she likes her tea, I realize. I just made it the way I make it for myself. I should have asked. Now she'll have a horrible cup of tea that she can't even drink and maybe that'll be the only thing she'll remember about me and our relationship. I'll be the girl she kissed who smelled like henna and made her horrible tea and made her sit in a terribly uncomfortable chair through an even more uncomfortable silence because conversation was too difficult for her.

"I think—" I say at the same time that she says, "I've been thinking—"

We both pause. Catch each other's eye. Smiles spread across our faces simultaneously.

Flávia reaches her hand across the table until her fingers find mine. She laces them together. Our hands fit perfectly together. Hers is still cold from outside. Mine is warm from the tea.

"I've been thinking about what happened today and . . . I'm sorry. I should have come to you. Spoken to you. Texted you. Something. I mean, it wasn't Chyna, but she wasn't exactly sad about it. She's been saying stuff about you for a long time now." She grips my hand tighter. "It's just that I've been so afraid they'll all turn around and do the same to me if I speak up. That they'll know. I'm . . . not ready for anyone to know yet."

I exhale. My decision pieces together in my mind, like a puzzle finally coming together.

"I understand."

"You do?" She raises an eyebrow.

"I do, but . . . "

She sighs. "There it is."

"I just don't think I can deal with it right now. Not with everything going on and . . . with Chyna being your cousin . . . I just . . . I can't pretend and hide. I can't sneak around for you. I can't—"

"I'm not asking—"

"I know." I cut her off because I do know. Flávia should tell them when she's ready. When she wants to. When she thinks it's her time. She should tell them for her, not for me. But that doesn't change how I feel. I can't take back the fact that Ali has outed me. I don't want to take it back. And to go into hiding with Flávia would be a step back, not a step forward. "I just can't deal with it, I guess. Being with you but . . . having to deal with them. When they don't know. And the things they'll say . . . about me and my family. I can't take it."

She nods. Her hand squeezes mine for a moment. The warmth of her spreads through me.

Then she pulls back her hand. The distance between us

seems miles long all of a sudden. It's unfathomable that just a moment ago we were touching.

"I get it." There's a waver in her voice I wish I couldn't hear. "I should go."

"Flávia."

"You're right. Please don't say anything else." She gets out of her chair, and I watch. There's nothing else I can say, really. Reassuring her wouldn't make things better. And it wouldn't be honest.

"Can I . . . " She stops and looks me in the eye. "I want to pull out of the competition. Everything that's happened . . . it's all wrong. I see it now and I should have seen it before. You were always right and I always knew it. I just . . . I didn't want to see it."

I shake my head. "I don't want to win because you let me," I say. "I want to win because I earned it."

"Even if everything is stacked up against you?"

I shrug. "Even if everything is stacked up against me."

"I'm sorry."

"I know."

She hesitates for a moment, taking me in. I think she's going to protest. Or say something. But she doesn't. With a wave of her hand, she turns and disappears from sight. I hear the front door click open and shut, and only then do I start breathing normally again. My chest hurts so much with all the anxiety I've been holding in.

I stare at the full mug of tea Flávia left behind. Untouched.

All I can think is that at least she won't remember me as the girl who makes terrible tea.

31

"What did she want?" Priti asks when I come upstairs and slump down on my bed, taking a deep breath, like that will make the events from the past few weeks disappear from my mind.

"We . . . broke up." It feels strange to say it aloud. Especially since I never really said aloud that we were together. Our relationship was shorter than Kim Kardashian's last marriage.

"I'm sorry." Priti lies down on the bed next to me and wraps her arms around me. It's super awkward because half her body is on me, but it's a nice gesture, I guess.

"Thanks," I mumble, extracting myself from her slowly. "But you don't have to pretend that you're not happy about it."

Priti turns to me with a frown. "I'm not *pretending*," she

says, like I've accused her of doing something horrendous. "I know I was resistant to her, but . . . " Her shoulders rise in a shrug. "If she made you happy . . . that's the most important thing."

I sigh, and turn to my side so Priti and I are face-to-face. "She's Chyna's cousin."

"Yeah, that part is *weird*," Priti agrees, scrunching up her nose. "Is that why you broke up?"

I take a deep breath. "Not exactly, but it played a part. Mostly, it's because Flávia doesn't want to come out and . . . I don't want to have a secret relationship. Plus, I can't imagine being with Flávia when Chyna is saying awful things about me being a lesbian."

"I'm sorry, Apujan," Priti says again, laying her head against my shoulder. I pull her closer and close my eyes. "You know . . . you should tell everyone that Ali sent the text. You don't have to protect her."

"I'm not protecting her," I scoff. In reality, I'm trying to protect Priti. It's hard enough losing your best friend of many years to something like this. Letting it fizzle out into nothingness instead of blowing it up to the entire school seems like the better option.

"We're not friends anymore, so you should tell everyone." Priti says it confidently, but I can see the hurt behind her eyes. She hasn't been quite the same these past few weeks.

"I think losing you as a friend might be the worst punishment she could ever have."

"I can think of a few others," Priti mumbles.

I roll my eyes. "I think we should put all of those shenanigans behind us. We were pretty terrible at them."

"I told you you aren't James Bond," Priti says, nudging me with her shoulder. I have to laugh, because I'm not sure why I ever thought sneaking around and sabotaging *Chyna* of all people would actually get me any positive results.

Ammu calls me into her bedroom on Saturday morning. When I show up at her doorway, Ammu is sitting on her bed with a bottle of coconut oil and a hairbrush by her side. Abbu is on the rocking chair by the bed, reading a book about the Bangladeshi War of Independence.

"Come here." Ammu pats the spot on the bed in front of her. When I scoot into position, she pulls me closer and begins running the hairbrush through my hair. It tugs a little at my tangles. It hurts, but only slightly.

When we were kids, Ammu used to brush my and Priti's hair every night before bed. We loved it so much that we always fought about who got to go first, until Ammu worked out a system: we would each go first every other day, so it was always fair.

"When was the last time you put oil in your hair?" Ammu asks accusatorily, running her fingers through the strands. "Look, your hair's gone all dry. Once it all falls out there's no getting it back, you know."

"My hair isn't going to fall out, Ammu."

"You never know. You have beautiful hair, like I had when I was young. And now, look." I don't know what she's talking about, because Ammu's hair is still long and thick and black as ink. "Don't cut off your hair, okay?"

I frown. "Why would I do that?"

"I don't know. Sometimes girls like you cut their hair short," she says.

"Girls like . . . me?"

"You know."

Lesbians. She's talking about lesbians. There's a weird comfort in hearing her—well, not say it exactly, but . . . recognize it. Out of the corner of my eye, I see Abbu fidgeting in his chair like he's not really paying attention to his book.

"There are a lot of lesbians with long hair, too," I say.

"Where? There's that woman, you know? Helen DayJinnraas. Her hair is so short, she looks like a . . . a lesbian." Ammu's voice dips low when she says the word *lesbian*, like it's not meant to be said aloud.

"Well, she *is* one. Her name is Ellen DeGeneres, by the way. And her wife has beautiful, long hair."

"And her wife is a lesbian, not a bisexual?"

I turn around so fast at that that the hairbrush is left swinging from my hair, pulled out of Ammu's hand.

"What are you doing?" She tries to get a grip of the brush again.

"Why do you know what a bisexual is?"

"I've been reading."

"About lesbians?"

"And bisexuals. And paansexuals." She says "pansexual" like they're people attracted to paan, the food, not people who feel attraction to people of all genders. "And . . . what is it called? Transgender. Like hijra, right?"

"Pansexual, Ammu," I mumble under my breath, though I'm impressed she knows even this much.

"Paansexual, that's what I said." She finally turns me back around and puts the hairbrush away. For a while, we sit in silence; I'm trying to figure out what I should say next while she begins to part the strands of my hair to rub oil into my scalp.

When she's finished, she pats me on the head like I'm a pet.

"You know, when I told your Nanu and Nana about me and your Abbu I didn't understand why they were so angry. He had such great prospects in front of him. So did I. It made no sense. Later, I realized that I was supposed to have lied about it, that that would have made it better. If

I had pretended I had never spoken to him before, never known him, that he was a stranger who I liked the look of and nothing more, then nobody would have spoken about us in hushed whispers like we were shameful. Amma and Abba would have been able to hold their heads up high, because I would have made the right choices."

"You said you regret what happened. You feel ashamed." That conversation is imprinted onto my mind and I'm not sure if I can ever forget it.

"I did. I do. I . . . " She trails off. "At the time, I didn't understand. I thought I was supposed to be honest with my parents. I thought I *had* made all of the right choices, so why was I being punished for one wrong thing? I was angry, you know. At the wedding, wearing my red saree and mehndi and jewelry, I couldn't be happy because I kept looking out at the sea of faces and thinking of what they were probably saying about me. I didn't want you to go through that, Nishat."

I push back the strands of my hair and blink up at her. I can't wrap my head around her words.

"But that's how you've been feeling anyway, isn't it?"

I nod, feeling a lump rising in my throat.

"I was just trying to understand. I don't . . . understand it, Nishat. I've never met someone like that before." There's a slight waver in her voice. "I thought . . . it was just something that happened here. Not to Bengali girls.

Not to my daughter."

"It's not something that happens, Ammu." I rub at the tears running down my cheeks. "It's something that I am."

"I know." She reaches out, wrapping her arms around me. "I know."

When Ammu and I pull away, we're both rubbing at our eyes. Even Abbu has put down his book and has red-rimmed eyes—like he's been not-so-secretly crying too. He rubs at his nose when he catches me looking, like he's embarrassed that I've seen him.

"Hey . . . " Priti's voice jolts us all out of our teary emotions. She's standing in the doorway to the room, taking us all in with wide eyes. "Um . . . what's going on?"

"Nothing." Ammu sniffles once, rubs away the last of her tears and settles into position in her bed again. "Come here, let me put oil in your hair."

Priti looks at us all skeptically for a moment before sitting down right beside me on the bed. She gives me a questioning look as Ammu begins to brush her hair back.

"Can I play a song?" I pull out my phone and start scrolling through Spotify.

"Rabindranath Sangeet." We all groan at Abbu's suggestion—even Ammu.

"Play something Bollywood," Ammu says. "Something upbeat that your Abbu can't sing along to."

"Play 'Tum Hi Ho.'" Priti bounces a little as she says

it, but Ammu pulls her down by her hair and she settles again immediately, mumbling, "ouch," under her breath.

"'Tum Hi Ho' is old, and it's super depressing."

"Play 'Amar Shonar Bangla,' we can all sing along."

"Abbu!" Both Priti and I groan. Singing our patriotic national anthem is definitely not what I had in mind.

Finally, after scrolling through my Spotify for too long and battling away awful suggestions from my whole family, I put on a Bollywood song that everyone—including Priti—complains about. I roll my eyes and sigh, leaning against Ammu's shoulder as she puts oil in Priti's hair. But really, inside I am bubbling over with happiness.

32

Two weeks of applying henna, of hard work, of accounting and of business plans pass. Despite my trashed stall, I manage to pull things together. It helps that Jess and Chaewon make me a brand-new poster with the colors of the lesbian flag. They even laminate it for good measure, so that nobody can rip it up.

But at the end of the two weeks our final presentations are due.

Ms. Montgomery told us about it the week before, calling us into her classroom at the end of the day on Friday. We all took seats as she stood at the top. She gave me a secret smile, like I'm her favorite to win; maybe that means something? That I have a chance? I seriously doubt it though.

"Next Friday is the last day of the competition," she

said in a booming voice that immediately shut everyone up. I caught sight of Flávia in one corner of the room. She was sitting beside Chyna, but she didn't look happy about it. She shot me a weak smile.

"We'll have your stalls set up all day, but because the judges will be coming around, you'll also need to have your portfolios to present to them when the time comes," Ms. Montgomery continued. "You'll have to show them your accounts, your business plans, everything you've been keeping a record of. It's not just the business with the most profit that'll win, they'll also be looking for the most innovative, the most eye-catching ideas. There are a lot of different criteria that go into the judging, so make sure your portfolios are up-to-date and ready."

She went around to each group, going through what we had prepared so far and what we still needed to do. It didn't sound too difficult. I had everything all set up, basically, since I've been keeping up with everything since the very beginning. I'm the daughter of a business owner, and I've been using Abbu's work as an example every step of the way, and I'm Priti's sister, which means she's micromanaged everything. I'm kind of thankful for that now.

When presentation day comes I am fully prepared, but I still feel butterflies fluttering around in my stomach.

Chaewon: *TODAY IS THE DAY!!!!!*

Jess: *ahhhhhhhhhhhhhhhh*

I keep typing and erasing, typing and erasing. I'm not sure what I can say, and I'm not sure what I feel. I'm excited, but also relieved. Today is the day all of this stops. The whole mess of me and Flávia and Chyna started with this henna business, after all. Maybe some semblance of normalcy will return to my life after today. Though after everything that's happened, I seriously doubt it.

Jess: *meet you guys at my locker before school?*

Chaewon: *yes!!*

Nishat: *see you there*

We gather at our lockers with excited grins. It feels like Christmas has come early for everybody involved in the competition. We've been working so hard—each and every one of us—and today is the day we get to show the world what we've accomplished. We get to claim the fruits of our labor—or try to, anyway. We spend the first class setting everything up once again, all of our stalls and banners and posters. I put up the poster Jess made me—the lesbian flag with all of its different shades of pinks and whites and reds. I can feel the others in the hall eyeing me with disdain, but I don't care.

Flávia catches my eye from the other end of the hall as I put it up. I smile and she smiles back, waving at me. I feel my heart speed up and I take a deep breath. I have to keep my feelings in check.

My phone vibrates in the pocket of my shirt. Two

messages. From Flávia. I glance around, trying to catch her eye again, but she's in an animated conversation with Chyna.

Flávia: *good luck*

Flávia: *hope you win :)*

My stomach plummets. I have no idea what to say back.

Me: *thank you, good luck to you too*

It's the only thing that feels sincere. I want to tack on an *I miss you*, because I desperately do; I even type in a heart before deleting it.

Chaewon and Jess come up beside me as I slip the phone back into my pocket. Chaewon hooks her elbow with one of mine, and Jess takes the other. They both smile.

"Ready?"

"Ready."

After the judges have had a chance to speak to all the contestants, fake smiles and clipboards in place, they take their spots on the stage that's been set up at the top of the hall. The rest of us gather around. An excited chatter builds in the hallway, broken only by a loud shriek from the microphone as Ms. Montgomery takes hold of it.

"Oh, sorry," she mumbles, holding the mic up to

her lips and smiling down at all of us. "Um. Welcome everyone. And a very special thank you to our judges, Mr. Kelly and Ms. Walsh, for joining us today. We're so delighted that we got the chance to participate in this competition this year. It brought out so much dedication in our young Transition Year students, and I'm sure in a few years we'll be seeing some of them up here on stage with us."

As she hands the mic over to Mr. Kelly, I feel a presence a little too close to me. When I turn around, I find Flávia smiling down at me. She slips her hand into mine and leans close.

"I'm nervous," she whispers, her lips grazing my ear and sending a shiver down my spine.

"Me too," I whisper back. She edges closer, and I can smell her sugary-sweet perfume.

"There are a lot of excellent business ideas and executions in this school this year," Mr. Kelly announces into his mic from the top of the hall. He's wearing a plain black suit and tie. The judge next to him, smiling through bright red lips, looks more relatable. In an all-girls school I think she should be the one running the competition. She should be the main judge, to show girls that they can make it in the business world.

"But unfortunately, there can be only one winner." As Mr. Kelly says this, silence spreads over the entire hallway.

We all wait breathlessly to hear who the winner is.

Flávia's hand squeezes mine at the same time Chaewon finds my other hand.

"And the winning business belongs to . . . Chaewon Kim and Jessica Kennedy!"

I gasp out loud, but it's drowned out by the sound of the hall bursting into applause.

Chaewon and Jess have the biggest grins on their faces. I wrap my arms around both of them before shoving them through the crowd. They walk up, looking at the stage in awe. They obviously didn't expect to win, but if anyone deserves it, it's definitely them. They've been working hard through and through. No games. No sabotage.

My heart fills with pride as I see them up there, accepting their award from Mr. Kelly and Ms. Walsh. Their smiles are so wide it's contagious.

"It's funny, isn't it?" Flávia leans down to whisper while everybody is still clapping.

"What's funny?"

"That this was all about the business competition. That's how it all started out and now . . . "

"I know. Neither of us are up there."

Flávia heaves a sigh and turns away, trying to find someone in the crowd of people. "I better go . . . Chyna doesn't look too thrilled with the outcome. Talk to you later?"

I want to tell her to stay, but I just shrug and say, "Sure."

Jess and Chaewon can't stop smiling after they've come down from the stage. I envelop them both in hugs, before admiring their trophy.

"I can't believe we won," Chaewon whispers. "I can't believe we won."

The trophy is translucent glass shaped like a diamond. In the very middle it says YOUNG ENTREPRENEUR'S AWARD in glittering gold writing.

"You guys deserved to win," I assure them. "You've worked so hard for this."

Chaewon wraps me up in another hug so tight that I can feel her ribs poking at me.

"Okay, okay. Wow, let me breathe." She lets me go and rubs at her eyes, like she's trying really hard not to cry.

"Chaewon." Jess rolls her eyes and pokes her until Chaewon does begin to sob a little bit, but also to laugh. And then we're all giggling together and I'm not sure why, really. But it feels like a huge weight off my shoulders. It feels like the most normal thing to happen since Ali outed me to the entire school. Like at the end of the day, none of that really mattered. Not Ali, not Chyna, not even the business competition. Because I'm still here and I have my friends, my sister, my family. And things will be okay.

It feels odd to be stripping my stall. Like it's the end of an era, even though the competition only lasted a couple of weeks. I carefully roll up the banner with the lesbian flag and tie it up with a rubber band. I'm thinking I'll stick it up on the wall of my bedroom.

" . . . her mom basically did all the work for her." A hushed whisper comes from the girls in the stall beside mine. I place my banner aside carefully. Soundlessly. So as to not attract any attention.

"That's why Chyna even did henna as her business. These days, if you're white, people don't even want to consider you."

"Right. The trendy thing is to be 'diverse' or whatever."

I can't even hear the speakers' next words, because I'm feeling that simmering of anger inside me again. *Of course* even when Chaewon and Jess win the competition Chyna still does everything in her power to manipulate the situation.

I catch sight of her and Flávia packing up their stall next to Chaewon and Jess's. The next thing I know I'm marching right over there and staring Chyna in the face.

"Nishat." Her lips are pressed into a thin line. "What do you want?"

"You can't stand that someone else gets attention even for a second, can you?" The words tumble out of me before they've even formed in my mind. It's like I'm working off adrenaline.

Her lips get thinner somehow. "What are you talking about?" she asks at the same time that Flávia shuffles over with wide eyes and says, "Hey, Nishat."

I barely register her. All I can see is Chyna, with her wispy blonde hair and blue eyes—trying to manipulate a victory for someone who deserves it, just like she tries to manipulate everything. Like she manipulated our friendship to make herself out to be kind of person who fits in, and me to be the "other."

"Telling people that the only reason Chaewon and Jess won the business competition is because being diverse is trendy?" It's an effort to get out the words in a remotely calm and collected way. The way Flávia is looking back and forth from Chyna to me makes me think maybe I'm not as composed as I think I am.

Chyna has the gall to sigh, like this conversation is boring her. "People like new things. It's not exactly a reach. Whatever Korean stuff they were selling is something we haven't seen here before so yeah, it's trendy and nothing we have is going to be new in the same way."

"Like henna is trendy?"

Chyna rolls her eyes. "Yes, like henna is trendy. That's why we did the whole henna thing. That's how business works, Nishat." She says it as if she has a master's degree in business and I'm someone who needs to be schooled.

There is more anger in me than I know what to do

with. But before I can say anything more, Flávia's hand is on my shoulder. Instead of sending me into a tizzy like it normally would, it actually calms me. I feel like she's on my side for once.

"Flá, come on, we have to finish packing up," Chyna is already turning away and I realize that a bit of a crowd has gathered around us. I must not have been as quiet as I thought I was being. Chaewon and Jess are looking at me from their almost-packed stall with wide eyes. Chaewon gives me a weak smile when I catch her eye.

"Chy, do you think it's trendy to be Brazilian?" Flávia asks this softly enough, but it seems to ring out across the entire hall. More and more students are stopping in their tracks to listen in on this conversation. I don't think Flávia cares.

Chyna turns back, brushing a lock of blonde hair behind her ear and heaving another deep sigh. "What are you on about, Flávia?"

"You come to our Brazilian barbecues every summer. You eat our food. Do you think it's trendy?"

"No . . . yes . . . I don't know. That's just something we do. Not a trend."

"Neither is being Korean," Chaewon says from the other side of us. "Or wanting to sell something that's Korean. It's just something I do."

"Or henna. That's just something that's a part of my

culture. Just like our food is—you know, the food that apparently gives everyone digestive issues?" I shrug. "One you thought was trendy, the other you didn't, so you used it to spread rumors about my family."

"That's . . . different," Chyna says, but for once she doesn't sound like she actually believes what she's saying.

Flávia shakes her head and says, "Imagine someone said the same stuff about me that you said about Nishat. Imagine they excluded me because I eat Brazilian food and speak Portuguese."

"That would never happen," Chyna chimes in immediately. "Flávia, that's not . . . Nishat hasn't given you the whole story. Nishat has her own friends, and her sister. I've never had anything against her."

"You spread rumors about her for being a lesbian." It's Jess who volunteers this piece of information, and I wonder if it's going to make Flávia back off. But it doesn't. Her grip on my shoulder tightens, and I'm not sure if it's to help her or to help me.

"Because being gay makes her different?" Flávia asks, and I'm not sure if anyone else hears the tremble in her voice but I do and it sends an ice pick through my heart.

"I didn't spread any rumors about anyone," Chyna says, with less and less conviction. "I really don't know why you're ganging up on me like this."

Flávia takes a deep breath and says, "Come on, Nishat."

She slips her fingers through mine and leads me away from Chyna and the hall full of girls in our year. All of them seem a little stunned by what's just passed. If I'm honest, I'm also more than a little astonished. The most I expected was to get rid of some of my anger by telling Chyna what was what. I never expected this.

"You didn't have to do that," I say to Flávia once we're outside the school building. The place is deserted. Most people have already gone home. It's only our Business class left now.

"I think I did."

"You didn't have to do it for me."

Flávia smiles. "I did it more for me than for you, Nishat."

We sit down on the steps beside us. They're near the front entrance to the school but far enough away to obscure us from view.

"Do you want me to go get your stuff from inside?" I ask. My bag and all of my henna supplies are still strewn across my table; I'm hoping Chaewon or Jess will grab them.

"It's fine. I'm sure . . . Chyna will take care of it."

"Are you okay?" It's the only question I can think to ask even though it doesn't feel quite right.

She shrugs and says, "Are you okay?"

I smile. "I guess it felt kind of good to stand up to Chyna for once."

"Even though you were standing up for someone else

and not yourself?"

"I guess it's easier to stand up for someone else. Plus . . . Chaewon and Jess don't deserve that kind of slander. They worked hard. They didn't play any games. They won fair and square."

"I feel like I've seen a new side of Chyna these past few months." Flávia sighs.

"Did you know her as a nice person before?"

Flávia lets out a small laugh, like thinking of Chyna as a nice person is maybe a little bit too much to ask for. "Chyna . . . has always been competitive and strong-willed. It can come in handy, like, when our whole family gets together and we play games together or whatever. I always hope I'm on Chyna's team because I know she's going to win. Whether we're playing soccer in the summer or Harry Potter trivia in the winter."

"Chyna likes Harry Potter?" I don't know why that's the most shocking thing to hear—but it really is. I would never have thought someone like Chyna could be a Harry Potter fan.

"We watch the movies every Christmas when they're on TV."

I can't imagine it—Flávia and Chyna sitting in front of the TV marathoning Harry Potter of all things. I still only see Chyna as the girl who's been tormenting me and my friends for the past three years.

"It's funny because in my old school, when the girls sometimes said mean things to me because I'm Black, Chyna would get so angry. And now I'm not sure if she was angry because she knew it was wrong or because . . . it was me and I'm the exception to her rule. And is that good or is that bad?"

I definitely can't imagine Chyna having any kind of a moral compass when it comes to things like race, but I furrow my eyebrows and try to work through it. Try to work out what Chyna saw in me the first day we met, and then later at the party when everything fell apart.

"Maybe it's both?" I offer.

"Isn't that a paradox?"

"Maybe . . . sometimes people don't see the things they do as wrong, but they can see the wrong in what other people do—especially if it's done to someone they care about," I say. "When it happens to someone else, it doesn't feel as important as when it happens to someone we love."

Flávia thinks about it for a moment, with a frown on her lips that makes my heart do somersaults. I try to ignore them.

"I think I want to tell her. About me. Us. If there still is an us." She doesn't look at me as she says this, and she shuffles her feet around like she's really afraid there might not be an us. Like I could have forgotten about her and me and us in just the past few weeks. Like I haven't been thinking about her almost every single day.

"You don't have to—"

"I know." She turns to me and takes my hand in hers and I feel electricity pulsing through me. "It's just . . . I don't feel so afraid of it anymore. Like . . . my mom keeps telling me the news from Brazil, and the things that our president says about women, and Black and gay people, you know? And then these past few weeks, I've seen you up against what seems like the entire world. Or at least like half the population of our school. And you never let it phase you. I don't want to be . . . the kind of person that lets things pass by. I want to be the kind of person that does something, and stands for something."

"And you're standing for . . . coming out?" I ask.

"I'm standing for . . . me. For you. For us, I guess."

It doesn't seem like much. But sometimes just being yourself—really, truly yourself—can be the most difficult thing to be.

33

PRITI HAS HER HEAD BURIED IN HER BOOKS WHEN I GET home, but as soon as I catch sight of her through the crack in her door she perks up. Like she's been waiting for any sign of me to distract herself from studying.

"I heard Chaewon and Jess won!" she exclaims, bouncing on the bed. "I'm sorry it wasn't you."

I lean against her doorframe and say, "It's not a big deal. It wasn't like I thought I was going to win." Even though there was that small inkling of hope still inside me. "Something happened . . . after the awards, though."

"Oh?" Priti leans so far forward in her bed that I'm surprised she doesn't fall off the edge. "Something good or bad?"

I shrug because I'm still making up my mind about it. "Flávia says she's going to come out to Chyna."

"Whoa." Priti sits back, eyes wide. Like she's trying to process and can't quite make heads or tails of it all.

"Yeah." I sit down beside her, trying to process as well. What does this mean? What will it mean?

"She must really like you."

I turn to Priti with a frown. "What? She's not doing this for me."

Priti looks at me like she doesn't quite believe me, but says, "Oh, okay," in the most unconvincing voice I have ever heard.

"You really think it's because of me?"

"I think it's not *not* because of you."

"Do you think she'll be okay?" My heart feels heavy at the thought of Chyna's reaction.

Priti crawls close to me and leans her head against my shoulder. "I think no matter what happens she'll have you, and her mom, and her sister."

I wait anxiously by my phone for the whole evening. It feels strangely like that fateful day when I decided to tell Ammu and Abbu about me, and I realize that now I have to tell them about Flávia too.

When I wake up the next morning with my phone still cradled next to me, I have one new message from Flávia.

Can I come over?

Ammu and Abbu are in the sitting room, their eyes glued to the TV. When I peer around the door, I expect them to be watching a Bollywood film on Star Gold, or an Indian natok on Star Plus. What I don't expect is for them to be watching the *Ellen DeGeneres Show* as if their lives depend on it.

"You want to watch, Nishat?" Ammu pats the empty seat beside her, but doesn't take her eyes off the TV. On screen, Ellen DeGeneres is interviewing Ellen Page. It's probably the gayest thing in this house—and my parents are willingly watching it.

"Um, no . . . " I mumble, looking from the TV to Ammu and back. "Can I . . . Ammu . . . " I'm not sure how to phrase the question. Flávia is on her way over and we only get one chance to make a first impression. "Is it . . . okay if I have a girlfriend?"

Ammu finally looks away from the TV, her eyebrows furrowed and lips pressed together. She exchanges a glance with Abbu before asking, "Is it the girl from the wedding?"

"What wedding? What girl?"

"You know." Ammu waves her arms around as if that's an explanation. "Your sister showed me a picture. From the wedding. The Brazilian girl."

I have never loved Priti as much as I love her right at this very moment.

"Flávia . . . yeah. She's . . . coming over."

"Now?" Abbu sits up straight, like he is very unprepared for this.

"Yeah, now. Is that . . . okay?"

Abbu frowns at me, before turning to Ammu. "What will we feed her?"

"Can she eat spicy food? Is she staying for dinner?" Ammu actually turns the TV off and adjusts her urna over her chest. "What do Brazilians eat? She's not one of those . . . vegetarians, is she?" Vegetarians are the bane of existence for most Bengalis since most of our food is full of meat.

I try to gulp down the lump forming in my throat and shrug. "I don't think she's a vegetarian. She might stay for dinner."

"She has to," Abbu decides at the same time that Ammu shakes her head and traipses into the kitchen, clearly distraught about what she's going to feed Flávia.

I text Flávia as soon as Ammu and Abbu have disappeared into the kitchen.

Me: *You're not vegetarian are you?*

Flávia: *nope, why?*

Me: *My mom is freaking out about what she's going to feed you. It's a Bengali thing*

Flávia: *freaking out about food?*

Me: *pretty much!*

By the time Flávia rings the bell, Ammu has started prepping an entire feast and I'm not sure if I should be proud or embarrassed. I'm a little bit of both as I introduce a flustered Flávia to my parents.

I manage to drag her upstairs and away from their awkward, prying questions as soon as they've exchanged hellos and shaken hands.

"We have a lot of homework to do," is what does the trick. Because studying—of course—comes before everything else.

"Your parents have really come around," Flávia says once we're up in my room. "Are they really going to feed me dinner?"

"If I let you go home without having dinner, I think they would disown me," I explain. "You don't come to a Bengali person's home and leave without eating."

"This is a perk I can get used to." Flávia grins, before leaning forward and taking my hand in hers. "Also . . . all the other stuff, I guess."

I have to smile too, but tentatively because the question I've been wanting to ask since I got her text is still bugging me. "Was Chyna . . . I mean, did you tell her? Is she . . . ?"

Flávia sighs. "Chyna is . . . coming around."

"What does that mean?"

"It means . . . we're working it out."

I want to ask her a thousand more questions. I want her to give me a blow-by-blow about her conversation with Chyna; I want to know everything. But then Flávia leans in and presses her lips to mine, and I don't care about any of it anymore.

Monday dawns as dreary and dull as most Irish mornings. There's a constant drizzle of rain that makes it look as if it's not morning at all. Still, I couldn't feel more elated if I tried. I can't stop smiling, even as I pull my heavy French book out of my locker.

"Hey."

At the sound of Chyna's voice, I drop said French book right onto my toes.

"Ow. Um, hi." I pick up the book, trying to massage my toes through my shoes and definitely looking like a misshapen pretzel or something.

Chyna doesn't seem very sympathetic to my plight, unsurprisingly. She's looking around as if to make sure nobody's watching us have this conversation. It's only five minutes until the bell rings, so everyone is too busy to pay attention to our corner of the hallway. Except for

Chaewon and Jess, whose lockers are only a few away from mine. Out of the corner of my eyes, I can see their attempts at inconspicuously eavesdropping.

Chyna takes a deep breath and, with a pained expression on her face, says, "I wanted to tell you that it's okay that you're dating my cousin."

"Oh." She's still avoiding my eyes and I wonder if Flávia put her up to this. "Well . . . thanks."

She finally catches my eye and her lips press together in a frown. "I probably shouldn't have said what I did on Friday . . . " She trails off as the sound of the first bell fills the air around us.

"I should . . . " Chyna is already shuffling away from me, putting visible distance between us like I'm contagious with something she's afraid of catching.

Chaewon and Jess make their way over almost as soon as Chyna is out of sight. Their eyes are bulging out their sockets.

"What was that?" Jess asks, as if she just witnessed something otherworldly. She might as well have.

"I guess that was Chyna apologizing?"

"*That* was an apology?" Chaewon asks, eyebrows raised.

I shrug. "I think it's the most I'm ever going to get."

Even Chyna's non-apology apology can't ruin my good mood because when I wave goodbye to my friends and slip into French class, Flávia is sitting in a corner. She has her bag propped up on the seat beside her, and she's absent-mindedly twirling a curl around her finger.

When she sees me, her face breaks out into a smile.

Dimples and all.

Warmth spreads through me at the sight.

34

FLÁVIA HAS A THING FOR PUMPKIN SPICE LATTES. IT'S possibly the most white girl thing about her. So when she drags me into Starbucks one afternoon after school and buys me one of those spiced coffees, I have to pretend that I hate it, even though I secretly kind of love it.

I scrunch up my nose with every sip I take, until Flávia rolls her eyes and says, "I bet if I come here tomorrow, you'll already be in a corner cradling a mug of pumpkin spice latte."

"I can't believe you think I have such bad taste."

"You're a real food snob, you know that?"

I shrug. "I can't help it. It's the Bengali in me." She definitely never complains about me being a food snob when she's having dinner at my house.

But now she pokes me in the ribs and says, "Admit it.

You kind of like it."

A fresh flurry of butterflies flutters through my stomach. I don't think Flávia realizes what her touch still does to me.

"Okay, I guess it's not that bad," I concede.

She grins, and I reconsider whether she does know exactly what her touch does to me. I don't have much time to think about it though, because in the next moment she's looped her arm into mine and is resting her head on my shoulder.

"We should study," she sighs. That's the excuse we gave both of our parents to venture out for the afternoon. Neither of us make an effort to reach into our bags, though; I'm not even sure what books I have in mine.

Instead, I lean into her and we watch the way the cars and buses and the Luas zoom up Westmoreland Street. The sunlight begins to dim slowly.

"I want you to do my henna." Flávia's voice startles me out of my reverie. She sits up and says, "You never did it. That one time—I got henna all in my hair and you never finished."

"You're realizing this now?" It's still only been a few weeks, but it feels like an eternity has passed since the competition finished, since our first kiss, since Flávia and I began our more or less public relationship.

She frowns and turns all the way around so we're

directly face-to-face—like we're in the middle of a serious discussion and not just talking about henna.

"I've been thinking about this a lot," she says.

"About henna?"

"About . . . yes, henna. Kind of. I talked to your friends and your sister and—"

"Behind my back?"

She rolls her eyes. "Don't be dramatic, Nishat. It's a good thing. Think of it as a present."

"Are you feeling okay?" I wonder if this is a side effect of pumpkin spice lattes. They do have a very strong scent.

Flávia just smiles. She pulls her phone out of the pocket of her jeans and taps it for a minute before thrusting the screen toward me.

"I didn't know when was the right time to show you, but . . . I think we're ready."

The Instagram page that I disabled after the business competition stares me in the face, but I barely recognize it. The profile picture is brand new. In bright red cursive handwriting it reads *Nishat's Mehndi*, with the same written in faded Bengali script in the background.

"Jess helped me with the design and we even set up a website. And your sister says your dad will let you use his restaurant again." There's this bright gleam of hope in Flávia's eyes that I'm not sure I understand.

"My business kind of failed miserably last time," I say.

"I'm not—"

"But you like doing it. Love it, actually." She says it like it's a fact. "Your sister thinks so. So do your friends. And last time things went up in flames because of us."

"But—"

"You're really talented, Nishat." Flávia leans forward and cups my face with her hands. I feel myself flush. Feel the bloom of warmth in my chest. "And everyone should see that."

"I do still have leftover henna tubes," I admit.

"And you have an entire catalog of original henna designs."

I think of the design book collecting dust in the back of my bookshelf.

"Maybe," I say finally.

It must be enough for Flávia, because she leans forward and presses her lips to mine. But it's such a brief kiss that when she pulls away I'm still leaning into her and nearly topple over.

She's too busy digging into her schoolbag to even notice. For a second, I'm afraid she's going to pull out her French book and insist that we get serious about school. But she pulls out something totally unexpected—a tube of henna.

She lays it on the table in front of us and looks at me with her dimpled smile. "Okay. I'm ready for a Nishat original."

"Flávia."

"Please?" She looks at me with big, round puppy-dog eyes, and it's not like I can say no to those.

I grab hold of the henna tube and begin to squeeze a pattern into Flávia's palm while she beams at me as if this is the best day of her life. It feels kind of surreal: The warmth of her hand. The tenderness of her gaze. The way the setting sun illuminates her face.

The fact that I'm weaving my very culture into her skin.

This is one of those moments that I want to bottle up and keep with me forever. Not because it's extraordinary, or because it's the kind of thing you would find in a Bollywood movie.

But because it's the kind of moment I could never have dreamed of having in a million years.

acknowledgments

A BOOK IS ONLY AS GOOD AS ALL OF THE PEOPLE WHO come together to make it into a reality, and I feel lucky to have many incredible people in my corner.

Thank you to my amazing agent, Uwe Stender, for believing in me and this story, and for your endless enthusiasm and support.

Thank you to my brilliant editor, Lauren Knowles, for all of your hard work in making *The Henna Wars* into what it is today. A huge thank you to the incredible team at Page Street: William Kiester, Ashley Tenn, Molly Gillespie, Tamara Grasty, Lauren Davis, Lauren Cepero, and Lizzy Mason.

I definitely would not be here without my very own team Avatar: Alyssa, Shaun, April, Kristine, and Timmy. Thank you for all of the years believing me in me and my writing, and for shaping me into the person that I am today.

adiba jaigirdar

Go raibh míle maith agaibh to Amanda and Shona, for putting up with reading my writing since I was a teen, and for the tea, cake, and tapas. And to Gavin for letting me vent to you endlessly, for being a supportive friend, and an amazing person.

This book would not exist without my incredible and talented friend Gabhi, who was the first person I turned to with the idea. Thank you for shouting at me to go and write the book, for always believing in me, and for everything you have done to shape this book into what it is.

To my Bengali Squad, Tammi and Priyanka: I don't know what I would do without the two of you. I can't thank you enough for all of your help throughout this entire process. For holding my hand from first draft all the way until now, and for always knowing the perfect Bengali word when I'm stuck.

To my brilliant and talented friend, Faridah: Thank you for putting up with all of my venting and anxiety, and always believing in me and this book. Thank you also for putting up with the creepy Jack Nicholson gif (it's not going away anytime soon, sorry).

Thank you to all of the fantastic people who have beta read this book, given me invaluable feedback, and have continued to support it with so much enthusiasm and love that I can hardly believe it: Terry, Tas, Maria, Cass, Francesca, and Fadwa. You are some of the most amazing people ever, and I am so grateful that I get to call you friends.

Muito obrigada to Lia for all of your enthusiasm, your support, the Flávia doll, and your friendship.

Thank you to my amazing friend Alechia: You talked me through so much while I was taking my first steps in this industry, even though you barely knew me at the time. I'll never forget your selfless generosity and everything you have done for me since. I'm so glad to call you a friend.

English teachers can play such a huge role in the life of a writer, and I have been extremely lucky in having some of the best ones, but none as amazing as Mr. Fallon. Your encouragement and enthusiasm have meant the world to me since I was a kid.

Thank you to my family, who still don't understand publishing but are trying their best: to Mamoni, Abbu, Bhaiya, Biyut Apu, and Labiba.

To every single person who has supported me and this book in any shape and form: I don't even have the words to thank you. Just know that every time I see a message of excitement or support, my heart fills up and I cry ugly tears.

Lastly, thank you to you, the reader, for picking up this book and giving it a chance.

about the author

ADIBA JAIGIRDAR WAS BORN IN DHAKA, BANGLADESH, and has been living in Dublin, Ireland, since the age of ten. She has a BA in English and History, and an MA in Postcolonial Studies. She is a contributor for Bookriot. All of her writing is aided by tea, and a healthy dose of Janelle Monáe and Hayley Kiyoko. When not writing, she can be found ranting about the ills of colonialism, playing video games, and expanding her overflowing lipstick collection. She can be found at adibajaigirdar.com or @adiba_j on Twitter and @dibs_j on Instagram.